I Am Quinn

McGarvey Black

Print ISBN 978-1-912986-33-0

This is dedicated to my husband, Peter Black,
who listened and encouraged each and every day.

"When someone shows you who they are,
believe them the first time."

— **Maya Angelou**

Chapter One

One thing I know is true, you find out who your real friends are after you're dead.

My name is Quinn Delaney Roberts. Friends called me Quinnie except on the days I was a little full of myself, then I was known as the 'Quinntessa'. The part that gets me is that everyone moved on with their lives practically the day after I was buried. That was almost a bigger a surprise than dying. Almost.

Attending my own funeral was strange. Over the years, I'd been to plenty of wakes – car accidents, drugs, and cancer: lots of cancer. But when it's yours, it's a whole different story. It's not sad exactly, it's fascinating and kind of bizarre. Questions that haunted me when I was alive disappeared. A therapist once told me 'with healing comes clarity'. I guess that's true. Suddenly, I know everything in the universe, except for how and why I'm dead. Did I slip in the shower and crack my skull open on the porcelain soap dish in my tub? Did I choke to death on a chicken bone because I was alone and no one was there to save me? Every other day of my life is crystal clear except for the last one. Things are upside down and make no sense.

I always figured I'd live to be a hundred. My grandparents on my mother's side lived into their nineties. Dying at age forty-four was unexpected and, if I might add, incredibly unfair. I wasn't done with my life or ready to leave my husband, Alec and my two children. My kids both tower over me, which isn't hard to do since I'm just over five feet tall. No matter what, they'll always be my babies. My daughter Hannah is only twenty and Jack, just twenty-one. They weren't ready to lose their mother. Not yet.

Growing up, my friends dreamed of big careers or traveling by train through Europe. All I wanted was to be a mother and have lots of kids. Even when I was little, I'd pretend my Barbie was a housewife and mother cooking dinner and playing with her children. My doll was always dressed like a suburban soccer mom acting out storylines that involved family picnics and Girl Scouts. I suppose it was odd, but it's who I am — who I was.

Leaving my kids before they were fully formed bothers me the most. There were still things I wanted to teach them, like making fresh pesto from a basil plant or how to play the ukulele. Except for the B chord, I was pretty good on the uke. Sure, I sang off-key sometimes, but always with confidence. Enthusiasm makes up for a lot of sour notes. I wanted my kids to learn that, too.

My life didn't turn out the way I expected. It was supposed to be amazing. Everyone had such high expectations, including me. Now, there's one question that keeps reverberating in my head, did I do something to myself?

Part One

THE WEEK I DIED

Chapter Two

Other than the time Quinn Roberts' sink backed up, and those two messages she left saying she thought there was brown mold in her bathroom, Joan Hemmerly hadn't heard a peep out of her new lodger in the six months since she moved in. Quinn Roberts paid her rent on time and didn't make any noise, the ideal tenant.

Hemmerly's son, Ronny, did the maintenance work on his mother's rental properties since his father passed away. Her son was the one who fixed Quinn Roberts' clogged kitchen drain. He thought the lady was 'real nice', especially after she told him he could bring his dog, Cooper, inside instead of having to leave him out in the car. While he snaked her drain, the woman played with his dog while she made the handyman some herbal tea. She even gave his grateful hound a dog biscuit.

'How come you have dog treats when you ain't got no dog?' Ronny asked.

'I always keep some in my coat pockets in case I run into someone walking their pooch. I love dogs,' said Quinn with a big smile.

The next day, Ronny stopped by his mother's house.

'You get that sink fixed?' his mother asked.

'Yeah, it's all clear,' he said. 'That Ms. Roberts is nice, Ma. Real pretty too, a definite MILF.'

'What the hell is a MILF?' his mother asked.

Just hearing his mother use the acronym made her son laugh.

'It means Mother I'd Like to F, Ma,' Ronny said, snorting while he laughed.

An expression of horror crossed his mother's face, and she shook her head. She'd never heard that one before and wondered where the hell he got that stuff.

'Listen to me,' she said to her twenty-eight-year-old son, 'you stay away from her. She's practically old enough to be your mother.'

'That's the whole point,' he said as he chuckled. She warned her son a second time and then wondered if anyone ever thought she was a MILF. Probably not, she decided.

About a week later, on a dreary Saturday, the phone rang as the landlady was finishing her lunch. She tucked a loose strand of overly processed platinum blonde hair behind her ear and reached for the phone. A woman identified herself as Viv DeMarco and said she was a good friend of one of her tenants.

'I've been trying to reach Quinn for five days,' Viv said. 'I'm standing out in front of her apartment right now, and she isn't answering the door. Her Subaru is parked in the driveway.'

'Maybe she went for a walk,' Mrs. Hemmerly said, a little annoyed. 'What are you calling me for?'

'Look,' Viv said. 'I'm one of her closest friends. She always calls me back. I've left her twenty messages. Please, I drove all the way here from Avon. Something is wrong.'

'What do you expect me to do? I can't force her to call you back. I'm her landlady, not her mother.'

'Quinn might be hurt or unconscious,' Viv said, becoming agitated. 'Her kids haven't heard from her in over a week. We need to get in.'

'I can't just bust in…'

'She talked about killing herself,' Viv blurted out.

Oh boy, thought the landlady, that's a game changer. She told Viv she'd be there in ten minutes and called her son, Ronny. He had been in the hospital the previous week, but he was back at work today painting one of her other apartments in the same neighborhood.

'Put down your brush,' the landlady said when her son answered. 'We might have a problem over at Brookside with Ms. Roberts' place. Meet me there in ten minutes.'

When the landlady pulled up in front of the building, a heavy-set woman with tangerine-colored hair and oversized matching red-orange glasses was pacing out front.

'You Viv DeMarco?' she shouted to the woman as she got out of her car. Viv nodded emphatically. 'You're sure about this? Ms. Roberts really talked about killing herself?'

'Yes,' Viv said, out of breath. 'Quinn is on all sorts of medications. She has so many pills.'

The landlady told Viv they'd have to wait until her son arrived before they could go in. Who knew what they were going to find and she wanted to have a big guy with her, just in case. Ronny wasn't the brightest bulb, but he was big and strong, just like his daddy.

A minute later her son and his friend, Jeff, both covered in white paint, came strolling over with Ronny's terrier mix, Cooper, trailing behind.

'Do you have to bring that dang dog everywhere?' the landlady yelled at her son. 'Never mind, let's go in, and don't be getting no paint on anything.'

The four walked up the front steps of the house. Joan Hemmerly rang the bell to Apartment B ten times to be certain no one was home. As the landlady unlocked the front door of the building, Viv started breathing funny.

'I'm sure everything will be okay,' Joan said as she pushed the creaky wooden front door open and stepped into the dark green foyer. 'Maybe she just went on a trip somewhere,' she said over her shoulder.

A massive pile of Quinn Roberts' mail lay inside the hall. The landlady noticed the foyer walls were scuffed and the wooden floors needed cleaning. She made a mental note to put that on her son's punch list. Swooping down, she picked up the mound of letters and the group proceeded to climb the stairs to the second floor. As they mounted each step, the old wooden staircase wailed under their weight. When they reached the top, the landlady knocked loudly on the door of Apartment B and waited for a response. Viv, Ronny and Jeff stood behind her, while Cooper scratched and sniffed at the apartment door. The landlady pulled out another key, shoved it into the lock and then pushed the door a quarter of the way open. Cooper ran in and disappeared. A putrid stink engulfed them, penetrating their clothing and every opening on their bodies. The place reeked. The landlady knew that smell. Something was dead in this place, and she secretly prayed it was just a mouse or squirrel trapped between the roof and the ceiling. That sometimes happened in old houses.

'Ms. Roberts,' the landlady called out loudly in a sing-song voice through the open front door. 'It's Joan Hemmerly, your landlady. I've got your friend Viv here with me. She was a little worried about you.'

They heard Cooper bark from one of the back rooms as they moved further into the apartment. With each step, the foul odor grew stronger, but no one acknowledged it, all fearing the worst.

The place was clean but messy and the temperature in the apartment was oddly colder than it was outside. A kitchen chair was turned over and lying on its side. The cabinet doors were all open as were the kitchen drawers, as if someone had been looking for something. Ronny closed all the doors and drawers and picked up the kitchen chair and put it back in its proper place. Unwashed dishes lay submerged in dirty water in the sink.

'Quinn,' Viv shouted, as the group moved into the living room. 'It's Viv, honey. Are you here?'

The persistent smell intensified the closer they got to the back hallway, making each one of them feel nauseous and gasp for clean air.

'We have to check the bathroom and bedroom,' the landlady said, starting to fear the worst.

'Ma, you want me to go first?' Ronny said.

His mother shook her head. 'Ms. Roberts might be unconscious, or she might not be dressed. I'd better go first.'

The bedroom door was ajar, and the awful smell of putrefied fruit and something indefinable grew stronger with each step. As the landlady pushed open the bedroom door, she knew it wasn't going to be a happy ending. The room was dim because the curtains were closed but she could still see the bedroom was in shambles. She flipped on the wall switch, and that's when she saw her. Quinn Roberts was lying on the rug next to the bed, eyes wide open. Hundreds of pills in every color of the rainbow lay scattered on the floor looking as though someone had dropped a garbage bag filled with jelly beans. Dozens of pill bottles with caps off were strewn around her body and in all corners of the room. Cooper was contentedly licking the dead woman's feet. When the landlady saw that, she threw up right on the white bedroom rug.

'Ma,' shouted Ronny as he and Jeff walked into the bedroom and saw his mother retching. 'What's wrong?' Then he saw Quinn Roberts slumped on the floor.

'Cooper, get away from her,' he shouted at the dog.

'Oh, my God,' said Jeff grabbing for the wall to steady himself.

'I've got to get out of this room,' the landlady said, hyperventilating, and walked back into the living room. Viv was standing where they had left her, frozen, clenching her hands, eyeglasses askew, tears streaming down her face.

'Is Quinn dead?' Viv whispered.

'Yeah, honey,' the landlady said gently. 'There are pills everywhere. Looks like you were right. You might not want to go in there.'

'Are you sure she's dead?' Viv asked again.

'I'm afraid so,' Joan Hemmerly said, shaking her head. 'Such a waste.'

Jeff, Cooper and Ronny, with his hands full of pill bottles, came out of the bedroom.

'She had so many different kinds, Ma,' he said, holding up some of the empty containers. 'Xanax, Wellbutrin, Lamictal, Depakote. Maybe she didn't kill herself on purpose. Maybe she got confused and took too many. She might have accidentally overdosed.'

'We've got to call the police,' the landlady said, feeling a bead of sweat trickle down her back.

'What am I going to tell her family?' said Viv.

They all stood silently in the living room for a moment. Viv started to sob as she told them that Quinn was only forty-four and had two kids in college.

'She was so young,' said the landlady. 'It's awful her kids losing their mother like this.'

She was about to call 911 when one of her other tenants from downstairs, Mr. Jenkins, walked in through the open apartment door.

'What's going on here?' he asked 'It reeks out here like a landfill on a hot Sunday in August.'

'Someone died,' the landlady said flatly. 'The woman who lived here committed suicide.'

'Quinn? She's dead?' he said. 'She always smiled at me when she was getting her mail. Sometimes we'd talk for a few minutes about the weather or the news. She told me she was getting divorced. Where is she?'

Ronny cocked his head towards the bedroom door.

With that, the old man walked towards it.

'I wouldn't go in there if I were you, Mr. Jenkins,' the landlady called out.

'I want to see her,' said the old man. 'I want to say goodbye.'

A minute later he came back ashen and with tears in his eyes.

'I straightened her arms out so she'd be more comfortable and covered her up with a blanket so she would be warm,' he said. 'She used to say she was always cold in this place.'

It was time. The landlady punched 911 into her phone while she said a little prayer for Quinn Roberts' soul.

Chapter Three

Balancing a coffee in one hand and a bacon, egg and cheese in the other, fifty-one-year-old Detective John McQuillan, known around the station as 'McQ', nearly had a car accident when the dispatcher's announcement crackled over his car radio. At first, he thought it was only a false alarm – another cat up a tree – until he heard that one word. Suicide.

'Call from The Glades; female, aged forty-four; landlord ID; possible suicide,' said the female voice.

He took a few sips of his tasteless, lukewarm coffee and devoured the remainder of the greasy sandwich. He needed to soak up all the beer he'd consumed the night before at his brother's fiftieth. The last round had been his idea and a colossal mistake and now he was paying for it. The taste of the salty meat combined with the scrambled and cheddar sent calming and happy signals to his brain, and he sighed with relief.

Five minutes later, belly full, McQuillan put the flashing light on top of his unmarked car and headed to The Glades, the high-end section of Newbridge and usually the quietest part of town. Nothing happened in that neighborhood, good or bad, it was painfully, peacefully dull. Most of the big old Victorian homes in the area had been converted into two- and three-family rental apartments inhabited mainly by professionals who worked downtown or over in Rochester. The detective steered his vehicle up Brookside Drive and stopped in front of #1404.

An empty black and white SUV with its light bar on top still flashing sat parked across the street. The front door of the police car was ajar and already attracting a crowd. A middle-aged, heavy-set woman wearing oversized glasses waved her arms frantically.

Her face was almost as red as her Flaming Hot Cheetos-colored hair. Visible tear tracks mixed with mascara streaked down her cheeks.

'Quinn's dead,' shouted the redhead.

'Are you the person who called?' said McQuillan to the agitated woman.

'It was the landlady who called. I'm Quinn's friend,' she sobbed. 'She's dead. I can't believe it. I drove over here from Avon. I knew something was wrong.'

'Why did you think that?'

'A couple of months ago, Quinn told me she wanted to kill herself. When she didn't call me back this week, I got worried,' she said, her voice catching. 'The landlady said there were hundreds of pills on the floor around her body.'

'Did Ms. Roberts use drugs?'

'Quinn wasn't into that. Her drug of choice was margaritas,' said Viv, sniffling. 'The last time we talked, she was better, but when I didn't hear back from her all week, I got scared. She said once that she wanted to buy a gun.'

'What did she want the gun for?'

'She said she wanted to blow her head off,' Viv said, crying softly. 'I thought she was just being a drama queen; she could be like that sometimes. We used to call her the Quinntessa.'

The detective walked towards the entrance of the building and immediately noticed something was wrong.

'Where's the goddamn yellow tape?' he muttered to himself. He pushed open the front door, and the stench hit him hard. It was unmistakable. Death. Inside the foyer, civilians swarmed like ants: upstairs, downstairs, on the stairs. Several older men sidestepped the detective as he ascended the steps.

'Is there a police officer here?' McQuillan shouted out to no one in particular.

On the second level, an older woman with platinum blonde hair pinned up on top of her head leaned over the dark wooden railing.

'I own this building,' she hollered, 'I'm the one who called. Your other officer is up here.'

The detective continued wearily up the creaky steps.

'It's so sad. That poor woman,' the landlady wailed as the detective got closer. 'I'll never be able to rent this apartment when people find out someone killed herself in here.'

McQuillan reached the top step out of breath and promised himself he'd reinstate his expired gym membership.

'It's going to take me weeks to get this place cleaned up,' said the landlady as she pushed open the front door of Quinn Roberts' apartment. 'I don't know how I'm going to get that smell out of this place.'

Chapter Four

Three middle-aged men deep in animated conversation barely noticed McQuillan when he entered the vestibule. Officer Yancy stood a few feet behind them taking a statement from a white-haired man.

'What the hell is going on here, Yancy?' said McQuillan angrily as he pulled the young cop aside. 'Who are all these civilians and why are they in the middle of my crime scene? It's like Grand Central Station at rush hour in here. And, where's the fucking barricade tape?'

'I thought I had a roll in my trunk, but I guess I didn't. I've been trying to get everyone out, McQ but...' Yancy started.

Out of the corner of his eye, McQuillan saw a dog dart through the living room, sniffing and poking its nose into every crevice.

'This is an active crime scene, you idiot,' the detective barked, unconcerned that he might be overheard. 'Why is there a goddamned dog in here?'

'That's my son's dog,' the landlady interjected, pointing to a young guy in painter's clothes outside the front door. 'I told him to come over, in case there was a problem.'

Two additional cops in uniform arrived just as McQuillan addressed the crowd. 'Anyone not a member of law enforcement, leave the building immediately.'

There was some grumbling as one of the uniformed officers herded the nosey neighbors out. When the floor was cleared, McQuillan walked towards the back. The minute he crossed the living room threshold, the stench hit him hard. For the second time that day, his stomach did a flip, and he once again regretted his choices from the night before. He reached into his pocket, pulled out a tiny jar of Vicks VapoRub and put a dab under his nose to camouflage the overpowering smell.

Nearing the back hall, he braced himself. He'd seen dead bodies before. Some cops took it in their stride, 'corpses were part of the job, not a big deal'. For McQuillan, every single time was awful. He was always mindful that the victim wasn't just a lifeless body. Somebody once loved them. Sometimes they looked like they were only sleeping, but other times it was gut wrenching. It was especially bad if they were young. The condition of a body depended on a couple of things; how long before it was found and the weather. Natural chemical decomposition mixed with heat and humidity made a potent combination. Together, they did terrible things to human flesh.

He took a deep breath and held it while he turned the knob on the bedroom door and opened it. Scanning the contents of the room, he was forced to inhale again, and the putrid stink made him cough.

The dead woman was on the floor next to the bed, covered by a white knit blanket. Her shoulder-length black hair cascaded around her face obscuring most of it. He made a mental note of the position of the body. It struck him as odd. Hundreds of pills and dozens of prescription bottles littered the floor. His nose and twenty-five years on the beat told him she'd been dead for a few days.

He pulled out his little black book and a pen and drank in the scene. It was an ordinary woman's bedroom and it was a mess; bottles tipped over, magazines, newspapers and mail scattered about the room. The windows were shut tight, curtains and blinds akimbo. There were photographs in frames, maybe of her kids, in every corner of the room. The top of the white dresser was covered with cosmetics, jewelry, hairbrushes, and other assorted girl junk. Shoes and clothes were strewn across the floor.

A clear liquid pooled on the wood floor in the corner of the room. McQuillan dipped his finger into it and smelled his hand. The all-encompassing odor already in the room made it difficult for him to tell what it was. He guessed it might be urine. A small pile of vomit lay on the white rug near the body. He wondered if the dead woman puked after she took a handful of pills. Maybe it wasn't suicide, he thought, it could have been an accidental overdose. He hoped that was what it was, for her family's sake.

He needed some fresh air pronto and went back into the living room to fill his lungs. A police tech team was bagging samples while the photographer snapped pictures.

'You called it a suicide,' McQuillan said to the landlady, who was still standing by the front door.

'Her friend told me my tenant threatened to kill herself,' said the landlady. 'That's the only reason I came over here. I don't barge in on my tenants. When you pay Joan Hemmerly your rent, you get your privacy.'

'Everything gets labeled and bagged,' he shouted over the landlady's shoulder to one of the lab technicians. 'Make sure you get a sample of that liquid on the floor in the bedroom and the puke on the rug.'

McQuillan scratched his ears as Yancy and another uniformed cop approached.

'I've been doing this a long time,' he said to the two young cops. 'This place is hinky. How many people were in here today? Was anything moved?'

Yancy began to stammer. 'W-well,' he said, squirming as he read from his notebook, 'there were the landlady, her son, the son's friend, the dog, the victim's friend, Ms. DeMarco, the downstairs neighbors; a Mr. Jenkins and a Mr. and Mrs. Rubin. Also, a middle-aged couple who lives down the street and three men who live next door stopped in. The mailman came in to deliver mail, but only for a minute.'

McQuillan felt his blood pressure rise. His head started to ache as if someone had jammed an ice pick in his skull above his right eye.

'See that old guy over there,' Yancy said, oblivious to the effect his comments were having on the older detective. 'He might have gone into the bedroom and put a blanket over the victim's body. He also might have moved her arms a little.'

McQuillan, mouth open, stared in disbelief at the incompetence of the young officer.

'It seemed like a clear case of suicide, McQ, so I wasn't that concerned about people being in here,' said Yancy.

'You weren't that *concerned*?' McQuillan said, his volume increasing. 'It's not your fucking job to decide that. Your only job was to secure this goddamn apartment and wait for me.'

'I didn't think I needed to…'

'It's a crime scene, Yancy, until I say it isn't,' said McQuillan, peering out the window at the flashing police car below. 'And turn your goddamn lights off when you get out of your car. Half of Monroe County is standing outside because of your vehicle.'

Yancy's face turned bright red, and he abruptly turned and left the apartment.

McQuillan pushed Yancy's monumental screw-up out of his mind in order to focus on the situation at hand. Given the relative orderliness of the home, the vast number of pills and all the corroborating statements, McQuillan conceded, it looked like suicide. Still, he had to be sure. Never assume anything, he reminded himself. Assumptions are for amateurs. He checked around for signs of a forced entry and found everything secured.

An attendant wheeled a gurney through the living room while two other techs prepared to bag the body. The photographer took a few final shots as a red-faced Yancy returned to the scene.

'The first rule of police work,' McQuillan said, leaning over to the young officer, 'secure the premises.' Yancy nodded wearily, tired of McQuillan's endless lecture. The detective knew the kid was pissed off, but he didn't care. He wasn't running a kindergarten, and he couldn't tolerate stupid, lazy or sloppy. Yancy had been guilty of all three.

Moving downstairs and out to the front lawn, McQuillan fielded questions from over fifty visibly rattled residents. After the Q&A, he talked to the landlady's son who told him he had been inside Ms. Roberts' apartment a few times to fix things. The seasoned cop sized the son up pretty quickly; the kid was strange and not the brightest bulb. Something about Hemmerly made the detective uneasy, but he couldn't put his finger on what it was.

Back in the bedroom, Yancy sorted through piles of papers.

'Crack a window,' said McQuillan as he entered the room. 'Suicide note?'

Yancy shook his head.

'Nothing,' the young cop said as he surveyed the room. 'Look at all this crap. This lady must have been a hoarder or something.'

McQuillan took a final pass through the apartment while he analyzed what they had learned about Quinn Roberts. She had been found lying in a sea of multi-colored capsules. She had a history of significant mental health issues, possible bipolar diagnosis, including hospitalisations and threats of killing herself. The conclusion — her death was probably self-inflicted. But if it wasn't, he was royally screwed. The DA would never take the case to a grand jury once they learned half the neighborhood had been traipsing around an unsecured apartment.

The dark gray zippered body bag containing Quinn Roberts was wheeled out of the bedroom on the gurney, carried carefully down the stairs and then moved out to the street.

'Look,' the detective said, turning back to Yancy, who was still licking his wounds, 'it was most likely a suicide, but you never make decisions based on first impressions. Everything stays on the table until it's ruled out. If I've learned one thing from my two and a half decades on the force, you never know what the surprises are until you're surprised. Then it's too late. That's why you have to do everything by the book. And if you don't, you'd better CYFA; cover your fucking ass. Did you cover your ass, Yancy?'

The young officer hung his head in silence.

'Yeah, that's what I figured,' said the detective as he walked away.

Chapter Five

Viv walked out of the small apartment building, slumped into the front seat of her car and shut the door. Tears flooded into her eyes as she asked herself if she could have done more. Could she have prevented what happened?

When Quinn first talked about killing herself, Viv and their other friends, Kelly, Margo and Nina went into panic mode. Each woman separately tried to reason with Quinn; they'd cajole or prop her up when she was down. Keeping their friend alive became a full-time job for all of them. Some days Quinn was buoyant and rational. But there were times, as Nina would often say behind her back, 'Quinn was a train wreck'. The girls did what they could, but when Quinn spiraled downward and became increasingly needy, their own lives took precedence and they pulled away. It might have been out of self-preservation, or maybe they got tired of being her keeper. When Quinn moved forty minutes away to Newbridge, her 'friends' rarely saw her and kept in touch only by phone. Over time, even the supportive calls diminished.

Viv blew her nose and punched Kelly's number into her phone. She started to sob again when her friend answered, spitting out a string of nonsensical words.

'Slow down, Viv, I don't understand a word you're saying,' Kelly said. 'Start over. What happened?'

'It's so awful,' said Viv, hyperventilating. 'Quinn's dead. She overdosed on pills.'

'Are you sure? Did you see her?'

'Not exactly,' Viv said. 'The landlady went into her room. She found Quinn on the floor in the bedroom. I couldn't go in, I just couldn't.'

'She finally did it,' said Kelly. 'She always said she would. Her poor kids. Do they know?'

'No,' said Viv. 'I mean, I don't think so, it just happened. We should have done more.'

'What could we have done, Viv?' said Kelly, her voice getting louder. 'We called her when we could. You know as well as I do that she didn't listen to any of us. She was on a self-destructive path. We did everything friends could do.'

'The last time I talked to her was three weeks ago,' said Viv, sniffling. 'Her divorce was moving forward, and she was in a pretty good mood. She even called Alec a "dickhead" so I knew she was feeling stronger. Her lawyer was finalizing the financial terms, and she said they were close to wrapping things up.'

'She told me that too,' said Kelly. 'She wanted to fix up her new apartment and take some classes at the community center. She said she wanted to learn how to blow glass.'

The last comment made both girls giggle for a second.

'Quinn could be so random,' said Viv, laughing and crying at the same time. 'I really thought she had turned a corner. We should have paid more attention to her.'

'Are you forgetting all the fire drills she put us through?' said Kelly. 'Let's be honest, Quinn had become a huge burden for all of us. We have our own families to take care of. Don't forget, we're the ones who got her to go to a therapist and get on medication. And we helped her move into two other apartments before this one. Something was always wrong with Quinn. We were good friends to her. I have no guilt.'

'Remember that time we all met for lunch and she told us her pills were making her fat? She said they made her feel like crap and announced she was going off them for good,' Viv said.

'That's when she started playing pharmacist, mixing up pills instead of what the doctors prescribed,' said Kelly. 'We never knew what version of Quinn we were going to get after that; happy and feisty or suicidal and depressed. None of this is our fault.'

'You're right,' said Viv, fighting back tears. 'We *were* good friends to her. We did try to help her all the time, didn't we? It wasn't our job to fix her. She had her own family. It wasn't our responsibility. Still, it's really sad. I'm going to miss that crazy girl.'

Chapter Six
QUINN

I got to know a bunch of moms in Avon, and we formed a little 'party posse'. Those girls filled the gaping hole created years before when I had to leave my own sisters and friends back in New Jersey, another sacrifice I made.

As our kids grew older and required less hands-on mom attention, this group of Avon women invited me to join their book club. We met once a month at one person's house for wine, cheese and gossip. After a few years, we moved the meetings to a local bar. Eventually, we did away with the literary component entirely and rebranded our meetings, 'Avon Ladies' Night Out'. Monthly book club turned into a weekly party night, and the Avon Ladies knew how to rock it. Those girls were my salvation, for a while.

Considering all the nights out we spent together, their lack of interest in my death and finding out what happened has been surprising and a huge disappointment. For seven years, I spent nearly every Wednesday night with those four women and regarded them as my closest friends. They had opinions on everything and let you know it. That was one of the reasons I liked them so much. Viv, Margot, Nina, and Kelly. We had each other's backs. Didn't we?

Now, it appears they didn't have my back at all. Not even Viv, who was never afraid to tell you where she stood on any issue. They all got busy with their own stuff right away. I get it, people have to get on with their lives, but these women moved on within days of me going into the ground. Not one of them called my husband, sisters, or the police. They never tried to find out what happened to me. Once, Viv texted my sister, Erin. One text hardly counts.

When my family put up a Facebook memorial page, the Avon Ladies all joined. Occasionally, they'd write platitudes about how much they missed me and how much they loved me and 'what a beautiful person' I am – was. Whenever my sister posted a new picture of me, the Avon Ladies would 'like' it or post a little crying emoji. In my opinion, Facebook words are cheap and emojis even cheaper. A little sad face isn't going to find out why I died. How about using your outside voices to make some noise, ladies? I've seen all of you start a riot when you thought your wine glasses hadn't been filled up enough. How about raising a little hell to find out what happened to me? How about that, bitches?

Chapter Seven

Detective McQuillan called the coroner to let him know a body was on its way over and he needed an autopsy, fast.

'McQ,' said a weary Dr. Metz, 'You're killing me. My son is playing in a soccer game this afternoon. It's the finals. I was going to leave early. Can it wait until tomorrow?'

'Unfortunately, Doc, it can't,' the detective said. 'We've got a situation, and I need to know what I'm dealing with.' Metz sighed and said he'd stay. A few hours later, he called McQuillan.

'According to your police report,' said Dr. Metz, 'the deceased kept her apartment very cold and used multiple dehumidifiers because of a mold problem. The cold condition in the apartment, combined with closed windows and doors and multiple dehumidifiers could possibly slow decomposition. Makes time of death harder to pinpoint. It may have happened much earlier than we thought. Or not. Hard to tell.'

'So how many days are we talking about?'

'Don't know exactly, we have a swing time of somewhere between three and five days,' the coroner said. 'From the looks of her, rigor mortis set in several days ago.'

'Several days? That's a big time window, Doc,' said McQuillan.

'Also, something funny, her right arm was frozen in an odd position not consistent with the police notes and pictures. I made a memo to myself to ask you if the body had been moved.'

'Unfortunately, that would be a yes, Doc,' McQuillan said, getting angry at Yancy all over again. 'Apparently, one of her neighbors moved her arm and covered her up.'

'That explains it,' said the coroner. 'Here's what I've got. The deceased was a forty-four-year-old female who otherwise appeared to be in good physical health.'

'So, it was either an accidental overdose or a suicide?' McQuillan said.

'I didn't say that,' said Dr. Metz. 'Blotches in her eyes and on her face told me she didn't die from a drug overdose. I checked her vertebrae and windpipe and confirmed my suspicions. This woman didn't commit suicide or accidentally take too many pills. Someone strangled her. Quinn Roberts was choked to death. The lady was murdered.'

'Shit,' said the detective as he hung up the phone. He walked upstairs to the forensics lab. The big open room was buzzing like a beehive with half a dozen officers working silently on computers. This was where all the evidence was examined, parsed, re-examined and eventually labeled and sent to storage. McQuillan tapped one of the guys on the shoulder.

'Branson, you cataloguing the stuff we collected this morning from Brookside?' he asked. The officer nodded.

'We've got a little wrinkle,' said McQuillan. 'Just heard from Metz. Not suicide. The lady was murdered.'

'No shit,' said Branson. 'You're kidding? We were only focused on evidence to support suicide.'

'I know. Now, I need you to take a team back over to Brookside and do another sweep, tonight,' McQuillan said. 'Every surface gets swabbed again. Every follicle collected. Every speck of paper bagged. And, Branson, no one besides police enters the place. Clear?'

Branson was already on his feet.

'Open up every book and magazine and shake them out. Maybe the lady kept a diary or a calendar,' the detective said. 'We need to catch a break. Right now, we've got a mess.'

Chapter Eight
QUINN

I'm pretty sure it was the baby thing that made me fall for my husband. We met on one of those gorgeous, warm, sunny spring days where temperatures were well above normal for New Jersey in May. The guy on the news predicted it might go over eighty and, for once, he was right. The sudden break from the cold and rainy spring threw us head first into summer, and everyone was in a good mood.

It was nearly four o'clock when the wedding guests arrived for the cocktail hour. They were ravenous and practically feral. I straightened my gray and white waitress uniform and pushed open the door from the kitchen with one arm while balancing a huge silver tray of jumbo-sized shrimp cocktail with the other. All eyes were on me as I made the twenty-yard walk towards the hungry crowd. In seconds I was surrounded by 'food paparazzi', and my tray was picked clean. With the appetizers gone, my popularity vanished as quickly as it had come. I turned to go back to the kitchen to refill my tray and start the dance all over again. On my way, I passed another waitress heading out to the crowd carrying a full plate of little hot dogs.

'Be careful out there,' I yelled with a laugh, 'or you'll lose a hand. You'd think all those people had never eaten before.'

As I got closer to the kitchen, the intoxicating salty smell of pigs in blankets heating in the oven surrounded me. That's when I met Alec for the first time. I couldn't see his face, but from behind, I could tell he was tall and kind of skinny, with thick black hair and tan skin. I had never seen him before.

'Hey, new guy,' I said, 'I need a refill, pronto.'

He turned around slowly. A single shrimp stuck out of each of his ears and two more protruded from his nostrils curling upwards. He looked like he had a pink handlebar moustache and hoop earrings. I'm not sure if it was the fish in his nose, the deadpan expression on his face or what he said that cracked me up the most.

'Bond, James Bond,' he said with a straight face.

I laughed so hard I nearly fell over and dropped my tray on the floor. Who was this crazy guy?

When the reception was over, we cleaned and packed up the equipment. I walked with some of the other kids to the parking lot, and suddenly Alec was right beside me. One by one the other servers got in their cars and left, but Alec and I continued talking for two more hours. I noticed he wasn't half bad-looking, now that he had no shellfish on his face. Not classically handsome, but there was something exotic and kind of cute about him. And he made me laugh, hard.

We talked about the bride, the groom and the wedding we had just worked – shop talk.

'When I get married,' he announced, 'I'm going to have a have a house full of kids. I'd like at least five, maybe six.'

I'm not going to lie; that comment was like catnip for me. A young guy wanting kids was like finding a unicorn. Most of the college guys I knew were busy partying and hanging out with their bros. If you asked them what their future looked like, none of them would have mentioned children. But he did, and I was hooked.

We dated until we graduated from college and got married the following fall. We had a formal wedding mass at St. Gabriel's. My older sister, Erin, was maid of honor. My younger sister, Colleen, and my best friend, Liza, were my bridesmaids. They were all dressed in blue, to match my eyes. The reception was at the best country club in town, in a room filled with cascades of white roses. We had champagne toasts and three choices of entrée. The eight-piece band played the entire night, and people danced until after one in the morning. We were both twenty-two and madly in love. Was I too young? Maybe, but I didn't think so at the time. Now, if my daughter, Hannah, told me she wanted to get married at twenty-two, I would be completely against it. Do what I say, not what I do.

Alec treated me like a queen, like the Quinntessa I was meant to be. I could do no wrong. I was perfect. Maybe that should have been my clue but I liked being up there on that pedestal, it was nice, it felt good. I didn't see any of it then. Maybe I didn't want to.

Chapter Nine

Sitting in the back seat of Grandpa George's car as it sped along the highway, Hannah was vaguely aware her grandmother was talking but couldn't process a word she said. Every few minutes the older woman would tear up, reach for another tissue and ask her granddaughter if she wanted one. Hannah didn't. She had no tears. She was numb.

'I don't know how this could have happened,' said Grandma Linda, her voice breaking. 'This doesn't happen to people like us. Your poor mother. Dear, sweet Quinn. It's all so awful.'

'You doing okay back there, Hannah?' her grandfather asked, looking at his granddaughter in the rear-view mirror.

Hannah couldn't answer. She couldn't find where her voice was and only nodded her head. She wasn't doing okay. She wasn't even in her own body.

Two hours earlier, she had been in her dorm room painting her toenails orange. She and her roommate, Meredith, had been getting ready for an off-campus party at one of the frat houses. Meredith had put an avocado mask on her face and was doing a yoga pose when the Resident Advisor from their floor softly knocked on their door. Whenever the RA showed up, it was usually because Hannah and Meredith were up to no good; playing their music too loud or the hallway outside their room smelled of weed even though the girls had shoved towels under the door saddle, opened the windows and turned on their fans. Hearing the RA's voice when they weren't committing a crime took them by surprise.

'Hannah, you in there?' said the RA as she turned the knob slowly and walked in. Hannah noticed immediately that the student leader had a strange look on her face.

'There are some people here who need to speak with you,' she said.

Grandma Linda and Grandpa George stepped awkwardly into the small dorm room. A police officer was behind them waiting in the hall. Grandma Linda's eyes were red. Without speaking, her grandmother gave Hannah a hug.

'What's going on?' asked Hannah.

Grandma Linda started to cry. That was the cue for Hannah's roommate. She grabbed a towel, wiped the green mask off her face and left the room.

'Why are you here?' Hannah said, starting to panic. 'Did something happen to Dad? Did he have a heart attack?'

Then they told her. Her mother was dead.

'No, she's not,' said Hannah. 'My mother's not dead. I would know if she was.'

Hannah's mind sifted through a million thoughts. Mom had been depressed. Sometimes she talked about killing herself, but she wouldn't have done it. She was just sad and wanted attention. *She wouldn't have left me. She loved me. My mother would never leave me. I know that for sure.*

'Hannah, there's more,' said her grandfather, taking her hand. 'The police think someone killed your mother, that maybe someone bad got into her apartment somehow. Might have been a drug addict looking for money or something like that. We don't know yet.'

Hannah stared at her grandparents. None of what they said made sense. She was sure her mother wasn't dead.

'Where's Dad?' Hannah asked. 'Why didn't Dad come?'

'He went to get Jack,' Grandma said. 'We're here to bring you home. Your father and brother are going to meet us at our house.'

The police officer asked Hannah a few questions as they walked to the parking lot. Later, she had no memory of what he had asked her or what her answers were.

The hour drive back to Avon wasn't long or short. Hannah had no sense of time or her surroundings. She repeatedly tried calling her mother's phone, but it only went to voicemail. When her mother answered, Hannah would prove to her grandparents that they were wrong.

As the car sped along the highway, Hannah stared out the window trying to make sense of it all. She needed to see her brother, Jack. He would straighten everything out, she told herself. My grandparents are wrong. They're old and confused and they never liked my mother.

Chapter Ten

He didn't want anyone to touch him but people kept hugging him. He wanted to be left alone and go to sleep and stay asleep, forever. Everything around him was spinning out of control. Jack Roberts couldn't feel his torso, arms or legs. He was just a giant head filled with horrible thoughts.

They told him his mother was dead. He felt a mixture of grief and relief. Sometimes he hated her, but she was still his mother. He had said some mean things to her, and now he couldn't take them back. He wished he could do things over. *Let it be yesterday, Mom was still alive; crazy, but breathing.*

In one day, his whole life had changed. His father had showed up unannounced at his college apartment just as he was coming back from lacrosse practice. He was carrying his sticks and a gym bag when he saw his father standing in front of his building talking to his roommate. When Jack approached, his roommate punched his arm gently and walked away.

'What's going on?' Jack asked. 'What are you doing here?'

'Let's go inside, Jack,' his father said.

'What's happening?' Jack asked again as he closed his apartment door. Then his whole life blew up.

His father said, 'something bad had happened' and 'he was there to take him home'. Grandma Linda and Grandpa had gone to get Hannah.

'I'm just going to say it, Jack, because there's no way to sugar-coat this. Your mother's dead.'

'No, she's not. She wouldn't have done that. I know her,' said Jack. 'She just wanted attention.'

'You don't understand. The police don't think it was suicide. Someone killed your mother. I don't know much more than that. We have to go to Newbridge later and talk to the cops,' said his father. 'I promise you, Jack, we're going to find out who did this.'

'Why do they want to talk to me?' Jack asked. 'I don't know anything.'

'Of course, you don't,' his father said. 'Neither do I. They talk to everyone. That's the way it works.'

His father's girlfriend, Alison, was waiting in the front seat of the car. She got out and gave Jack a hug, and they started for home. The rest of the ride was a blur.

In the back seat by himself, he looked out the window as the world streaked by. His father didn't say much during the trip back to Avon. Jack's face and shirt collar were wet from the constant stream of tears. He wanted it to be last week when his mother was alive, and everything was normal – or at least, normal for them. Nobody was in trouble, nobody was dead. He looked at the back of his father's head. Was it his imagination or did his father not seem that upset? Dad didn't look like he had even cried. That pissed Jack off. He needed to be mad at someone, and decided it might as well be his father.

'You act like you don't give a shit that Mom is dead,' Jack blurted out from the back seat.

'That's unfair,' Alec said, taking his eyes off the road for a second to look at his son in the mirror. 'Your mother and I were getting divorced, but you know I still cared about her. We just went in different directions. It happens. That's life.'

'That's bull,' Jack said. 'The minute she got sick you bailed on her. You might be able to fool everyone else, but I know the real truth, not the shit you spin.'

'Hey, I don't need this kind of crap from you right now,' his father said, raising his voice. 'I'm going to let it go because I know you're in shock.'

The remainder of the ride was in stony silence. When they arrived at his grandparents' house, several cars were parked out front on the street. Grandpa George's car was in the driveway. That meant Hannah was inside and Jack wanted to see his sister more than anyone. She was the only person in the world who knew exactly how he felt.

When he entered the house, he was surrounded by teary faces and arms that wrapped themselves around him like vines. It didn't register who the arms belonged to, and they kept coming, touching him, engulfing him. He didn't deserve their love. Every touch felt like a burn. He only wanted to see his sister. He spotted Hannah standing in the kitchen, leaning against a wall looking the same way he felt. Their eyes locked and he went over to her. They hugged and sobbed for a long time. Her touch was the only one that felt right.

'We're going to find out who killed Mom, Han,' Jack said to his sister. 'I promise.'

'I just want her back,' Hannah said through her tears. 'I want Mommy.'

A few hours later, Alec and Jack walked into the red brick building that was home of the Newbridge Police Department. An officer ushered them into separate rooms. A lanky homicide detective in his forties introduced himself to Jack as Detective Crews, one of lead detectives assigned to Quinn's case. He told the kid he was sorry for his loss. Yeah, okay, whatever, thought Jack, save it.

Crews asked him a bunch of basic questions like his name, age and address. Then there were a whole lot of questions about where Jack had been over the past week and how he got along with his mother.

'My mother hadn't been well. She had good days and bad,' he said. 'Sometimes she embarrassed me when she'd drive up to my campus and wander around saying crazy shit. I'd get mad at her, but I still loved her.'

'How long ago did your father and mother separate?' the detective asked. 'Did they get along? Your mother ever express concerns about your father?'

'My dad can be a pontificating jerk,' said Jack, 'but he wouldn't kill anyone. He's a talker, a college professor with a PhD in History. He rebuilds antique cars, takes pictures of butterflies and has a vegetable garden in our backyard with a compost pile. He grows tomatoes and zucchini. Give my father a minute, and he'll give you a thesis on almost any subject. He can be annoying and suck all the air out of a room, but he wouldn't kill my mother. He would never do something like that.'

Jack answered all of the detective's questions, mindful of how his answers sounded. His father could be an asshole, but he was still his father and the only parent he had left.

He didn't dare mention the times his mother was off her meds, and his father screamed at her and locked her out of the house. Sometimes, Jack thought, when she was like that, she kind of brought it on herself. His mother knew exactly how to push his father's buttons. His father didn't know what else to do but lock her out when she got crazy and combative. He and Hannah used to hear them fight from their bedrooms.

Jack knew he probably should have gone in and helped his mother, but he never did. He didn't want to get in the middle of whatever was going on. He just shut his bedroom door, turned up his music and closed his eyes.

Chapter Eleven
QUINN

Six months after my wedding, surprise... I was pregnant. Sure, it was sooner than we had planned, and maybe I wasn't so careful with my birth control. Maybe I 'accidentally on purpose' forgot to take my pill for a few months. Alec and I had agreed we'd wait for three years before having a baby. That seemed like an awfully long time to me. The plan was, I was supposed to work while he went to grad school. He wanted to get his masters and then his PhD in History and teach at a university. He had big plans, but I had my own ideas.

The arrival of our son, Jack, changed everything. Alec wound up going to grad school at night so he could work during the day and I could stay home and take care of our baby. It took him a little longer to get his degree, but it was worth it because we had our beautiful son. A year later, our daughter, Hannah, arrived. Oops, again.

Before Hannah was born, Alec received an offer to teach at Pondfield College which was just outside of Rochester. More than six hours by car from all my family and friends in New Jersey, I had to leave everything I knew to be a supportive wife. We packed up and moved to a small community called Avon. Alec promised we'd return to New Jersey within a year.

Why do I only have two kids if I wanted tons of babies so badly? There were complications during Hannah's birth. There was a C-section, lots of blood, detached uterus. Hysterectomy. The doctors said it couldn't be helped. I found out I couldn't have any more children moments after they placed my new baby girl in my arms. For weeks, I was depressed. What's that saying? When life gives you lemons, make lemonade. I decided to focus on the two kids I had and be the world's best mother possible.

I baked and sewed, volunteered at their schools and put a homemade hot meal on the table every night. Dinner was always ready right after Alec arrived home and we ate together as a family. That was important to me, to us. The kids' Halloween costumes were made from scratch. I taught them how to ice skate and ski in the winter and in the summer, I took them on nature walks in the woods pointing out plants, trees, and birds. And, of course, I sang to them from the minute they were born. My kids were mostly happy, and I was proud and fulfilled being their mother until things started to change.

Chapter Twelve

Erin Delaney Danzi was taking an afternoon nap when her husband, Mike, turned on the lights in the bedroom and gently woke her up. She looked over at the clock.

'Why are you waking me up now?' she said, confused and annoyed her sleep had been disrupted. 'I could have slept for a few more minutes.'

'I need to talk to you, sit up,' Mike said.

Something registered in a remote part of Erin's brain that her husband looked funny. Something was wrong.

Before he could speak, Mike started to cry. He tried to get the words out, but they kept catching in his throat.

'Mike, you're freaking me out, what's going on?'

'There's no good way to say this,' he said, his voice cracking. 'Quinn is dead.'

Something hard hit her stomach and knocked all the air out of Erin's lungs. She couldn't breathe and started to fall over as her husband caught her. They had been dreading something like this for close to a year. Quinn went up and down, and when she was down, it was almost impossible to reach her. Once, Erin even called some radio psychologists to see if they had any answers. They didn't and now, it didn't matter.

'She finally got her way,' said Erin, as tears rolled down her cheeks. 'My sister said she was going to kill herself all the time, but I thought she just wanted attention. I didn't think she would really do it.'

'Her landlady found her,' Mike continued.

'She didn't use a gun, did she?'

There was a long pause as Mike silently cried and stared at his wife.

'Quinn didn't commit suicide, Erin. She was murdered.'

It took Erin nearly a full minute to respond to the new information. The initial shock of learning her sister was dead was devastating, but murder took it to a whole new level. Murder happens in the movies, she thought, not to my family, not to Quinn.

'How did she die?' Erin asked barely able to get the words out between sobs.

'The police think someone strangled her.'

Chapter Thirteen

QUINN

Erin, why can't you hear me? I'm right next to you screaming into your ear. I'm here! Promise you'll look after my kids. Watch out for them and for Alec. He's hurting, too. He was still my husband, and I didn't tell you this, but he was seriously thinking about the two of us getting back together. I was planning to surprise him and cook him his favorite dinner to celebrate his birthday. I think everything was going to be okay between us and we'd go back to the way it used to be.

I don't know where I am, Erin. I see people, but no one sees or hears me. Sometimes, I find myself at the playground, the one we used to go to when we were little, down the street from Mom and Dad's. I like to go on the swings because it feels good. I'm not sure why; maybe because it's familiar. Back and forth, up and down. Like flying. Remember, Erin, how we used to swing for hours? We'd try to see who could go the highest? We soared like birds, remember? We always went higher than everyone else.

There are others like me here at the playground. They go on the swings, too. We each wait for our turn. When you see empty swings moving by themselves, it's not the wind. It's us trying to fly up to the sky.

Chapter Fourteen

When McQuillan arrived at work the next morning, he knew they had to scramble. Precious time had been wasted documenting a suicide and now that the tables had turned, they were a full day behind the eight-ball. Statistically, there was a far better chance of catching a killer within the first seventy-two hours of the crime. After that, each day that passed, each hour even, made solving it more unlikely.

He called the Chief and apprised him of the new development and officially moved the suicide over to homicide on the war room whiteboards. His team would have to pull an all-nighter to play catch-up on the investigation. From a preliminary phone interview with the victim's brother-in-law, Mike Danzi, McQuillan learned that Quinn Roberts and her husband had been in the middle of a contentious divorce. When it came to murder of a woman, ninety-six percent of the time, it was the husband or the boyfriend who was good for it. Of course, there was still the possibility that the son could have been involved or a yet to be identified stranger. They had to rule everyone out. McQuillan had one, and only one, objective that day: he had to get the husband to talk and rule him in or out. If it wasn't the husband, he and his team needed to get busy real fast.

Six hours later, Alec Roberts was seated in one of the police interview rooms. A cold cup of coffee sat on the table in front of him. He appeared relaxed, like he was waiting for a movie to start. McQuillan peered at him through the video monitor down the hall and then walked briskly down the corridor to meet Roberts in person. After five minutes in the same room with the victim's husband, McQuillan had formed his opinion. He had seen

Roberts' type before but had to remind himself that just because the guy was an asshole, didn't mean he was a killer.

Gaining Alec Roberts' confidence was critical. The detective let Roberts think he was on his side and offered just the right amount of support and sympathy. If Roberts was guilty, his own arrogance would do the detective's work for him. Perps always forgot that cops interrogated criminals for a living. Detectives did it every day, all day, and they were good at it. Alec Roberts, on the other hand, had probably never been interrogated by a police officer in his life. The professor was in uncharted waters but so convinced of his own intellect, he didn't know his ship was way off course.

'Mr. Roberts,' McQuillan said. 'Where were you last week?'

'It's Dr. Roberts,' Alec replied. 'I have a PhD in History.'

'My mistake, Doctor. May I call you Alex?'

'It's Alec, with a "c", not an "x",' he said.

'My apologies again,' McQuillan said, looking down at his papers. 'Got it, Alec, with a "c".'

'It's okay, officer, everyone makes mistakes,' said Alec.

McQuillan's inner cop radar was blinking red, and his ears were hot and itchy.

'So, Alec,' McQuillan said, with an emphasis on the 'c', 'let's start with where you were last Monday.'

'It's always the husband, isn't it, Detective?' Alec said. 'You can be more imaginative than that.'

Piss me off a little more, you arrogant little jerk, thought McQuillan, and I'll nail you to the wall.

'You're not a suspect,' McQuillan said politely. 'We're talking to everyone. It's extremely early in the investigation. You want to find out who killed your wife. My job is to get all the facts and eliminate people, so we can find your wife's killer and put him or her in jail.'

'I know how this goes,' Alec said, still smiling. 'Let me save you some time, Detective. I didn't touch my wife. If you're acting all chummy with me hoping I'll confess to something, you're going to be waiting a long time.'

'Is there something you want to confess?' McQuillan asked.

'My wife and I were getting divorced, that's no secret,' Alec said. 'We didn't live together any more. I don't know what happened to her. I haven't seen her in months.'

'Let me go back to my original question,' McQuillan said. 'Where were you last Monday?'

Alec stared at the detective with cold, dark eyes and smirked.

'Where I am every Monday; at the University of Rochester.'

'UR? My older sister went to UR,' McQuillan said, 'but before your time, good school.'

'Yes, it is.'

'There would be people who could confirm that you were teaching that whole day, correct?' McQuillan said.

'About two hundred. I have a full load of classes on Mondays,' Alec replied. 'I also chair the History department meeting every Monday at five.'

'Can you give me the names of some of those people?' McQuillan said, as he passed Alec a yellow legal pad and pen. Alec nodded and wrote down a few names and numbers. 'How about Monday night?' the detective asked. 'Where were you Monday night?'

'At my house,' Alec said. 'I usually stop in at LA Fitness on my way home from school and work out. I like to stay in shape, you know what I mean?'

'Oh yeah, that's very important,' McQuillan said, looking down at his own expanding gut hanging over his belt and promising himself he'd start working out again. 'Is that the LA Fitness near Avon?'

'I go to one near the university,' Alec replied.

'About what time did you leave LA Fitness on Monday? Did you go directly home?'

'My workout usually takes about ninety minutes,' Alec said. 'My department meeting went until a little before six, and I got to the gym by six fifteen. I worked out until about seven forty. Then I went directly home.'

'About what time did you arrive home?' McQuillan asked.

'I don't know. Maybe eight fifteen.'

'And then?'

'I watched a game,' he said. 'Monday night football.'

'I saw that too, good game.'

The police still didn't know the exact time or day Quinn Roberts had been killed. It could have been Sunday, Monday or even Tuesday. The wide window on time of death presented McQuillan with an unwieldy playing field.

'Did I forget to mention,' said Alec with a cocky expression on his face, 'my girlfriend, Alison Moore, was with me Monday night? We had lobsters.'

McQuillan wanted to slap the smug look off the professor's face but kept his cool and just nodded, making a note of the girlfriend's name, address, and phone number.

'Would Ms. Moore verify that?'

'Why wouldn't she?' Alec said, visibly proud of himself.

'Did you see anyone on Tuesday night?' McQuillan asked.

'Actually, I did,' Alec replied. 'First I went to the gym until about eight thirty. You can check the time clock at LA Fitness. Later, my girlfriend Alison came over. She stopped by to drop something off around nine thirty but only stayed about two hours.'

'She drove to your place late at night and then left? According to your written statement, you said she lives all the way over in Milford. That's a long drive late at night.'

'I left a work folder at her place and desperately needed it for an important presentation I had the next day. She offered to bring it to me.'

'She must be a nice person to make that long drive so late at night when I presume she also had to work the next day.'

'She is very nice, Detective, that's why she's my girlfriend. We usually get together only on weekends. For some reason, last week we saw each other every day,' said Alec, pausing to think for a moment. 'Guess that's lucky for me.'

'Very lucky. So, you're saying you were teaching each day and that Ms. Moore was with you every single night last week,' McQuillan continued.

'That's what I'm saying.'

The questioning went on for another hour. Alec thought he was running the table and the detective let him believe that. If McQuillan needed to stroke Alec to get him to crack, he'd gladly do it. No skin off his nose. That was how the game was played.

'Tell me how you felt about your wife.'

'You ever get divorced, Detective?'

'Yeah.'

'How did you feel about *your* wife?' he asked.

'She was a bitch.'

'Exactly,' he said, with a smile on his face.

He may have been in the middle of a divorce, thought McQuillan, but Alec Roberts was just too freaking cheerful, given that his wife and the mother of his kids had just been murdered. Something was off.

An hour and a half after their session started, Detective Jimmy Crews walked into the room. Crews, a division one guard back when he played college basketball, was tall, lanky and sharp as a tack. He and McQuillan had partnered on a lot of cases over the years and knew each other's every thought. It was apparent Crews had a chip on his shoulder when he sat down and introduced himself, spitting out a slew of insinuating questions in rapid fire. Alec's body language changed and he began to bristle.

'Hold on there, Detective,' McQuillan said. 'Dr. Roberts has been through a lot today, and so far, he's been extremely cooperative.'

'Sounds to me like you're stonewalling, Roberts,' said Crews. 'We don't have time to waste with bullshit. Every minute that passes, the killer gets further away.'

'You've got it all wrong. Dr. Roberts has provided a lot of good information.'

Alec's head cocked slightly, and there was a glimmer of recognition in his eyes. He smiled and began to clap slowly.

'I get it,' Roberts said. 'You're playing good cop,' he said, pointing at McQuillan, 'and you're the bad cop,' pointing at Crews. 'You're both quite good. Bravo. You missed your calling.'

The two detectives remained expressionless and kept their eyes fixed on Alec.

'Please, continue with your theatrical production. I can't wait to see how Act Two ends.'

'I'll tell you how it ends,' McQuillan said. 'Spoiler alert; the killer is arrested, tried and convicted then spends the rest of his life rotting in prison, no parole.'

'I hope that's exactly what happens, Detective. My wife didn't deserve this. No one does.'

The two detectives asked Alec if he would agree to take a lie detector test and let them do a DNA swab.

'Sure, I've got nothing to hide. If it helps rule me out and will get the police focused on finding my wife's killer, I'm happy to help in any way,' Alec said with a smile.

Aside from statistical data that overwhelmingly pointed to a significant other when it came to murder, Alec Robert's last comment was what signaled McQ's gut and told him the killer was probably sitting right in front of him. McQuillan moved Dr. Alec Roberts to the top of his list.

Within five minutes, a DNA technician had swabbed Alec's cheek and sent his sample to the lab. The lie detector session was scheduled for the following afternoon.

'Thank you for trying to find my wife's killer,' Alec said, shaking the detectives' hands. 'The sooner we can get all this behind us, the better. My kids are in bad shape. I'm sure you can understand. Now, it's got to be about my kids.'

As it turned out, Roberts didn't return the next day to take the lie detector test. He left the police station, lawyered up and never spoke to the cops again. Ever.

Chapter Fifteen

Riding in two cars, the Delaney family made the long drive from New Jersey to Avon, NY for the funeral of their sister, daughter, and friend, Quinn Marie Delaney Roberts. Meetings with the Newbridge police were to take place after the service. Erin and Colleen decided due to the nature of their sister's death that it was too traumatising to pull their kids out of college, so none of the cousins attended. Quinn's father, Ed, just plain refused to go.

'I don't need to stand in front of a wooden box to remember my daughter,' he said to his wife. 'She's in my heart. And I don't want to see him. I don't know what I'd do if I were in the same room with that son of a bitch.'

Eileen Delaney knew that guys from South Philly settled things with their fists. As much as she wanted her husband with her, she gave him the space to grieve on his own terms.

Quinn's mother and sister, Colleen, along with Colleen's husband were in one car. Mike, Erin and three of Quinn's high school friends, Cathy, Liza, and Molly were in the second. Each passenger clutched a damp wad of tissues while trying to make sense out of it all. They had six hours in the car to process that she was gone.

Mike's car was eerily quiet for the first thirty minutes with only sounds of sniffling and noses being blown. At one point, he turned on the radio to drown out the screaming silence and country rock music filled the car. After a few minutes, the festive nature of the songs felt wrong, given where they were going and why. He soon turned off the radio, and the car was painfully quiet again until Liza spoke up.

'Remember how much Quinn loved mustard?' she said suddenly to break the silence. A relieved group chuckle filled the car.

'Oh, my God,' said Cathy, laughing and crying at the same time, 'she was abnormally obsessed with mustard. She put it on everything. Celery, cookies, crackers, meat, apples, cheese. I once saw her put mustard on spaghetti and meatballs.'

'Ewww,' groaned the group as they laughed with tears in their eyes.

'Once when we were little, Quinn put mustard on her peanut butter and jelly sandwich,' Erin said, smiling.

'Ewww,' everyone chorused again.

Over the next few hours, they shared stories about Quinn, some funny, some sad. They had all lost something precious and took comfort in being together. Without saying anything, each person was aware that there was still a huge elephant in the car.

Halfway to Avon, the conversation lulled as everyone retreated into their own grief. They rode in silence until Mike blurted out loud what everyone had privately been thinking.

'We all know Alec did it, right? We agree, he killed Quinn.'

'We don't know that,' Erin said, hitting her husband on the arm and starting to cry again. 'I just lost my sister. I can't go there right now. I won't accept that my brother-in-law is responsible for her death. We've spent every Christmas with him for over twenty years. I'm reserving judgment until we talk to the police.'

'He locked her out of the house and cheated on her year after year. He screwed with her head every chance he had,' said Mike.

'I know,' Erin sobbed.

'He did everything he could to break her spirit,' said Mike, 'and keep all his money for himself.'

'Okay, you're right, he's a bastard,' Erin said. 'But it doesn't mean he killed her.'

'You think Quinn's life sucked so bad that when she finally got free of him, a total stranger randomly broke into her apartment and killed her?' asked Mike. 'You said yourself that she didn't know anyone in Newbridge, that she'd only been there a few months and spent most of her time with her lawyer and therapist. You even worried she had no friends there.'

'I know.'

'The police don't think she was robbed and there was no evidence of a sexual assault. You really think some random intruder broke in and killed her for the hell of it?' Mike said. 'That's a bridge too far for me, especially when you know Alec and Quinn's history.'

'I know it looks bad, but…' Erin said, starting to cry again.

'He's the only one with a motive,' Mike continued. 'He didn't want to pay her alimony, and like magic, now he doesn't have to. Convenient.'

Mike's sharp words rang true to everyone in the car. Quinn had told each of them separately that Alec had asked her to waive her rights to alimony and his pension, all the while trying to convince her that she was selfish for saddling him with spousal support. 'If you really love me,' Alec had said to her, 'you'd only take alimony for six months and then stand on your own two feet.'

'You're jumping to conclusions, we don't know anything yet,' Erin said to her husband.

'Let me line this up for you,' Mike continued. 'Quinn was hospitalized twice, had a documented mental illness and had been a stay-at-home mom for over twenty years. Her lawyer told her that any judge would order permanent alimony because of her medical condition. Alec went nuts when he heard that.'

'That's true. Quinn told me he was furious about the alimony,' Erin said.

'A few weeks later,' said Mike, 'Quinn ends up dead and Alec's financial problems miraculously disappear. Like I said, convenient.'

'He probably did it,' Erin said softly.

'Mike, do you really think Alec is capable of doing something like that?' Liza asked.

'He's a fucking psycho,' said Mike after a long pause.

Chapter Sixteen

One party you never want to be invited to is your murdered sister's funeral. Erin spoke to Quinn's kids the night before and let them know their mother's family was driving up from New Jersey in the morning. Erin had one mission. She wanted to put her arms around Jack and Hannah for her sister and let them know she would always be there, just like she had promised Quinn.

She asked Jack to arrange for the Delaneys to have some private time with Quinn before everyone else entered the room at the funeral home. Erin didn't want to face Alec while she said goodbye to her sister. Even if he hadn't killed her, he had treated her terribly while she was alive and Erin couldn't forgive that. They were to arrive twenty minutes early, and the funeral director would let them in.

The two Delaney vehicles pulled into the parking lot of the Barton Funeral Home. Over a hundred people waited outside for the doors to open. Most of them were young, college-aged kids who Erin assumed were friends of Hannah and Jack. Quinn's house had always been the 'hangout house' for all of Jack and Hannah's friends – until she got sick, then no one came around.

When Eileen Delaney got out of the car and took her first step, her legs gave out. Colleen caught her just in time and held her up. Erin raced over to her mother and quickly linked arms. She and Colleen walked their grieving mother slowly to the door of the funeral home, bypassing the waiting crowd. They were on the one VIP line you never want to be on.

Hannah and Jack stayed with their father on the opposite side of the parking lot while the group from New Jersey filed into the main receiving room. The large mourning space was filled with rows of empty chairs and numerous arrangements of flowers from friends and family. Big blown-up photos of Quinn were scattered around the room on metal easels. A light wood closed casket was situated at the far end of the room.

Erin looked at the pictures of her sister. One was of Quinn hiking in the woods, sun on her face, not a stitch of make-up, young, healthy, beautiful. Another was of Quinn playing her ukulele, mouth open, strumming in front of the Christmas tree, entertaining the whole family. Erin remembered everyone had been so happy that day. She could still hear her sister singing off-key, and it made her smile. Across the room was a portrait of a radiant Quinn in her wedding gown. A lump the size of a golf ball lodged in Erin's throat as she looked at the beautiful images of her baby sister. Her stomach ached, her body temperature was high, she was sweating, but somehow, she was freezing. Her heart pounded in her chest, and her ears were ringing. Every part of her ached, and her legs felt like they were going to collapse underneath her. For a terrifying moment, she thought she was having a panic attack and then she realized what it was. Grief. To calm herself, she took a few deep cleansing breaths. Keep it together, Erin, she told herself.

A giant picture of a smiling Quinn and Alec on their wedding day hung at the back of the room. Seeing that image of marital bliss infuriated Erin. Alec was mocking her sister's memory. That picture made it look like they had a loving relationship. Erin wanted to rip it down and tear the image into a thousand pieces. She glanced out the window at Alec in the parking lot talking with her niece and nephew. He should be in that wooden box, instead of Quinn, she thought. It should have been him.

Erin kept her eyes from going to one place in the room. She couldn't look over at the casket. *My little sister is inside that wooden box, and I am here for her funeral.* It was surreal. Erin's attention shifted as a commotion was heard across the room when Eileen Delaney became hysterical. Seeing her mother fall apart set Erin off and she sobbed uncontrollably and lost her balance. Standing next to her, Mike quickly put his arms around his wife and held her up. Colleen and her husband took their mother to a seat in the back of the room to calm down. They only had a few more minutes before the doors would open for everyone.

'Let's go say our goodbyes to your sister,' said Mike to his wife. The two of them walked stoically towards the casket and knelt down in front of it. Liza, Cathy, and Molly followed and stood behind them as they all cried and prayed together. Erin questioned her own faith for the first time, screaming at God from inside her head. *Why did you take her? Why is my sister dead?*

A moment later, the funeral director whispered in Mike's ear. Mike nodded.

'It's time. They're letting them in,' Mike said gently to his wife.

Erin braced herself as people quietly filed in and a long line formed, snaking out the front door and around the building. A moment later, there was a crowd by the entrance as Jack, Hannah and Alec, followed by Alec's parents and his brother and his wife, entered and walked up to the casket.

The Delaneys watched the Roberts family each take their turns on the kneeler. As Alec knelt, Erin examined the back of her brother-in-law's head. His hair was thinning severely and that made her slightly happy. She hoped all his hair fell out and tried to bore a hole in the back of his balding head with her eyes.

For the Delaneys, the rest of the wake was a blur. They didn't know most of the people attending and stayed by themselves, refusing to acknowledge Alec in any way. Jack and Hannah eventually came over, and Erin gave them each a big hug, telling them she would always be there for them.

When her niece and nephew moved away to talk to others, Erin looked over at her husband. Mike was laser-focused on Alec, wouldn't take his eyes off of him. She could feel the hatred coming off her husband. Alec must have felt it too because he kept stealing glances at Mike who never broke his icy stare.

The Avon Ladies gave Erin their condolences. It had been a few years since Erin had seen Viv, Kelly, Margot, and Nina, but she remembered them well. Viv was the unofficial ringleader.

'You four were important to my sister,' Erin said. 'She used to talk about you all the time and valued your friendship. She loved being an Avon Lady.'

Truthfully, Erin didn't think the 'ladies' had paid much attention to her sister after she got sick. When Quinn started having emotional problems, her 'good friends' all but disappeared. Once Quinn stopped being a good time, the 'ladies' couldn't spare time for her.

'We loved Quinn,' said Viv. 'She was the best, so much fun.'

'The best,' echoed the other three women simultaneously.

After the 'ladies' walked away, Alec's parents moved towards the Delaney group. Alec's mother swept in and wrapped her arms around Erin, causing Erin's entire body to stiffen like a stone statue. *The mother of the man who possibly killed my little sister is touching me.* A wave of nausea overtook Erin. Linda Roberts had done nothing to support her sister while she was alive. The second Linda Roberts released her grip, Erin backed away and shook her head. Linda said something about how terrible this whole thing was and how sad they were. She said they loved Quinn and mentioned how traumatic it all was for Quinn's kids.

While watching the awkward scene between Alec's mother and Erin, Mike's rage grew and a mask of hatred spread across his face. He knew Alec's parents had never lifted a finger to help Quinn and they had no right now pretending they cared. They were fakers just like their son.

Mike and Erin now knew that Quinn had hidden a lot of things from the Delaney side of the family. But Alec's parents lived in Avon, less than two miles from their son's house. They knew what was going on. They knew how their son betrayed and mistreated his wife and they did nothing to help her.

Mike was sure of one thing. He believed the entire Roberts family was complicit in Quinn's death – and wondered if her kids somehow played a role?

Chapter Seventeen

QUINN

There were so many people at my funeral, must have been more than two hundred. Impressive. My kids' friends all showed up. There were tons of flowers, and big pictures of me all around the room. One of them was my wedding picture. I loved that photo. I looked pretty.

Lots of people were pouring into the chapel, and everyone was crying. All the Delaneys and my New Jersey friends were on one side of the room. The Avon contingent including Alec and my kids, along with the Avon Ladies, were on the other. Most of the girls from Hannah's high school lacrosse team were there and I even saw a few of her old teachers. Guess all the volunteering I did at Avon High paid off. It was very nice of all of them to show up.

Some professors from the University of Rochester stopped in to show support for Alec. I didn't know his colleagues very well. He hadn't brought me to a UR event in a few years. I wondered if Alec's girlfriend, Alison, would be there. I wasn't sure what she looked like. He wouldn't bring his new girlfriend to my wake, would he? That would be kind of tacky. My brother-in-law would lose his mind if Alec did that. I'd known Mike since we were kids and he was more like my big brother and protector. Nobody messed with any of the Delaney girls when Mike was around. There sure were a lot of people in the funeral home. Lines of mourners went out the front door and all the way around the building. I went over to my daughter. She looked sadder than I had ever seen her.

'Everything is going to be alright, Hann,' I whispered in her ear. 'I'm alright. I'm still here with you.'

A single tear trickled down her cheek.

'I love you, Hann,' I said, blowing her a kiss, wanting to believe she heard me. I moved towards my son. He looked as though he wanted to sink into the floor.

'Don't be sad, Jack,' I said. 'I'm okay. You'll be alright, too. I'm not exactly sure where I am, but I'm still here looking out for you. Promise me, you'll take care of your sister. That's what big brothers are supposed to do.'

My New Jersey family huddled together in the back of the room. I didn't see my father. Where was he? My mother, sister, Mike, Liza and my high school friends were all together, but not my dad. Did something happen to him? I stood in front of my mother and shouted as loud as I could.

'Where's Daddy? Please don't cry, Mom, I'm alright,' I yelled, but she couldn't hear me.

I moved towards the Avon Ladies, my party posse, all clutching their tissues as they reminisced about the good times we'd had together; the book club, the nights out, the partying.

'She was so great,' said Viv sniffling. 'I'm going to miss her.'

'Me too,' said Margot, laughing and crying at the same time. 'She was so much fun. Remember her with the ukulele or when she made us do the cancan on top of the bar in Metaire with our shirts off.'

The Avon Ladies all laughed. I laughed along with them. I remember that cancan escapade; that was a wild night. The bartender bought us several free rounds of tequila shots, and we got a little naked, but only just a little.

'She was one of a kind,' said Nina. 'It must have been awful for you, Viv, finding her dead like that.'

'It was horrible,' said Viv, blowing her nose. 'She was just lying on the floor. It was the worst moment of my life.'

'I thought you said you didn't actually see her,' said Kelly.

'I didn't,' said Viv, 'but I was in the building when they found her. It was still traumatising.'

The Avon Ladies formed a group hug around Viv.

'Look,' said Viv, 'Quinn dying is a horrible thing, but nothing we do is going to bring her back. We have to accept that we're going to miss her. In time, it won't hurt so much. I know Quinn wouldn't want us to be sad forever. She'd want us to move on and go out and party.'

What? No, I would not want you to go party, Vivian DeMarco. I wouldn't want that at all. What I want is for you to find out why I was killed and who did it and to harass the police until they do. I want you to watch out for my kids. And, don't be so touchy feely with my husband like I just saw you being. This time it's about me, Viv, not you.

Chapter Eighteen

During the funeral service, Alec felt Mike and Erin staring at him. He couldn't stop himself from turning to look. It was an itch he had to scratch. No matter how hard he tried, he had to steal a glance.

His conscience was clear. He and Quinn had been married for over twenty years and he had taken care of her when she went off the rails. *Nobody knew what I went through. Her judgmental family has no clue what it was like for me.*

After he got back from that first meeting with the Newbridge police, his father had pulled him aside.

'You need to hire an attorney, Alec, to protect yourself,' his father said firmly.

'I've got nothing to hide. I gave the cops my DNA. That will clear me,' Alec said.

'Talk to a lawyer before you do anything,' his father said. 'There are a lot of innocent men in jail. Every year you hear a story about some poor schmuck who spent thirty years in prison for a crime he didn't commit.'

His father reached into his wallet and pulled out a business card.

'Call this guy, Steven Stern,' he said. 'He's supposed to be an excellent criminal attorney.'

'I don't need some high-priced lawyer,' Alec protested. 'The local police are idiots, anyway. I can handle them with my eyes closed. Besides, I don't have the money for another lawyer after all the funeral expenses.'

'Don't be such a stubborn ass, Alec. I'll pay for your goddamn lawyer,' said his father in a tone that told him it was not up for debate.

The next morning, Alec met with Steven Stern, Esq. The lawyer was smart and cocky just like his potential new client and Alec decided they were both cut from the same cloth.

'It's not that they always accuse the husband, Alec,' Steven Stern said. 'Statistically, when it comes to murder, the spouse or significant other is most often the guilty party. Naturally, that's where the police look first.'

'I already gave the cops my DNA,' Alec said.

'That was a mistake. I would have advised against that,' said Stern. 'From here on in, don't speak to the police. I'll do all the talking for you.'

Alec nodded.

'You're certain there's no possibility they'll find your DNA in your wife's apartment?'

'No chance,' Alec replied. 'I've never been to her place. I haven't physically seen my wife in six months. All communication between us was by phone or text.'

'I'm going to ask you the question that I ask all my clients. Your answer is protected by attorney-client privilege, okay?'

'Okay.'

'Did you kill your wife, Alec?'

'No. I did not.'

'Okay, that's all I needed to know. Unless the police want to charge you,' Stern said, 'you're under no legal obligation to talk to them again. From now on, be like a mime. Complete silence. Clear?'

'Absolutely. My DNA will rule me out,' said Alec confidently.

Stern picked up the phone and called the Newbridge Police Department to let them know he was now representing Alec Roberts and his client had nothing more to say. He also told them Alec would not be returning to take the polygraph test either.

It had been a long few days and Alec was bone tired. He wanted things to go back to normal. Years of coping with his wife's mental illness, and now he had to protect himself from a murder allegation. He felt himself getting angry. *Quinn tried to drown me when she was alive and now she's reaching back from the grave to pull me in with her.*

Chapter Nineteen

The two detectives canvassed half of Newbridge and then did the same with every shop in downtown Avon. McQuillan took one side of Main Street and Crews the other. Armed with a photo of Quinn Roberts and his little black notebook, McQuillan was looking for anyone who had spoken to or seen the victim in the weeks leading up to her death. At this point, they had no idea how she'd spent the last days of her life.

Some of the people in the stores recognized Quinn Roberts from the news. A lady at the thrift shop said Roberts used to come in all the time but couldn't remember when the last time was. The guy in the liquor store and the lady at the fruit and veg market also said Ms. Roberts had been a regular customer but hadn't seen her in a while. Apparently, Quinn Roberts liked tequila, chardonnay, and mangoes.

McQuillan pushed open the door of a small jewelry store called Bling. The owner, Joelle Lester, an attractive middle-aged woman with short blonde hair, stood behind the counter.

'I'm with the Newbridge PD,' McQuillan said, flashing his badge and handing her Quinn Roberts' picture. 'Ever see this woman? She lived here in Avon until fairly recently.'

'Her husband did it,' she said, without looking at the picture.

'What makes you say that?'

'You'd be surprised what a jeweler knows. We keep a lot of secrets,' she said. 'It was her husband. I'm very intuitive.'

McQuillan felt his ears getting warm.

'Ms. Roberts was a customer of yours?'

'She'd been in my shop a few times. I get to know local people pretty well,' Joelle said. 'The ladies in town drop by to try on a necklace or a pair of earrings while they're out shopping. My store is kind of a sanctuary for them, a place where they can try on pretty things that most of them can't afford.'

'Why did you say her husband did it?'

'About three years ago, this middle-aged guy comes into my store. Said he was looking for a birthday gift for his wife,' Joelle said. 'Based on his age, I showed him a few pieces in gold. After he looked at the price tags, he said he wanted something less expensive, so I showed him silver. He decided on a silver necklace with the letter "J" charm on it, and we added a large carved green bead to the chain for her birthstone.'

'The letter "J"?'

'He paid for it with Visa. When I ran the card, it said "Alec Roberts", but I didn't make the connection to Quinn at the time. Roberts is kind of a common name.'

'Why did you say Alec Roberts killed his wife?'

'I'm getting there. About a month later, Quinn comes into my shop to chit-chat,' Joelle said, 'and she tries on one of my hammered gold chains. She said she needed to get her husband, Alec, to come down to buy her something special. That she deserved it, after all she had to put up with.

'That's when I realized that Alec Roberts was Quinn's husband and I thought to myself, uh-oh. Her husband bought a "J" charm necklace for his "wife's" birthday,' Joelle continued, making air quotes with her fingers. 'Clearly, it wasn't for his wife. Look for someone whose name starts with a "J", Detective.'

'You're sure about this?'

'Oh, I'm sure. Wait, it gets better,' Joelle said. 'A few months after that little fiasco, this young blonde in her twenties comes into my shop to get the clasp fixed on that very same "J" necklace with the green charm. It was definitely the same one because I only had that one jade bead. I bought it from an estate sale. It was one of a kind. The blonde said her "husband" bought it for her,' Joelle said, making air quotes a second time. 'When I heard about Quinn Roberts' murder, all I could think of was that green bead.'

The detective gave the woman his card as he considered what she had told him. It didn't definitively nail Alec Roberts for the murder of his wife, just proved he was a cheater. McQuillan knew he had a lot more work to do.

The next day, Crews and McQuillan drove six hours south to Cranbury, New Jersey, to interview people who had attended Quinn's twenty-fifth high school reunion a few weeks earlier. The main person McQuillan wanted to talk to was Quinn's old boyfriend, Mark Miller.

'Let's just say, we were old friends, that's all. I hadn't seen her in twenty years,' Mark blurted out before either detective could ask a question.

'You and Quinn Roberts dated all through high school?' asked Detective Crews.

'She was Quinn Delaney then. Yeah. We went out for a few years. Broke up when we went to college.'

'Had you been in touch with Ms. Roberts?' McQuillan asked.

'We kind of had a bad break-up, and then I met someone, and she met someone. The one and only time I saw her was at the reunion.'

'Your classmates told us that you two were inseparable at the party,' said Crews, 'that you were by her side the entire evening and you left together.'

'We had a lot to catch up on after twenty-five years,' Miller said.

'People said you never took your eyes off her the whole night,' McQuillan said.

'She was still beautiful, what can I say?'

'And you left the event with her?' Crews asked again.

'The lady needed a ride home. I'm a gentleman.'

While McQuillan's money was still on the husband, Mark Miller had emerged as the first runner-up. The two detectives remained silent, hoping Miller might meander his way into a confession.

'Look, I'm married,' he continued. 'I gave her a ride to her parents' house. Is that a crime? It was no big deal. Like I said, we were old friends.'

'Except,' McQuillan said, looking at his notes, 'according to Ms. Roberts' sister, that night you told the victim that you were still in love with her. You said you wanted to leave your wife and start up with her again. Her sister said she turned you down. That might make a guy get pissed off, going out on a limb like that and getting shot down.'

'You've got to be kidding me,' Miller said indignantly. 'That's a total lie. I never said that. Everyone knew Quinn Delaney was damaged goods. People said she had a screw loose. She might have told her sister I said it but it never happened. She probably made it up to make herself feel important. She was always high up on her horse, even back in high school. I'm married. Quinn Delaney was attractive but she was delusional. I wouldn't jeopardize my marriage for someone that unhinged.'

Chapter Twenty

QUINN

Why, Mark Miller, I believe you just told those detectives a big fat lie. I'm glad you still found me attractive but 'delusional'? I remember exactly what you said to me that night, Mark. You said you wanted to dump your fat wife and ride off into the sunset with me. Truthfully, I thought you were the crazy one, and I felt sorry for your wife. Don't you know that a marriage built on lies is bound to unravel? Take it from one who knows. You're in for a whole lot a pain.

Chapter Twenty-One

McQuillan had lost count of how many doors he had knocked on in Quinn Roberts' old neighborhood in Newbridge. It was a quiet part of town. You could hear birds chirping and an occasional dog bark; everything was nice and peaceful. That's why a woman being brutally murdered and no one seeing or hearing anything didn't jive. If a person didn't belong here, like a crazed drug addict, for instance, somebody would notice.

Frustrated, he and Crews had gone house to house and talked to countless numbers of people. For all their effort, they still had nothing. An elderly lady who lived across the street from the murder scene said she saw a blue van parked there one day that same week.

'I keep a watch on this whole neighborhood. You can never be too careful. The guy driving the van looked strange, like he was on drugs or crack or something,' the old woman said. 'He had long hair in a ponytail and maybe a tattoo. I didn't like the looks of him. I think he had Vermont plates.'

'Where were you when you observed the vehicle?' McQuillan asked.

'I watch everything and everyone from the window in my dining room,' said the old woman. 'I'm pretty sure that van was parked out there last week.'

After almost thirty years on the job, McQuillan had gotten pretty good at separating fact from fiction. The blue van and ponytail screamed fantasy and McQuillan didn't have time to chase down false leads. He asked the woman a few more questions about the 'drug addict', and inconsistencies in her story made him confident there was nothing to it. He crossed it off his list. Seemed nobody knew nothing.

Even the people who lived in the same building provided little. Scott Rubin, a middle-aged tax attorney and his wife, lived underneath the victim offered almost no help.

'We're private people,' said Rubin. 'We don't want to know anything about our neighbors, and we don't want them to know anything about us.'

What a delightful guy, McQuillan thought.

'I'll say "hello" to you or lend you my snow shovel, but that's about it,' Rubin continued.

'I get it, Mr. Rubin, you like your privacy,' McQuillan said, jotting down a note. 'Did you hear or see anything last week?'

'Her damn footsteps on my ceiling,' Rubin said. 'That woman walked around at all hours of the night. This is an old building, the floors creak. Her pacing made our ceiling squeak all night long, every single night. I had to use earplugs. She drove my wife nuts. I'm sorry she died, Detective, but we don't know anything.'

'Do you remember what days you heard Ms. Roberts walking around?'

'She did it every night. Definitely Sunday cause I was trying to watch a movie. And maybe Monday too. Not sure about Tuesday.'

After the police interviewed all of her classmates, neighbors and family members, they determined that Quinn Roberts didn't appear to have any enemies. She was close with her parents and sisters, and most everyone said complimentary things about her. She was a good mother, involved in the local schools and at least up until the past couple of years before she developed some emotional problems, she was well-liked and had a good sense of humor.

In the three weeks since the murder happened, it had been front page news, and everyone had an opinion. McQuillan's challenge was to determine what was speculation and what was reality. A lot of people reported their theory to the police as a fact.

He entered a hair salon in the center of Newbridge and flashed his badge along with a dog-eared photo of Quinn Roberts.

'I know her,' said the hairdresser, her eyes tearing up. 'I did her hair the week before she died.'

McQuillan's ears turned bright red and started to itch.

'Really,' he said, trying to stay calm. 'When was that?'

The hairdresser checked her book. 'Three weeks ago, on a Wednesday,' she said. 'She came into my shop on Tuesday.'

'You just said you did her hair on Wednesday.'

'Stay with me. She first came in on Tuesday and told me she had passed my shop a hundred times. Said she wanted to do something new with her hair,' said the stylist. 'It looked like it hadn't been cut in a while and it was flecked with strands of gray. She looked kind of lost. I knew I could make her look so much better, but my schedule was jammed.'

'So, you didn't do her hair?' McQuillan asked.

'I was about to tell her I couldn't take her for at least a week when my empathy gene kicked into overdrive,' said the woman. 'I'm a very empathetic person, which is a blessing and a curse. I told her to come back the next day at eleven, and I'd squeeze her in. She really needed a haircut, and I was dying to get rid of that gray.'

'Did she come back?'

'The next day, which was *Wednesday*, she shows up a few minutes before eleven. She looked more pulled together than the day before. I wrapped her in a plastic cape and took a hard look at her hair and face in the mirror. We were about the same age, and we both have black hair. Her skin was fair like white porcelain, and she had these pretty light blue eyes. I, on the other hand, am Sicilian, dark eyes, dark hair. In Disney princess speak, we were like Princess Jasmine and Snow White.'

'Then what happened?'

'I cut and colored while she talked. Something about my chair; they all tell me their secrets. She said she was getting divorced but that she didn't want to and now it seemed her husband wanted to get back together. She said she had plans to have dinner with him for his birthday and wanted to look really good. Something about the way she said it made me wonder if she was telling the truth or if it was only magical thinking on her part. I kind of got the feeling she wanted to have dinner a lot more than he did. It didn't sound like a firm date to me. Don't ask me why, just a gut feeling. I'll tell you what though, when I finished with her hair, she looked like a cover girl. That was the last time I ever saw her.'

McQuillan wondered if the birthday dinner between Quinn Roberts and her husband ever took place and made a note to follow up on that. When he got back to the station, Crews was sorting through hefty bags of papers and other assorted items collected from Quinn Roberts' apartment. Everything was in the process of being separated into organized piles.

'From the looks of it, the lady didn't throw anything out,' said Detective Crews. 'You think she was a hoarder like the people on that TV show? She saved gum wrappers, empty cereal boxes and old jars.'

The two detectives sifted through stacks of junk mail, bills and promotional letters selling car insurance and services to clean chimneys. McQ wondered why Quinn kept chimney cleaning mailers when she didn't have a fireplace. There were prescriptions never filled and dozens of shopping lists, mainly for cleaning supplies.

They found a tiny scrap of paper with Quinn Roberts' address handwritten in block letters in blue ink. That little bit puzzled McQuillan. The paper looked like it was torn from the corner of a newspaper and it had the date printed on it. The date was from a week before they found Quinn's body. Next to the date was a big letter 'C' and small 'a' printed in old English style type. Why would Quinn Roberts have her own address handwritten on a piece of newspaper dated from the week before her death? She'd been living in that apartment for over six months. Maybe it was nothing, he thought, but possibly it was something. Beyond that, the rest of what they collected was mainly garbage, except for the stacks of letters and cards from her mother, sisters, and friends in

New Jersey trying to cheer her up. Sad, he thought as he read each letter. This woman had been deeply loved.

For the next few weeks, McQuillan and his team pieced together the framework of Quinn Roberts' life. At their Thursday morning briefing, McQuillan reviewed where they were with the hard evidence, what had been collected and what they were still waiting for from the lab. He then wrapped up with the personal details that had been uncovered through the dozens of interviews.

'Looks like the husband was a serial cheater and wanted out of the marriage for years,' said McQuillan. 'Not sure when his wife became aware of all of his extracurricular activities. According to her friends, despite learning about his other relationships, she didn't want the marriage to end. Go figure.'

'We've found out the husband liked college girls,' said Crews. 'And, we got a bunch of the lab results back and ruled out a few neighbors and the landlady but there were still a couple of samples that we haven't identified yet.'

'We may never get a match,' McQ said. 'So, it's going to boil down to thorough police work if we're going to crack this thing. Everyone clear?'

The following day, the two detectives spent some time nosing around UR and talked to a lot of students. They learned that Alec Roberts had a nickname with some of the female students, 'Dr. A'. According to some of the girls, all you had to do was put out once or twice and you could move your grade point average way up. They said some of their classmates deliberately signed up for his courses with that in mind.

'Last year,' said one student, 'I knew this girl who was a senior, and she wanted to get a job with Google when she graduated. She was worried her GPA wasn't high enough. She registered for two of Dr. Roberts' classes her first semester senior year and did what she needed to do. Now, she works in marketing at the Google headquarters in New York.'

Jesus Christ, thought McQuillan, my daughter's in college. She gets all C's. I guess that means she's not sleeping with her teachers. The more McQuillan learned about Dr. Alec Roberts, the more convinced he was that there was something off about the guy. The two cops walked around the school looking for more information when someone directed them to a young woman with a long blonde ponytail. She was sitting at a picnic table deep into a book.

'Excuse me,' McQuillan said. 'Are you, Chrissy Goodwin?'

She nodded. The two detectives pulled out their badges and flashed them. She was nonplussed.

'I'm Detective McQuillan, this is Detective Crews, Newbridge PD. We're working on the murder investigation of–'

'Dr. Roberts' wife?' she interrupted with an affected accent. McQuillan nodded. 'Everyone on campus is talking about it. So tragic.'

'We heard you have a close relationship with Dr. Roberts,' Crews said.

The young woman stared at the detectives for a moment. They could see she was a lousy liar before she even opened her mouth.

'He's a good teacher,' she said slowly. 'I took his class last year.'

'I'm going to cut to the chase, Ms. Goodwin,' Crews continued. 'Some of your classmates reported you were romantically involved with Dr. Roberts.'

'Then they should mind their own business. Yeah, I went out with him, it was no big deal. At first, it was kind of a rush, you know, he was my professor. I thought he was smart and he worked out a lot. He was in good shape for an old guy. He was married, but that wasn't my problem. I wasn't breaking my wedding vows. Besides, I figured it would help with my grade.'

'Did it?' the detective asked.

'Look,' she replied. 'It was fun in the beginning, but then it got icky. Dr. Roberts had this idea of a woman in his mind, and he wanted me to be her. He got super intense about how I dressed, too. He loved trashy.'

McQuillan nodded as he wrote in his notebook.

'Then he started to creep me out,' Chrissy continued. 'One day he said he wanted us to make a sex video. Wasn't really my thing but YOLO. I may have slept with my married professor, but I'm not a slut. When the semester was over, I ended it. I got what I wanted, an A in History. Guess he got what he wanted, too.'

'That guy is a real creep,' McQuillan said to Crews as the two detectives walked across campus. When they parted ways at the main quad, McQuillan cut through the student center on his way to his car. That's when he saw them.

A row of cream-colored metal stands lined the walls of the main hallway. Inside the bins were stacks of the free UR student newspaper, the *Campus Times*. McQuillan picked up a copy and stared at it. Something was familiar, but his brain wasn't quite there yet.

Come on, McQ, think. Why does this seem familiar?

His eyes focused on the title. The title, *Campus Times*, was written in an old English style type. He covered up most of it with his hands, everything except for the 'C' and the 'a'. Bingo. The color and type of paper along with the logo was identical to that torn scrap of paper with Quinn's address scribbled on it in blue ink that they had found in her apartment. The date printed on it was from the same week Quinn Roberts was murdered. Now he had concrete evidence linking Alec Roberts or at least the University of Rochester to Quinn Roberts' apartment. Who else would have had access to the UR newspaper? It had to have come from Alec Roberts. But how it got there, McQ didn't know.

He drove directly to the district attorney's office to plead his case to the Assistant District Attorney, Bernie Gonzales', in person. He and Gonzales had worked on a number of investigations over the years and the ADA owed him a favor. McQ hoped to cash in one of them and convince the prosecutor to reconsider ruling out all evidence found in Quinn Roberts' apartment. That tiny piece of paper he had just identified could be the game-changer.

'Sorry but that still won't fly,' said Gonzales after he heard McQuillan out. 'I'm not messing up my conviction record. The DA doesn't let us take cases we don't think we can win, even if we know the defendant is guilty. It's a waste of taxpayer money. You know the drill.'

'But this is different. What's the problem?'

'Half of Monroe County was walking around your crime scene.'

'The first responder let things get a little out of control,' McQuillan said, 'but only for a short while. Once I got there, I assure you, everything was done by the book.'

'We heard there was a stray dog stepping on and sniffing around the body,' Gonzales continued. 'The coroner found a dog hair on the lady during the autopsy. Your guys sent a urine sample to the lab that turned out to be dog piss and vomit that wasn't from the victim but from the landlady. Your investigation is a mess.'

'There were a few missteps, but now we've finally got solid evidence,' McQuillan said.

'A scrap of newspaper is your solid evidence?'

'It had to have come from the husband,' the detective said. 'He's a professor at UR. How else would it have ended up in Quinn Roberts' apartment? That issue of *Campus Times* was printed a couple of days before we found her. If Alec Roberts hadn't been to her place, maybe he wrote her address down so he could find it.'

'Have you checked the handwriting?' asked Gonzales, shaking his head.

McQ pulled out the scrap of paper and showed it to the attorney.

'It's only a few block letters, our handwriting guy said it would be impossible to identify it. Alec Roberts wrote it down and then went to find and kill his wife. What do you say, Bernie?'

'It's possible, but I still can't use it.'

'You're killing me.'

'Roberts' defense attorney would have a field day with how everything was collected,' said Gonzales. 'Unless you find some evidence not retrieved at the scene or a new witness, I hate to tell you, this investigation is headed to Cold Case.'

'Come on, Bernie,' McQuillan begged.

'If I know about the holes, then Roberts' lawyer knows about them,' said Gonzales as he turned to walk away. 'Everything your people recovered, physical, DNA, would all get tossed. Sorry, McQ, I can't take this to a grand jury. Get me something new that hasn't been compromised.'

Part Two

HOW MY PERFECT LIFE STARTED

Chapter Twenty-Two

Eileen Delaney often joked that her oldest daughter, Erin, was like a football; 'you could throw her across a field, and she'd bounce into the end zone all by herself'. Her youngest, Colleen, was the quiet and independent one, preferring to be alone and focused on a project, even when she was a toddler.

Her middle child, Quinn, was the one Eileen needed to be extra gentle with. Only five-and-a-half pounds when she was born, Quinn just wanted to be held. Whenever Eileen turned around, Quinn would be there, her little arms in the air, begging to be lifted.

'Pick me up, Mommy,' she'd plead.

While her older sister was off making friends and the younger one happily playing in her crib, Quinn would cling to her mother's legs and sit as close as possible, like a lap dog.

'You should have been born a kangaroo, Quinnie. Baby kangaroos live in a pouch in their mommy's tummy,' said Eileen to her five-year-old middle daughter.

The little girl's eyes widened as she smiled at what she had just learned.

'Mommy, I would like being in your pouch. Then you could carry me around all the time,' Quinn said. Eileen laughed and shook her head because she knew her daughter meant it. *That girl hates being alone,* she thought.

From the time they could talk, Erin and Quinn were the best of friends. Colleen, who was so much younger, was often an afterthought for her two older sisters. Once in a while, they would *let* Colleen play with them but most of the time, they bossed the poor thing around until she cried and their mother had to come to the rescue.

With a house full of girls, Eileen's husband, Ed, was surrounded by a sea of pink, purple, and sparkles. Ed was a big, loud, burly guy. He was nearly six-feet-two and weighed two-hundred-and-fifty pounds and had a mop of thick black hair. Whenever Eileen saw Ed's big frame sprawled out on the living room floor playing dolls with the girls, it always made her smile. Her husband had figured out that the best way to win over his daughters' hearts was to play with Barbies. He was a tough guy on the outside but inside he was marshmallow fluff, and his girls knew that. Even when he'd bark at them, they never took him seriously.

'Girls,' he'd bellow. 'I want your bedrooms cleaned and your clothes picked up, now! We don't have maid service here, you know.'

'Oh, Daddy, please. Stop yelling, you're hurting my brain,' Quinn would say, rolling her eyes as she walked past him with her hands over her ears ignoring his commands.

Erin and Colleen were carbon copies of their mother, with green eyes, strawberry blonde hair and a sprinkling of freckles across the bridge of their noses. Quinn, on the other hand, took after her father with a fair complexion, dark almost black hair and bright blue eyes rimmed by thick black lashes. She had naturally red lips that made her look like she was wearing lipstick. Once when she was in kindergarten, a few of the mothers gossiped that five-year-old Quinn was wearing make-up to school. Eileen Delaney set them all straight right away.

'My daughter's red lips are a gift from God,' she said proudly. 'She won't ever need make-up like most girls.'

By the time she was fourteen, Quinn started developing physically, and the boys noticed. At first all the attention felt strange. She was more interested in playing with her friends or the family dogs but eventually, she came to appreciate and enjoy all the male admiration.

When Ed and Eileen saw what was happening, they laid down the law. No boyfriends until Quinn was sixteen. On the week of her sixteenth birthday, Quinn introduced her parents to her first boyfriend, and then another, soon followed by another. The parade of would-be suitors made her parents wonder if every boy at school had signed up for a turn to go out with their daughter.

At seventeen, and a junior in high school, Quinn started going out with Mark Miller. They dated for two years and she and Mark were each other's dates to the junior and senior proms.

Eileen liked Mark well enough and thought he was basically a sweet kid. Ed, on the other hand, didn't like any of the boys his daughters brought home; it was how he was wired. Nobody was good enough for his girls. He'd grunt when Mark came over to the house and Mark, to his credit, remained polite and tried desperately to converse. Eileen thought of pulling Mark aside and telling him not to try so hard with her husband, but part of her enjoyed watching their weekly death dance.

After high school graduation, Mark went away to college in Pennsylvania. Quinn decided to stay home in Cranbury and go to a nearby state school. She and Mark tried to keep their relationship going but like many high school romances, it had run its course. Turns out there were plenty of boys at college waiting for their turn to go out with Quinn Delaney.

The first time Quinn brought Alec home, her parents didn't know what to make of him. They had heard the story about Alec putting shrimp up his nose fifty times and failed to see why Quinn found it so enchanting. Alec was different from the other boys Quinn usually dragged home. Most of the guys Quinn dated were the star football player or student body president; confident, smart, athletic. Alec was tall, thin and tentative and Quinn's father made him visibly nervous.

Despite Ed's disapproval, Alec and Quinn's relationship flourished. They got engaged a few months before they both finished college. Eileen had wanted her daughter to wait, take her time and get married later. After much internal debate though, she kept her mouth shut, believing that every person was on their own journey and that meant her grown daughter was capable of making her own decisions. Anything Eileen said would likely fall on deaf ears anyway, she reasoned, because Quinn was 'in love'.

The wedding was set for the following October. The whole family got caught up in the matrimonial whirlwind. There was much to be researched and selected – dresses, flowers, invitations, photographers, favors, music, and food, and they pulled it off. For months the Delaney women powered through wedding magazines and marched into countless numbers of bridal stores looking for that perfect dress.

They finally found 'the one' at a little dress shop in Princeton. It was a fitted creamy-white gown with long lace sleeves that hugged her body in just the right places. When Quinn stood on the stand in the middle of the bridal store wearing her veil and gown and the most beautiful serene smile, Eileen thought her daughter looked happier than she had ever seen her, glowing from within. It reminded the mother-of-the-bride of the time Quinn and Erin were about six and seven and had found a box filled with old sheer white curtains in the basement. Using the contents, the two girls had draped themselves in the fabric and played 'bride' for hours. They continued that game for years. Now, it was for real.

For the four bridesmaids, Quinn decided on blue strapless gowns, a color all of them approved of. That September, Eileen, the bridesmaids, and Linda Roberts, Alec's mother, threw Quinn a beautiful bridal shower in the Delaneys' backyard. Quinn's future mother-in-law, Linda, was Korean-American. She painstakingly made hundreds of homemade Asian dumplings and dipping sauces for the party. Most of the attendees had never had Korean food before and the Asian delicacies were the hit of the event.

During the party planning, Eileen got to know Linda Roberts a little. They were very different types. Eileen spoke her mind and was a bit of a maverick while Linda was quiet and reserved, a follower. It was evident to Quinn's mother that Linda took the backseat in her marriage to her husband, George. George was a bit of a blowhard and Eileen noticed he was often dismissive with his wife. No matter, Eileen thought, it was none of her business. Her soon-to-be in-laws didn't have to be her best friends.

When Quinn's wedding train pulled out of the station, Eileen jumped on board to make the perfect day for her daughter but she noticed Quinn's father didn't have the same level of enthusiasm. At first, she thought it was just Ed being Ed.

'So,' she began one evening, 'you haven't said much about the wedding. It's coming up. When are you getting fitted for your suit?'

'I'll get to it,' he said not looking up from his newspaper.

'It's in four weeks.'

'I know when it is, Eileen. I'm goddamn paying for it.'

'You don't have to bite my head off,' she said. 'Is it the money?'

There was a long silence, and Ed finally looked up at his wife.

'I think he's a jerk. My sweet little girl could have anyone in the world and she picked a putz, and that makes me sad. I wanted better for her,' he said, shaking his head as he got up and walked out of the room.

Four weeks later, on a warm, sunny October afternoon, friends and relatives stood in St. Gabriel's and watched the Delaney girls walk down the aisle in a blaze of white and robin egg blue. Eileen told herself that Ed had been too tough on Alec. Quinn was happy, and that was all that mattered. Alec was her son-in-law now, and they all needed to act like a family and support each other.

When the priest said, 'You may kiss the bride,' the church burst into applause and cheers. Making a grand show of it, Alec cradled Quinn in his arms, leaned her back and lowered her down inches above the floor while planting a long dramatic kiss on her lips.

When he lifted his new wife up, she proudly held her flowers high over her head like a defiant Statue of Liberty holding her torch. The crowd in the church erupted. The music started and through their tears, Ed and Eileen watched their little girl, the same one who would cling to their legs, now hang on the arm of her new husband.

Minutes later, the wedding guests stood in front of the church while the bridal party posed for pictures. Through the crowd,

Eileen saw Alec's mother, Linda, and their eyes met. She could see Linda had been crying too and walked over to her with a welcoming smile.

'Well,' Eileen said, giving Linda a hug, 'they really did it. Our kids are married. Alec looked handsome in his tuxedo.'

'I know,' said Linda, smiling and wiping away another tear. 'He polishes up nicely, doesn't he? And Quinn, she has to be the most beautiful bride I've ever seen, and that includes the ones in the magazines.'

'Believe it or not,' said Eileen, 'she's been completely calm throughout all the wedding planning. There was no drama whatsoever. I was the wreck. Quinn has always been the most composed and cool-headed of all my girls.'

'That's good,' Linda said. 'I guess it helps her deal with my son's temper. I never knew how to handle him when he got so mad. She must know the secret.'

At that, Linda waved to a relative and moved away. Eileen felt a cold chill go down her spine and her stomach churn. What did Linda mean? Alec had a temper? She knew Alec could be opinionated, but Quinn never mentioned anything about a temper.

Eileen decided to keep the comment to herself. If Ed heard about it, holy hell would break loose. Besides, she might have misunderstood what Linda had meant. Maybe she was saying Alec could be a hothead from time to time. Eileen knew all about that. She was married to one. Don't borrow trouble, she told herself. Years later, after things got bad, she wondered if she should have told her husband about it.

Chapter Twenty-Three

They were only eighteen months apart, but Erin Delaney was definitely the big sister, and as far as she was concerned, that made her the boss of them. It worked because Quinn liked being the second banana, it suited her personality. She enjoyed being looked after, and Erin loved being in charge. Their mother used to joke that they were the perfect bookends.

Quinn was tiny; Erin was tall. Quinn was beautiful; Erin was cute. Quinn turned out to be fragile and Erin wasn't able to protect her the way she was supposed to. That was Erin's job.

Their mother put baby Quinn into Erin's arms when Erin was barely two, and that's where Quinn stayed. Always safe and protected, until the awful day. The sisters were each other's most prominent critics and fiercest protectors. Growing up, they shared clothes, jewelry, make-up, friends and sometimes even boyfriends, but never at the same time. They were, as the expression goes, 'in each other's pockets,' and mostly, they liked it that way.

When they were five or six, Erin favorite games were to play dress-up as Cinderella or Rapunzel, or coloring in her books. Quinn's idea of fun usually involved her baby dolls and pretending they were real. Sometimes, just to get under her sister's skin as sisters are known to do, Erin would refuse to play with the 'stupid dolls'. Quinn would look at Erin with her big sad blue eyes, hold her breath and pout. Invariably, Erin would give in, never able to say no to that sad pouty face. Quinn had Erin wrapped around her finger.

Until they were almost teens, their mother had dressed the two of them as if they were twins. Everything matched, clothes, shoes, hair clips, snowsuits. Same colors, different sizes.

'I buy two of everything,' Eileen would say to her friends. 'Identical clothes and nobody fights.'

When Erin turned seven and Quinn six, their parents gave them permission to go to the playground at the end of their street by themselves. They'd spend hours riding on the swings, slides, and seesaws. Quinn liked the swings the best, and two sisters would compete to see who could go higher, each encouraging the other to pump just a little harder.

'Come on, Quinnie,' Erin would shout, 'move those skinny little legs of yours or you won't catch up to me. Go higher, Quinn, higher.'

Quinn would pump her scrawny limbs even harder and get all red in the face to stay even with her bigger, more athletic sister as they both soared recklessly through the air, wind in their hair. They pretended they were birds flying through the sky. A few times they went so high, they were afraid they would swing right over the top, but they never did.

Erin was the comedian and Quinn her adoring audience.

'Do that funny voice again, Erin,' Quinn would beg. Without much encouragement, Erin would oblige and perfectly imitate a man they saw on the street that day or one of the teachers at school. Quinn would laugh so hard that tears would run down her face. Laughter was Quinn's Achilles heel. Make her laugh, and you owned her. That's how Erin got her sister to do almost anything.

The matchy-matchy clothing their mother insisted on was tolerated for a while, but once the girls hit their pre-teens, they demanded their own fashion identities. Saturday afternoons were spent shopping and walking around the nearby college town. Upscale Princeton, New Jersey, had a bustling downtown, an Ivy League university and was loaded with cute college guys who could be found loitering on just about every corner. On one of those Saturdays, Erin realized her fourteen-year-old younger sister had mastered the art of boy-talk. Erin watched Quinn effortlessly navigate conversations with countless numbers of guys and wondered how her sister had learned to do this. Quinn was so confident and masterful while Erin felt awkward and clumsy. Quinn knew exactly what to say to make every boy smile and come back for more.

In high school, the sisters snuck out for cigarettes between classes, got fake IDs to get into bars and were the popular party girls. The two of them had a blast and somehow managed to stay just to the right of any real trouble. They didn't always get along. They loved each other, but they had fights, too. Big ones.

'Why can't I go with you and your friends to the movies?' Quinn whined.

'Damn, stop being so clingy, Quinn, you can't go everywhere with me. Make your own friends for a change. You're so annoying.'

'I don't want to be by myself all day. I have nothing to do.'

'You're such a whiny baby,' said Erin.

'And you're such a bitch,' said Quinn. That's when Erin would pounce on Quinn, and the physical brawl would begin. Quinn was so small that Erin always won.

Sometimes their mother had to intervene before someone got hurt. The fights were usually short-lived, and after a few hours of mutual seething, one of them would apologize. It was usually Quinn who couldn't stand the idea of her big sister being mad at her. By the next morning, they were best friends again.

In the summer before her senior year of high school, Erin began dating Mike Danzi. Mike was easy breezy, adored Erin's sense of humor and playfulness and was also fiercely protective of her. No one hurt Erin on his watch and Erin knew back then that one day she would marry him.

Quinn's boyfriend, Mark, on the other hand, was cut from a different cloth. While he was cute and basically nice, he often wanted Quinn to 'quiet down' and sit next to him like an obedient dog. Quinn used to do it too, which never sat well with her sister.

Years later, Erin wondered if she had encouraged her sister to stand up for herself with Mark in high school, she might not have ended up with Alec. She might have been more independent. She might be alive. Erin vividly remembered the first day her sister met Alec.

'He put shrimp up his nose?' Erin had said incredulously. 'That's disgusting.'

'No, you don't understand. It was funny,' Quinn said, laughing. 'He's really cute, too,' she said with a sly smile. 'You'll see.'

Erin met Alec the following weekend when she worked a wedding with her sister. He wasn't what she was expecting, but there was something oddly appealing about him. He told silly jokes that made both Quinn and Erin laugh. It was evident to Erin and everyone else that Alec was crazy about her sister. He fawned over Quinn who could seemingly do no wrong in his eyes. Erin noticed that Quinn lapped up his adulation. It irked her that her sister basked so shamelessly in Alec's admiration.

'You're being the Quinntessa, again,' Erin reminded her sister one night after they had seen Alec.

'I am not,' Quinn yelled over her shoulder, running to pick up his phone call. 'You're just jealous that Mike doesn't treat you that way.'

'You're just stuck up and blind,' shouted Erin.

Some people look at life through rose-colored glasses. Quinn's lens for Alec was deep red. Everything he did was funny, witty and original. Erin didn't get it, but as long as her sister was happy, she decided Alec was probably alright. She figured Quinn would move on to someone new in no time, like she always did before.

As Erin always knew, her boyfriend, Mike, eventually became her husband. Mike was not a fan of Alec.

'I guess he can be funny sometimes,' Mike said to Erin one afternoon when they were in their mid-twenties, 'but he's so arrogant, thinks he knows everything. He gets on my nerves.'

'He makes me laugh once in a while,' said Erin, defending her brother-in-law.

'Come on, but he's so full of himself,' said Mike wearily.

When Alec met Quinn's parents, they were surprised at their daughter's choice. Alec was ordinary and Quinn, most definitely was not. After spending half an hour with Alec, though he didn't say it, Ed Delaney wasn't impressed.

'That's Mr. Wonderful?' said Quinn's father to his wife.

'He's so thin. A summer breeze could blow him right over,' his wife whispered after Quinn and Alec left to go into town. 'He barely looks like he's eighteen. Still, Quinnie seems to really like him. I just don't get it.'

Eileen Delaney told her husband not to worry. None of Quinn's boyfriends lasted very long. Her daughter soon tired of them, needing a fresh injection of admiration from a new suitor. Her family fully expected she'd be on to her next conquest within a week.

Months passed, and surprisingly Quinn didn't tire of Alec, and he didn't disappear. A year later, he was seated at their dining-room table on Christmas Day. Even though the family's initial opinion of the loquacious Alec Roberts had been middling at best, he had grown on them, and they began to enjoy his offbeat sense of humor. Quinn was over the moon in love and one by one, Alec won each of them over, even Mike. Everyone, that is, except Big Ed.

In spring of her senior year of college, Quinn announced that she and Alec were engaged to be married and proudly showed her family the tiny diamond solitaire ring Alec had given to her. Erin had gotten used to Alec and even occasionally enjoyed his jokes but the thought of him marrying Quinn just didn't feel right. It occurred to Erin that from then on, until she died, Alec Roberts would be with them every Christmas, every Thanksgiving, every Easter, 'every-everything' and she wasn't sure how she felt about that.

Chapter Twenty-Four

The first time he saw Quinn Delaney wasn't the day he stuck shrimp up his nose. She thought it was. Alec had seen her on the college campus plenty of times but never had the balls to say anything. Every guy at school had a crush on Quinn Delaney because she was so freaking beautiful and she didn't act like she knew it – at least not most of the time. There were a lot of pretty girls there, but Quinn, she was in another league.

Alec Roberts didn't start to grow until the end of high school. Guys his own age treated him like an annoying little brother because of his size. The girls used to say he was 'adorable' but not in a good way, not in a boyfriend way. He took the jeers, he wasn't a baby, but sometimes it was hard. He never had a girlfriend until the middle of college. He was never even kissed until then.

The beginning of Alec's sophomore year was the first time he laid eyes on Quinn. She was walking across campus, laughing and joking with a bunch of other kids, in the center of the crowd. Even from thirty yards away, her shiny black hair and almond-shaped blue eyes sucked him in. That first glance so mesmerized him that he nearly walked into a parking meter in front of the library. For him, it was love at first sight.

After that, he was always on the lookout for his dream girl. He wasn't the only one; half the guys on campus tripped over themselves to flirt with her. Alec would watch from a distance while the queen held court in the cafeteria or on a bench under the giant oak tree in front of Tully Hall. Dozens of his male classmates competed for her attention. She handled them effortlessly, knowing precisely what to say to make each one feel special. Every guy hoped he might be the one she'd choose. They laughed and smiled at her every word, and she basked in all their attention.

For Alec, everything about Quinn Delaney was perfect. She was petite and small women made him feel big, strong and powerful. Her body was curvy, perfectly balanced in a tiny package like a fantasy Wonder Woman doll. Rumor had it that Quinn had been a model for a local newspaper when she was in high school. If you asked Alec and half the boys on campus, she could have been on the cover of *Sports Illustrated* or in a Victoria's Secret catalog. For all of them, she was the embodiment of the perfect woman. While he thought she was a modern-day Aphrodite, she had no idea he existed or that his heart raced every time he saw her.

Quinn was walking across campus carrying a brown Coronet Catering uniform over her shoulder when Alec spotted her from the second floor of the History Department building. He recognized the brown shirt because a kid on his baseball team had the same one and it gave him the idea. There had been a job posting for servers by Coronet Catering on the bulletin board outside the Uni Student Center. If he worked for them, maybe he'd finally get to talk to his dream girl. The next day he applied for a job and was hired.

The first Saturday, Alec worked a bar mitzvah. His job was to unload the trucks and set up the food stations. He had heard from another waiter that Quinn Delaney was upstairs serving hors d'oeuvres. Their paths never crossed the entire day.

The following weekend, luck was on his side. He and Quinn both worked the same wedding. Alec promised himself he would get her attention before the day was over.

He was in the kitchen reloading food platters with fresh pigs in blankets, shrimp cocktail, and Swedish meatballs when he saw Quinn in the distance walking towards him carrying an empty tray. This was his chance. He turned his back to her and went on autopilot. Without a plan, he grabbed the nearest thing to him, which turned out to be four jumbo shrimp.

'Hey,' Quinn said, out of breath, tapping him on the back. 'You new? I need a refill. I'm picked clean. You'd think those people had never had a meal before.'

His fantasy girl was talking directly to him. She knew he existed. Slowly, he turned around with shrimp in his nose and ears and calmly proclaimed he was 007.

She looked at him, stunned for a second and then burst out laughing. She laughed so hard she doubled over and almost dropped her tray as she bent over to catch her breath. Tears ran down her cheeks.

'What's so funny?' Alec said, without flinching or removing the fish from his face. His stoic composure made her laugh harder.

'Stop, you're killing me. Oh my God,' she said, trying to right herself as she wiped her eyes. 'You're crazy.'

'Actually, my name is Alec,' he said, removing the fish and extending his hand. She smiled at him with rows of sparkling white teeth and Alec's heart nearly stopped.

'Hi, Alec, I'm Quinn. Nice to meet you,' she said as she reached out her hand. When her fingers touched his, an electric current traveled up his arm and shot all the way to his shoulder. It was all over for him. At that moment he promised himself that one day he was going to marry her. A week later he asked her out.

By the third date, things got pretty serious. Alec kept Quinn laughing while she continued to charm and beguile him. His fantasy had come true. How often does that happen, he wondered. Never.

Within a month, they were in a committed relationship, and Alec made sure everyone on campus knew they were a couple. Being Quinn Delaney's boyfriend completely changed Alec's social status. He went from being a nobody to a somebody. To say the other guys were incredulous was an understatement. They used to treat Alec like a nothing. Now they all wanted to be him.

'Hey, Roberts, how the hell did you score with Quinn Delaney?' they'd shout out. Alec would smile and hold up his hands like it was a total mystery to him, too. In a way, it was.

They were all jealous, he decided. The hottest girl at school was in love with him, and he was mad, crazy in love with her. After all the abuse, all the teasing, he was the big winner. If someone like her had picked him, he must be a rock star.

It wasn't only her looks that made Alec fall for her. He wasn't completely shallow, he told himself. Quinn was also sweet and would do anything to help someone, even a total stranger. When it came to animals, if she could have, she would have adopted every stray dog and cat in the world. She couldn't pass a dog on the street without stopping to pet them. Quinn was a total marshmallow inside, just like her father.

Chapter Twenty-Five
QUINN

Right after our wedding, we rented our first apartment near my parents' house in New Jersey. Alec was going full time on his master's degree while working at a photography equipment company to pay the bills. That's where he learned so much about taking pictures, techniques of lighting and lenses. I waitressed four or five nights a week at a local pub called the Angry Turtle, and made great tips – especially if I flirted my ass off when groups of guys came in. Old guys were always good tippers, and I knew how to butter my own bread. Things were pretty perfect for Alec and me that first year. We didn't have a pot to piss in, but we were young and had our whole lives ahead of us.

A few months later, my life reached total nirvana. I was pregnant. Oops.

'We agreed we'd wait,' Alec said, visibly annoyed and upset when I told him the news. 'I was supposed to get my PhD first. Having a kid now messes everything up.'

Sure, it was sooner than we'd planned. Was the timing great? Not for him, but for me it was perfect. The road of life was littered with surprises. Alec needed to get over it. He would, eventually.

He stood by the window with his back to me processing the baby news.

'I can't do this right now,' he said. 'It's too soon. We just got married.'

'What do you expect me to do?' I said fiercely. 'I'm not having an abortion.'

'I wasn't suggesting that. I'm just upset.'

'You'll be a great dad. We'll make it work, you'll see,' I said, putting my arms around him.

After a few seconds, he turned around and hugged me, and I knew the angry moment had passed and everything was going to be alright.

'I guess I don't have much choice,' he said, finally smiling. Then he gave me a big kiss. All was forgiven. We were going to have a baby, and our lives would be incredible.

The day my son, Jack, was born was even better than my wedding day. My whole family came to the hospital to meet my new little angel. I finally had what I'd always longed for, my very own baby.

'I want you to be his godmother, Erin,' I said when my sister and I were finally alone in my hospital room. 'Promise me, if I die young, you'll watch out for Jack?'

'Stop being so morbid,' Erin said, making a face and rolling her eyes. 'You just had a baby, and you're talking about dying? Seriously, Quinn?'

I laughed and let go of the negative thoughts that had been with me all day. Erin always knew how to snap me out of a mood. She was right; this was a time for joy. Happiness is fleeting, you have to grab it and savor it, whenever you can.

A few months after the baby arrived, everything changed again. Alec came home with news that turned my world upside down.

'Pack your bags, Quinnie,' he said with a big grin. 'Your big deal husband just accepted an adjunct professor position at Pondfield College. It's right outside of Rochester.' He smiled proudly while puffing out his chest. 'I'm on my way to becoming a History professor. Now that my masters is done, I can go for my doctorate over at the University of Rochester while I'm teaching at Pondfield. It's my dream come true. Isn't this great? We're on our way.'

While I was happy about his job offer, the school was six hours away from where we currently lived, and everyone we knew. Alec had been trying to land a teaching job for a while, but he'd promised he'd only apply to schools in the NY metro area so we could stay close to our family and friends. In my opinion, six hours from New Jersey didn't qualify as close.

Now that I think about it, there's another commitment you didn't keep, Alec.

I didn't want to move to Rochester. The schools there were crappy, everyone had Lyme disease, it was freaking cold. I didn't know anyone up there. I stared at him, tears pooling in my eyes.

'Don't look at me that way, Quinn. Everything is going to be great,' he said. 'The college is even going to give us free housing for three months. Think how much money we'll be able to put away. We can save up for a house. I start in four weeks.'

We stared at each other in silence for a minute, each subscribing to the notion that whoever spoke first lost.

'How about "congratulations, Alec"?' he finally said.

I was incredulous. Did I have no say whatsoever in my future? Alec had decided for both of us and expected me to blindly follow him like a trained seal. A lump formed in my throat when it occurred to me that my son wouldn't know his grandparents.

'You promised you'd only take a job near New York or in New Jersey,' I said.

'Hey, remember when you told me you were pregnant?' said Alec with a look of superiority on his face. I stared at him, not knowing where he was headed and not wanting to open that can of worms.

'*I know it's not what we planned, Alec, but we'll be fine,*' he said, mimicking me. 'I got through that *little* change of plans, you'll get through this.'

He must have seen the look of quiet desperation on my face and changed his tactics. His smug expression faded away and was replaced with a look of empathy. He walked over, wrapped his arms around me and gave me a reassuring hug.

'It's only temporary, honey,' he said softly, looking into my wet eyes. 'We're young. Try to be flexible. This move will pay off for us down the road, you'll see. I need a year or two under my belt, I'll finish my PhD and then we can move back to a school in New Jersey. Maybe I'll even teach at Princeton one day. I'm smart enough for Princeton, don't you think? That would be cool. Professor Alec Roberts of Princeton University.'

I smiled back at him but on the inside, I was freaking out. I convinced myself that the move was only for a little while and soon we'd be back near my family and friends, before I had my next baby.

While I made peace with our move north, my parents were a harder sell. Mom cried when I told her. She loved being a grandma and had become a permanent fixture in our apartment from the day Jack came home from the hospital.

'I'll never see you or my grandson if you move that far away,' she said, wiping tears from her eyes. 'He won't know I'm his grandmother.'

'Mom, you're over-dramatizing. It's only for a year. Alec needs this teaching job, they're hard to come by. He guaranteed me, in about twelve months, we'll be back,' I said.

When I told my father, he looked sad and shook his head. It killed me.

'Eighteen months, max, Daddy,' I said emphatically. 'Alec swore to me. You can visit us, and Jack will still be a baby by the time we get back. I promise.'

Chapter Twenty-Six

While he wasn't ready to be a father, Alec rose to the occasion. He handled the new development like he did everything else: methodically. His biggest worry was whether his wife would look the same after she'd had a baby. Some women started blowing up right after the first kid and kept going. He hoped Quinn wasn't one of those and decided he'd have to watch what she ate to prevent a problem.

They were just getting into a regular routine with the new baby when Quinn announced she was pregnant again.

'How the hell do you get pregnant when you're on the pill?' Alec demanded, his voice getting louder. 'It's supposed to be ninety-nine percent effective.'

'I don't know,' Quinn said, looking away. 'I guess I'm in that fertile one percent.'

'The pill didn't work twice? You think I'm stupid? It's statistically impossible,' he snarled.

At twenty-four, he'd now have three other people to take care of, and he didn't like it. This was not his plan and he resented his wife for saddling him with all the responsibility. Most of his friends were still living the freewheeling single life in New York City and here he was with a wife and two kids.

By the time Hannah was born, they had settled in up near Rochester and Quinn fully embraced motherhood. She stopped dressing the way she used to. Make-up only came out on special occasions, and slinky dresses and short skirts were replaced with 'mom clothes' and sweatpants. Alec found it impossible to see his beautiful wife under layers of oversized clothing and encouraged her to dress differently.

'You still have a great figure, why don't you show it off?' he'd say. What good was it, he thought, to have a gorgeous wife when she was covered up in sweats or in her ratty old bathrobe with baby food stains on it? Did she think he found that attractive? He didn't marry that. He married a knockout and what he ended up with was a hausfrau. This wasn't the deal he thought he'd made.

'You need to take more time with your appearance,' he said. 'This is not a one-way street. You have an obligation to keep yourself looking good for your husband. I take care of myself for you. Spend more time with your clothes, hair and make-up. You should paint your nails.'

Quinn looked at him unconvinced, saying she didn't care about all that stupid stuff.

'I have two little kids who need me,' she said. 'I don't have time to waste getting dressed up every day. I'd rather do things with our children.'

'Yeah, well, what about me?'

'I'm a mom now,' she said, not paying attention to his complaints, 'not a contestant in a beauty pageant.'

But that was what he wanted. He thought he had married Miss America. If Quinn hadn't started looking like shit, he rationalized, he would never have looked elsewhere. She forced his hand. At least the college girls put on a little lipstick.

As time passed, Alec was surprised his wife changed the way she did. He grew resentful and decided she had misrepresented herself. She wasn't the perfect princess she had projected to the world. She trapped him with babies and lies. That's what forced him to seek other options, he told himself. There were loads of flirty girls on the UR campus looking for extra help, and he was more than happy to provide it.

Chapter Twenty-Seven

QUINN

Alec's promise to return to New Jersey was never kept. My daughter, Hannah, was born after an emergency C-section and whenever I brought up moving back to Jersey or closer to my parents, Alec shut me down.

'You're being selfish,' he'd say, his voice bristling. 'I'm doing the best I can to take care of this whole family. How about a little support instead of complaints for a change?'

'We have two kids,' she said.

'Whatever. I have to make money to support all of us. Right now, that means we stay in Rochester. You got a better idea?'

Was I being selfish? I didn't think so. I was taking care of two babies and a house, and he had promised it would only be for a year or two. I tried to sort everything out in my mind. Alec loved me and just wanted the best for me, check. He worked hard to take care of all of us, check. I didn't mean to find fault with him. He was my husband, and I loved him. Didn't I?

'I'm sorry,' I said, trying to smooth things over. 'I am grateful, and I know you work hard. I miss my family and friends, that's all.'

'We'll move back right after I become a full professor at UR and chair the History Department,' he said, warming up. 'Once I get to that level, I'll be able to earn a lot more money and things will be easier for us.'

The following year, with a little financial help from my parents, we put a down payment on a three-bedroom house on a leafy street in the center of Avon, a small suburb of Rochester. It was exciting to have our own home and move out of the cramped apartment we had been renting, but I knew once we bought real estate, the move back to New Jersey was further away. At least he promised we would always spend Christmas with my family in Cranbury, no matter what.

We hardly ever saw Alec's family. They were polite but reserved, not warm and noisy like mine. My father-in-law, George, was demanding and liked things his way, which required Alec's mother to acquiesce on everything in order to keep the peace. Once in a while, I'd see a little of Alec's father in my husband, and it scared me. I didn't want to end up like my mother-in-law.

Then the strangest thing happened. Alec's parents, who rarely visited, announced they were moving up to Avon from New Jersey to live near us. I was stunned. His parents had never taken that much of an interest in us before. If it had been my parents moving to Avon, I would have been doing cartwheels. My husband didn't care at all. I thought having my in-laws nearby would mean we'd have a few extra hands to help with the kids. Alec and I might be able to get out once in a while for dinner or a movie.

A few months later, Alec's parents moved to Avon. I guess the joke was on me. All those years they lived two miles from us, and the only time they ever watched our kids was when we were in a jam and literally begged. I thought they moved near us so they could be close to their grandkids. What I think now is they moved to Avon so we could take care of them as they got older. What was wrong with that picture? Everything. I read them all wrong. His parents never had my back. Not once.

Chapter Twenty-Eight

When she was four or five, Hannah convinced herself that her mother was a princess and her father, a prince. She was pretty sure it was true.

Her father called her his 'little pumpkin' and they'd go on adventures together, just the two of them. He'd often take her with him to the supermarket. Hoisted up on his shoulders, Hannah would point to things she wanted, items her mother would never buy. When they'd get home and unpack the groceries and her mother questioned all the junk food, Dad would wink at his daughter and pretend to be surprised to see all the cookies and chips in their bags. It was their little secret. Those shopping trips with her father were happy memories for Hannah. So was the summer her father taught her all about photography. He showed her which lenses to use and how to set up a shot. He taught her how to work with light and once in a while he even let her use one of his good cameras. He was nice then.

When her parents would go out for the night, Hannah loved watching her mother get ready; putting on make-up and fixing her hair. Quinn would sit at her vanity table with a glass of white wine and slowly apply different magical potions out of tubes and jars. Eyeshadow, lipstick, liner, mascara. With each stroke, her mother became more beautiful. Sometimes, she would let Hannah sit in her chair, and she'd apply lipstick to her daughter. Then she'd style Hannah's hair and fasten it with one of her faux-diamond clips. The back of Hannah's neck would tingle as her mother brushed and she wondered if was going to be beautiful like her mom.

Her mother taught Hannah to play the ukulele and how to cook. The two of them often baked cookies and cakes, and her mother showed her the proper way to knead bread and roll out homemade pasta.

By the time she was ten, Hannah had learned to make about fifteen different meals and started cooking the family dinner once a week. Whenever Hannah cooked, her mother called her 'zee little chef', doing a terrible French accent that would always make her kids laugh.

As the kids moved into their early teens, their father was rarely home, always over at UR with his precious students, even on weekends. Sometimes, when their mother knew their father was going to be away, she'd plan an overnight trip and take Hannah and Jack camping. It didn't cost much, and the kids loved it.

The three of them would drive up to the mountains, pitch their tent and her mother would light a fire and play her ukulele. The three of them would sing songs, toast marshmallows and dance around the flames before crawling into their sleeping bags. Those were happy times, and their mother was alright then.

Later, everything got dark and scary, and Hannah wound up cooking almost every night because there was no one else to do it.

Chapter Twenty-Nine

QUINN

For the longest time, I was lonely in Avon. I had my kids and our dog, but Alec was gone most of the time, always over at the college. He had his own social network at the university, and I wasn't part of it. I didn't really want to be, anyway.

Occasionally, he invited me to some official college event to honor a colleague or some other pomp and circumstance university bullshit. He'd be all up in my face for weeks leading up to the date. He wanted to know exactly what I was going to wear and insisted I get my hair done the day of the event. Before we'd leave the house, he'd inspect me from head to toe suggesting different jewelry or another shade of lipstick, like he was some expert on women's beauty products. My style was simple and conservative, but he always pushed me to look sexy. Tighter clothes, bigger earrings, higher heels. I complied to keep the peace. It wasn't really me, but it made him happy and got him off my back. Eventually, I started dressing that way all the time. It was easier than arguing and he'd smile more.

At some point, he started coming with me when I went clothes shopping under the guise of spending more time with me. He said he enjoyed helping me pick things out.

'Look at it this way, I'm another pair of critical eyes,' he said. 'I'll keep you from making a fashion mistake. Like a girlfriend.'

I interpreted his interest in my wardrobe as a sign of his love. I figured he must love me an awful lot if he cared so much about what I wore. We'd enter a store, and he'd pick out all the dresses, shirts and pants for me. Then I'd model each item for his approval.

He'd say, 'yes' or 'no' or 'I like it, but it's too big' or 'you look like an old lady' or 'that makes you look fat'. If I got upset, he'd say he was 'just trying to help me look good'. I always felt terrible after one of our little shopping excursions.

By the time Jack entered kindergarten, I knew our family was staying in upstate New York for a while. We owned a house and Alec was now chairman of the History Department, just like he had planned. His new responsibilities came with more money and financially, things had gotten more comfortable for us. I wasn't miserable.

I threw myself into being a great mom and wife. I took care of the house, grew fresh vegetables in my garden and cooked my family healthy meals every day of the week. Most importantly, I spent a lot of time with my kids.

When Jack was in first grade, he signed up for intramural soccer. There were two practices after school during the week and games on Saturday mornings. Alec often taught Saturday seminars, so I was usually solo at Jack's games and practices with my daughter in tow.

When my son had the ball, I'd scream at the top of my lungs to cheer him on. He was fast and agile and knew when to pass and when to take a shot. Whenever he'd get the ball and make it all the way down the field, I'd shout and clap so hard my hands would sting afterwards.

Halfway through the soccer season, I struck up a few conversations with some of the other moms. That's where I met the girls; Viv DeMarco, Margot Alexander, Nina Campobasso, and Kelly Bresnahan. They were fun and sassy and didn't take themselves too seriously.

'Do you like to read?' Margot asked me one afternoon.

'I never have time,' I replied.

'How about wine?' she said. 'You like wine?'

'Who doesn't like wine?' I said, grinning.

'She's in,' said Viv to the others.

'My kind of girl,' said Nina and she invited me to join their monthly book club. The next meeting was being held at Viv's house. The book for this month had already been selected, Jane Austen's *Sense and Sensibility*. I had never read any Jane Austen before and was excited to give it a try and more than that, to have some new friends.

Four weeks later, I knocked on Viv's front door with a bottle of chardonnay and a plate full of Muenster cheese, slices of apple, French bread, and some spicy hot mustard. I have always believed everything tastes better with mustard. Viv ushered me into her family room. Her husband, Frank, waved as he and her boys headed down to the basement to watch a game, obviously banished.

'When we have book club at my house, Frank makes himself scarce,' said Viv, pouring herself and Quinn a glass of wine. 'As long as I put beer, soda and chips in the basement fridge, they'll stay down there until I let them out. That way, we ladies have the run of the house.'

As the other women arrived, each with a dish and bottle in hand, we topped off our wine glasses and got comfortable on Viv's burgundy leather couches. It soon became evident that these girls knew how to party. A copy of *Sense and Sensibility* sat in the middle of the dark wood coffee table. The group chatted about the schools, the teachers, the comings and goings of people in town, who was getting divorced and who was cheating on who. After almost an hour, I wondered when we were going to talk about Jane Austen. Finally, Viv demanded our attention.

'Everyone, the Avon Ladies' Book Club will officially come to order,' said our host, taking a big gulp of wine.

'What do we do?' I asked. 'Does one person lead the discussion about the book?'

The four women looked at me incredulously.

'We never talk about the book, Quinn,' said Margot, seemingly stunned.

'You never talk about the book?' I asked, baffled. Had I misunderstood? I tried again. 'But this is a book club, right?'

'Yes, it is a book club,' said Nina jumping in, 'but we don't talk about the books.'

'We don't even read the books,' said Kelly. 'We just pick the book that we would read if we were actually going to read a book. Whoever hosts the meeting puts it on the table, and it feels like we read it. Then we drink wine and trash talk about celebrities and people we don't like in town.'

I was in heaven. These were my kind of girls. They were fun. They were crazy and irreverent. I had found my clique. I still missed my parents, sisters and friends in New Jersey but now with my new friends, Avon wasn't so bad.

For the next ten years until Alec and I split up, I spent many nights out with those girls. Eventually, we moved the 'book club' out of our houses and met in pubs and bars instead. We'd go to different places on Wednesday nights. Once in a while, we'd even do a barbecue or dinner party that included our husbands, although we had more fun when the husbands weren't around. They'd just put on a game and crack open a few beers, so they didn't have to talk to each other – typical guy social interaction. Alec didn't like most of their husbands, calling them 'dumbasses', his new word. Everyone was now a dumbass. The Avon Ladies became a big part of my life. Alec had the university, and I had the girls. At least I thought I did.

Chapter Thirty

Quinn was only his sister-in-law, but she reminded Mike so much of his wife that she occupied a special place in his heart. Their coloring was different, but you could tell they were sisters. They had the same voice, the same way of walking and they laughed at the same stupid things.

Mike thought himself lucky to have married a Delaney. Erin was his high school sweetheart, and he grew up with the family. Quinn and Colleen felt like sisters to him.

The Delaneys were all about big family events and made sure there were always parties and reunions with all the cousins. Erin's parents organized family trips to Florida and ski trips out West. Usually, Big Ed would pay for everyone, including the grandkids. Those occasional big family trips and Christmas week were when everyone got to see Quinn and Alec and their kids.

On five separate occasions over eighteen years, Erin and Mike drove up to Avon to visit Quinn and Alec. The first trip, all the kids were young and it was a good visit. They drank lots of beer, stayed up too late and everyone had fun. Alec took some terrific pictures of all the cousins. He was relaxed, and Quinn was happy keeping herself busy with her children, volunteering for school projects and chauffeuring the kids from one activity to another. Alec and Quinn seemed to be in sync then.

A few years later, the second time Erin and Mike visited them, it wasn't as good. Alec had just received his doctorate in History and was very puffed up about it. He wouldn't stop mentioning his new degree and congratulating himself. It started before Erin and Mike even walked through the front door.

When they pulled up in front of the house, Alec was underneath an old car parked in the driveway. Fixing old cars was his hobby. He'd take them apart, rebuild them and then sell them at a profit. He knew engines inside and out. His grandfather had owned a gas station; that's where he'd learned everything about cars.

As Mike got out of his car, Alec got up, wiped his hands on his shirt and gave Erin a hug.

'Good to see you, Alec,' Mike said, shaking his hand.

'Don't you mean, good to see you, Doctor,' Alec said with a sly grin.

Mike laughed at his joke. 'That's right, I heard about the PhD, congratulations, Dr. Alec,' he said. 'That's quite an accomplishment. Good for you.'

'Yeah, congrats,' said Erin. 'Quinnie told me about it. She's so proud of you. You got another degree and a new job at the same time, impressive.'

'It practically killed me,' Alec said. 'I was working on my dissertation at UR while teaching at Pondfield College. I was totally pumped when the University of Rochester offered me a teaching job. People kill for those positions. And, I'll be making about thirty percent more than I am now.'

Over the next three days, Alec dropped the 'Dr.' every ten minutes. He even suggested that they start calling him Doc instead of Alec. He later said he was only joking, but Mike thought he was deadly serious. It was a long weekend, and they were glad when Sunday came around so they could leave.

On the third visit to Avon, a few years later, Hannah and Jack were in their early teens, as were Mike and Erin's kids. Things were very different on that trip.

Alec was insufferable. There wasn't any subject where he didn't have the last word. At one point, Mike completely stopped talking while Alec pontificated for an hour on some whacky political theory. Mike let him speak and didn't say one word. He figured Alec was going to do it anyway, it was less painful for him to keep his mouth shut and allow his mind to wander. Erin spent most of the time out in the backyard with Quinn, giggling and sharing secrets. The sisters hardly ever got to see each other and needed that time together. Unfortunately, that left poor Mike alone with 'the doctor'.

On Saturday morning of that weekend, Alec, acting like a big shot, cracked open his first beer at ten thirty in the morning. Mike figured because they were visiting, he'd join him. When in Rome, he thought. A few minutes later, Quinn and Erin walked into the house and saw their husbands drinking morning beers.

'Whoa,' Erin said, laughing when she saw Mike with an open bottle. 'Starting a little early, aren't we?'

'Alec, we talked about this,' said Quinn sternly. 'What are you doing?'

'It's my house, and I'm entertaining my brother-in-law,' said Alec as he cracked open another beer.

A scowl crossed Quinn's face. Mike and Erin surmised that this had come up before.

'I'm only having this one, Quinn,' Mike said, trying to smooth things over, 'then I'll wait until the barbecue tonight.'

'You can have as many beers as you want, Mike,' Alec said, holding out another bottle. 'I pay all the bills here. It's my freaking house.'

Quinn, visibly upset, turned and went into the kitchen followed by Erin. Mike changed the subject and the rest of the afternoon was uneventful. Still, that was the day Mike and Erin started to wonder about Alec and what was going on between him and Quinn. When Erin and Mike got back to New Jersey, Alec's behavior was all they talked about for weeks.

Chapter Thirty-One

After hearing about the infamous Avon Ladies for years, Erin finally met them on their fourth trip up to Avon. She noticed that the 'ladies' looked decidedly different from Quinn's old friends back in New Jersey. Their clothes and jewelry screamed 'look at me', and each one needed to lose more than a few pounds. Erin didn't think her sister belonged with them. Quinn was clearly the jewel in their tin crown.

Later that night, when she and Mike went to bed, Erin still wanted to talk.

'I'm not a fan of Quinn's new friends,' said Erin. 'They're rough around the edges and look like they buy their clothes from a QVC sale event.'

Mike made a cat-claw gesture and meowed at his wife making her laugh.

'You know it's true,' she said, giggling and protesting at the same time.

'What does QVC look like?' Mike asked, clueless.

'Like them,' Erin said. 'Quinn's starting to dress the way they do. Did you see all the cleavage? My mother would die if she saw my sister dressed that way.'

'She looked fine,' Mike said.

'That's because she hasn't done a full QVC yet,' Erin whispered. 'Her top was cut too low, her pants were super tight, and then there was all that gaudy jewelry. She never used to wear stuff like that. She used to have style, now she looks cheap.'

Mike was tired, but he knew his wife wasn't finished, not even close, so he listened, nodding at appropriate moments acknowledging that Erin wasn't wholly wrong.

'Your sister was acting like a bit of a party animal,' he agreed. 'She never used to be like that.'

The next morning, Quinn and Erin's kids left for a day of bowling, pizza, and movies. The two sisters folded towels and sheets outside on the picnic table in the backyard while their husbands sat in lawn chairs drinking coffee and discussing college basketball coaches they didn't like.

In the middle of a sentence, Alec pulled off his shirt, walked over to the grass and began doing push-ups in front of his brother-in-law. Erin watched the scene from a distance. As Alec rounded out his twentieth repetition, he lectured Mike on the importance of fitness and outlined his weekly workout schedule. Mike's eyes met Erin's with a 'what a total asshole' look forcing Erin to stifle a snort.

For the remainder of the day, the two couples prepared the fixings for that evening's barbecue. The night's theme was to be Tex-Mex; margaritas, chips, guacamole, salad, and grilled skirt steak.

The Avon Ladies and their spouses arrived. The music was turned up, pitchers of margaritas were poured, and the men started getting frisky. When the party was in full swing, Quinn made her grand entrance on the deck. She was heavily made-up and wearing an extremely short skirt, skimpy tank top, and four-inch heels. Her shiny black hair was piled loosely up on top of her head, and sparkly dangling earrings grazed her shoulders.

Erin nudged her husband in the ribs. 'Mike, look,' she whispered. 'My sister looks like a trash bag.'

'She looks fine,' he whispered back unconvincingly.

'For a hooker, maybe. Who wears five-inch spiked heels to a barbecue?'

Alec looked up from the grill and saw his wife on the deck holding court. He smiled, put down his spatula and walked over and put his arm around her shoulders. He gave Quinn a kiss on the cheek and then on the lips, making a grand show of it.

'You look fantastic, honey,' he shouted while stepping back to admire her. 'You should dress like this all the time. Right, guys, my wife is hot.'

Catcalls and whistles erupted from the men in the crowd. Quinn flashed a big smile, picked up a frozen margarita and lit a cigarette. Erin hated when her sister smoked, and it bothered her that Alec didn't mind.

Two hours later, with very little coaxing required, Quinn brought out her ukulele and sang as if she were a country and western star. There were occasional gaps of silence when her fingers didn't move fast enough on chord changes but she laughed charmingly, and the crowd egged her on. While her sister entertained everyone, Erin noticed Alec leave the party with a scowl on his face and go into the house. When Quinn finished, everyone applauded, and she beamed. It was after she put the ukulele away, that Alec came back outside carrying a handle of Dewar's. He had changed out of his t-shirt and into a sleeveless tee, a wife beater.

'Look at Alec,' Mike whispered to his wife. 'He's so transparent. He wants us to notice his muscles.'

'Why did you change your shirt, hon?' Quinn asked her husband. 'Spill something?'

'I was hot,' Alec said with an edge. 'Got a problem with that?'

'No,' she said. 'Sorry I asked.'

'I'll wear what I want,' he hissed, pouring himself a tall glass of scotch. 'I stay in shape so why shouldn't I wear this? How much weight have you put on since we got married, Quinn? Ten, fifteen, maybe twenty pounds?'

'What?' she said.

'You heard me. You're not going to look good forever, Quinn. I can't wait until you get old, then no one will want you.'

Quinn's face got red and her eyes flooded with tears. Her sister and brother-in-law were the only ones in the yard close enough to hear the exchange. The other guests were oblivious, too busy downing cocktails and engaging in idiotic conversations to notice. Erin and Mike had heard the whole thing.

Chapter Thirty-Two

Nobody in the family said it aloud, but Hannah and Jack thought their father was a bully. Over at UR, his students, especially the girls, loved him. He was one of the most popular teachers. According to their father, his classes filled up faster than anyone else on the faculty. He was an entirely different guy with his own kids.

Most of Hannah's friends had their fathers wrapped around their fingers. Her best friend only had to look at a pair of shoes or a new bag, and her dad would hand over his credit card. Hannah had to work hard for every little thing. Her father called it 'training for real life'.

'If everything is handed to you on a silver platter, Hannah, what would that teach you?' he'd say. 'My job is to shape and guide you. If you want something, you work for it and maybe, you'll get it.'

Always the professor first and parent second, Alec Roberts insisted that his daughter and son prove themselves to him for even the most insignificant things. Every statement had to be backed up with facts and examples as if they were doing a term paper for one of his classes. Allowance money or the ice cream he had promised were often denied because they had forgotten one tiny detail and hadn't earned the prize. Their mother hated when her husband acted like this and secretly provided the extra money or treat when he wasn't around. It was a secret pact between the three of them.

At the start of Hannah's sophomore year of high school, she asked for some new clothes. Like he always did, Alec started hammering his daughter, wanting to know precisely how many skirts, shirts, pants and pairs of shoes she already had in her closet.

'Take inventory of everything, and then present your research,' said her father. 'Make your case, and I'll decide.'

Hannah did what he asked, but that night he shot her down.

'Hannah,' he said as he looked over her list, 'you have eleven skirts, eighteen shirts, nine pairs of pants and twelve pairs of shoes. There are kids in Africa or India who don't own a single pair of shoes. Did you ever think of that?'

Here we go, Hannah thought as she rolled her eyes, another lecture from Professor Roberts. Couldn't he just say yes or no? Every answer always comes with a speech and a life lesson.

'I'm afraid you haven't proven to me why you need more clothes,' her father continued.

After fifteen years of living with Professor Dad, Hannah knew the devil she was dealing with. She was expecting this response, and she was prepared. She put a second document in front of her father that broke down her entire wardrobe by age size, and condition of the garment. Bullet points identified five pairs of shoes that had been re-heeled more than once, with the soles worn through. Also, they all were a half size too small for her growing feet. Every pair of pants was too short, and one had a tear that couldn't be mended. While Hannah schooled her father in wardrobe details, her mother watched the whole exchange. 'Good girl,' Quinn said to herself under her breath.

'So, you see,' Hannah concluded with fanfare, 'more than half the things in my closet don't fit me anymore. I am growing, Dad. That's what teenagers do.'

'Hannah girl,' said her father with a smile. 'Well done. You thoroughly supported your argument. Bravo.'

Score one for me, Hannah thought as her father handed over a hundred and fifty dollars for new school clothes.

'Make it last, Hannah. Spend wisely,' he said. 'Don't come back asking for more money next month. The bank is closed.'

While she was thrilled to get the money, she knew a hundred and fifty dollars wouldn't go very far even if she did shop at Forever 21. Her mother slipped her another hundred and drove her to the mall.

It wasn't only money; their father debated his kids on grades, activities and even dietary choices.

'Your mother tells me you want to be a vegan,' Dad said with a slightly mocking tone one night at the dinner table.

'Yes,' Hannah said cautiously, 'I don't want to eat animals.'

'Break it down for me, Hannah,' said Dad with a 'gotcha' smugness in his voice. 'Explain the pros and cons of vegetarianism to me.'

Jack rolled his eyes and squirmed in his chair.

'I saw that, Jack,' Dad said, sneering. 'You got a problem?'

'I don't know what you're talking about,' Jack said. 'If she doesn't want to eat meat, she shouldn't have to.'

'I simply want your sister to support her position,' Dad said, puffing up. 'If she's that committed to it, she needs to be able to explain why.'

As usual, the conversation deteriorated and ended with Dad shouting, Hannah leaving the table, Jack going to his room and Mom trying to coax all of them to come out of their corners. Usually, when this kind of thing happened, Dad would turn his anger on their mother. That was the main reason why Jack and Hannah avoided getting into debates with their father. More often than not, their mother paid the price for their freedom of speech.

It was always that way. Dad, the stern argumentative ruler and Mom the marshmallow who wanted everyone to have fun and deluded herself into thinking they were the perfect family.

As Hannah got older, she learned to keep her mouth shut. If her father said black, she said black. If he said the ocean was red, she said, 'you're right, the ocean is red, just like a rose, Dad.'

Chapter Thirty-Three
QUINN

I wasn't completely clueless. I do have a brain.

It was winter and Alec had just returned from a week-long seminar in Minneapolis. As soon as he walked in the door, I detected something was different, but I couldn't put my finger on it. He was in a good mood, and I let my guard down. As long as things were going his way, he was nice and calm, most of the time.

'Good trip,' Alec said as he put down his bags and gave me a non-committal hug.

'Not a waste of time like you thought?' I asked brightly.

'It was a total waste of time, so I was able to work out in the gym and even used the tanning bed in the hotel a few times.'

That's what was different; my husband was tan in January.

Alec was very precise and neat about some things but putting his clothes away wasn't one of them. The contents of his overnight bag were draped over various pieces of furniture in the bedroom. While he was in the shower, I picked up some of his clothes including one of his nice sports jackets that was rolled in a ball next to his nightstand. I was about to hang it in the closet when I felt something in the breast pocket. It was an airline ticket folder. I don't know why I looked at it, I just did.

It was his plane ticket, but it was for a flight to the Bahamas. Confused, I examined it more carefully, checking the dates on the receipts. The ticket dates were for this past week.

But he went to Minneapolis, didn't he? He told me he just came back from a conference in St. Paul. I picked him up at the airport.

I heard the shower shut off and waited for Alec to come out of the bathroom. My head felt like it was going to explode as I tried to make sense of a hundred random thoughts. He probably had a good explanation. He always did. When Alec came out of the bathroom, towel around his waist, looking muscular and tan, I held up the ticket in front of his face.

'I found this in your jacket pocket.'

Without flinching, he looked at the paper in my hand.

'My plane tickets. Thanks,' he said, snatching them from me. 'I need them to fill out my expense reports.'

'The tickets are for a flight to the Bahamas.'

'That's right. There was a huge mix-up at the airport,' he said, putting the tickets into his top dresser drawer. 'Stupid airline had me on a flight to Nassau, almost missed my flight to Minnesota. That would have been a disaster.'

'You didn't go to the Bahamas?'

'Don't be ridiculous, Quinn. The conference was in St. Paul.'

'You have a tan.'

'I told you. I used the tanning thing at the hotel. Anything else?'

My husband had become a good liar, but I wasn't convinced. I'd lied about things, too. Guess it takes one to know one.

What do they say, the best defense is a good offense? That sure was Alec's strategy. The minute you called him out on something, he'd turn it around, and before you knew it, the barrel of the gun was pointed between your eyes.

You'd think after so many years I'd have gotten a clue, but I never saw it coming. Even after he'd criticize my appearance or intelligence and push me around. Sometimes he was heavy-handed with the kids. That bothered me more than anything.

I almost left him once.

'I'm out of here,' I had said as I pulled a suitcase out of the closet.

'You have no money, no job, no skills. Where are you going to live?'

'I don't know,' I screamed, throwing random garments into my suitcase. 'I'll figure it out.'

'Go,' he said, 'but let me be very clear. You leave, you can't come back, ever. You'll be all alone, and I won't let you see the kids.'

A few minutes later, I backed down. I couldn't risk not seeing my kids.

Every time we fought, the pain and humiliation festered inside me for weeks. Sometimes, I wanted to kill him, but I knew if I did that I'd be alone and that would be worse.

There was something else. Something I never told anyone. I don't know for sure, but I think Alec drugged me. A few times I woke up alone in bed and couldn't remember how I got there, my underpants were gone and I was all sore down there. I think he might have raped me. Whenever I brought it up and asked questions, he called me crazy. I'm not crazy. I'm just exhausted. I could never tell Erin and definitely not my father. He'd kill my husband and I wouldn't want my dad to get into any trouble. Also, I'd be too embarrassed to tell anyone. Alec's not mean all the time and he always apologizes after we have a fight. I know he loves me.

Chapter Thirty-Four

If there was a loud voice in a room, it was probably Viv DeMarco. No matter how much noise there was, you could always hear her. Everything about her was big and loud. Her hair was bright red, and her clothes had a definite point of view. Of what, most people were never sure. Viv was never pretty, not even cute and she knew it. The way she saw it, beautiful girls knew they were, and the plain ones knew they weren't. As she got into her forties and fifties, she put on more weight and rationalized that her looks weren't her calling card. She made up for not being pretty with three sets of brass balls and a biting sense of humor.

The first time Viv laid eyes on Quinn, she was standing on a soccer field. Oblivious that she was being examined, Quinn cheered and whistled for her son as he took a shot at a goal. Viv instinctually hated Quinn because of her perfect little figure and big blue eyes. She decided 'Little Miss Perfect' –a name she used to call Quinn before she got to know her – was probably a size four or maybe even a two. Whenever Quinn's son scored a goal, she jumped up and down, put her fingers in her mouth and made a loud whistle. When she did that, all the dads on the side lines would check her out. Bitch, thought Viv.

To Viv, Quinn was everything she wasn't. Quinn was the one who always had a boyfriend in high school; the cheerleader, the homecoming queen. Doors routinely swung open for her and opportunities were placed at her feet. Life was one big sundae with two cherries on top for girls like Quinn Roberts. Even after they surprisingly became friends, Viv was always a little jealous of her, until Quinn started to lose her grip. Then Viv just felt sorry for her.

The first time she noticed something was off was one night when the Avon Ladies were out partying in a noisy bar downtown. Quinn drifted in and out of the conversation. There were moments when it was clear she didn't comprehend the gist of what the girls were talking about. At first, Viv thought she was drunk but later realized Quinn had only had ginger ale that night.

A week later, Viv walked up to Quinn at a lacrosse practice. Quinn looked haggard as if she had just climbed out of bed, not her usual pulled together self.

'Are you okay?' Viv asked, trying to be diplomatic, which wasn't her strong suit. 'You look kind of tired.'

Quinn didn't answer and stared blankly ahead without acknowledging her friend.

'Quinn, are you alright?' Viv asked again, this time touching Quinn's arm.

Surprised, Quinn turned and looked directly at her friend.

'Viv,' she said. 'Sorry, I didn't see you.'

'Didn't see me? I'm standing right in front of you,' Viv said. That's when Viv first knew something wasn't right. She wondered if Quinn was drinking or doing drugs. That night she called some of the other Ladies and asked them if they had witnessed any weird behavior with Quinn. Everyone said they had. When it started to occur more frequently, the Ladies suspected something was seriously wrong.

Chapter Thirty-Five

'I don't need marriage counseling,' Alec said under his breath. 'I need a wife without a loose screw.'

Filled with renewed optimism that Alec had finally agreed to go with her, Quinn had made an appointment with a licensed therapist in Rochester named Naomi Sheridan. While Quinn thought meeting with a counsellor would be the first step to fixing their marriage, Alec intended the session would be a 'one and done'. He had no intention of wasting his time or money on months of psycho-bullshit. His wife was the one who needed therapy, he thought, not him.

'I'll go, but if I think it's stupid, I'm out of there,' he said to her.

'Things are so different between us now,' said Quinn. 'We have to work on our relationship.'

'Look in the mirror,' he said. 'I'm not the one with the problem.'

'Stop saying that,' she retorted. 'How would you know anyway? You're never here, and when you are, you're mean.'

Quinn and Alec drove in silence to Naomi Sheridan's office. From the second they sat down, Alec laid on the charm and soon won the therapist over. He could feel his wife seething next to him, and he enjoyed it.

'I chair the History Department over at UR. I'm away a lot because of my lecture schedule. My kids are off at college, and my wife has been experiencing periods of depression, loose thoughts and paranoia. I've begged her to get some help, but her response is always for "us" to get counseling.'

'What do you think about what Alec just said, Quinn?' asked Naomi.

Silence.

'Quinn,' repeated Naomi, 'what do you think about what your husband just revealed?'

'I don't know,' Quinn said without any emotion.

'How do you feel right now?' said Naomi.

Silence.

'Quinn, is there something you want to tell me?' Naomi asked.

'No. Everything's fine.'

'My wife insists there are medical versus mental reasons for all her problems,' Alec explained. 'Once she hit a mailbox with her car because she was so "distracted" so she got her eyes checked. If she can't get out of bed for a week, she claims she has the flu. And her big catch-all is Lyme disease. Every whacky thing she does, she blames on a tick bite.'

'Do you have Lyme disease, Quinn?' Naomi asked.

Quinn nodded.

'Maybe it is the Lyme,' said Naomi helpfully.

'At first, that's what I thought, too,' Alec said, 'but there were too many instances. She'd forget things and tell me she talked to people who I knew she didn't know. Weird stuff and it's been increasing. Some days she can't get out of bed at all.'

Alec told Naomi he had seen signs as far back as five years before, but over the last two, his wife had gotten much worse.

'No matter how much I pleaded with her,' Alec said, playing the noble, steadfast husband, 'my wife's response was to have a couple of drinks and have her ears or blood pressure checked at the walk-in clinic. She refuses to face that she has a serious emotional problem.'

'That's not true,' said Quinn.

'Tell me what you're thinking right now, Quinn,' said Naomi gently.

'It was my idea to come today,' Quinn protested. 'I made the appointment and had to beg him to come with me. Things have been difficult the last few years. He never talks and when he does, he just barks commands. I never smile anymore. He shuts me out and spends all of his time over at his precious school.'

'See what I mean? She places the blame for her problems on me, so she doesn't have to acknowledge her own crazy.'

'I'm not crazy.'

'No one said you were,' said Naomi.

'He just did.'

'We don't use that word in here, Alec,' said Naomi.

Realising he had overplayed his hand, Alec dialed it back.

'You're right, that was uncalled for, I'm sorry,' he said, looking at his wife. 'I just want you to get help. We need you to get better.'

'He's right,' said Naomi. 'The first step to getting well is admitting there's a problem. Alec said that you have mood swings and sometimes get very depressed, so much so that you can't get out of bed. Is that true?'

Quinn sensed the dynamic had shifted. Alec was so good at manipulating people and now the therapist was on her husband's side. It wouldn't matter what she said anymore, Naomi was on team Alec. By the time they ended their first and only session, Alec was off the hook for future marriage counseling. Naomi gave them the name and number of a psychiatrist saying she thought Quinn might benefit from medication.

Alec and Quinn drove most of the way home in silence.

'You weren't honest,' she finally said as they crossed the Avon town line. 'You told her it was all my fault. You exaggerated everything. What about what you do?'

'Like what?'

'Like the drugs or the women.'

'I don't know what you're talking about, Quinn.'

'You know exactly what I'm talking about. You think I don't know. You think I'm stupid. You might fool people like Naomi or your precious students but I know who you really are.'

'There you go again with your paranoia,' he said as he pulled the car into their garage and got out of the car. 'You are nuts. You need to get it together. One day you're going to wake up and I'll be gone.'

Chapter Thirty-Six

The last Christmas at the Delaneys' in New Jersey was strained. They made their annual pilgrimage to New York City to see the Rockettes at Radio City, a thirty-year Delaney tradition. They baked their favorite holiday cookies, strung popcorn and cranberries into garlands and sang Christmas carols, but something was off.

It snowed on Christmas Eve and all the grandkids, now in high school and college, got up early on Christmas Day and went sledding at a nearby park. Erin, Quinn, Colleen and their mother busied themselves in the kitchen preparing the big holiday feast. There was plenty of laughter and teasing going on in the room reminding Eileen of when the girls were young. After a while, she noticed not everyone was laughing. Quinn had barely said a word and had a peculiar smile frozen on her face. Her eyes looked sad. When Erin and Colleen left the kitchen to set the dining room table, Eileen pulled Quinn aside.

'Everything alright, honey?' she said to her daughter. 'You don't seem yourself.'

'I'm fine, Mom,' Quinn said quietly.

Her mother looked at her with a mix of concern and confusion.

'Really, Mom, everything's okay,' Quinn insisted.

Eileen Delaney knew something was wrong, but at that moment she was up to her eyeballs in cookie dough and chocolate mousse and told herself she'd talk to her daughter the next day when they were alone.

From the kitchen, Eileen heard Alec lecturing Mike, Tim and Ed on the correct way to assemble a bicycle. She and Ed had gotten used to Alec and his thinly veiled condescension, but lately, they both had to work hard at being cordial, especially when he was short with their daughter. He would get dismissive and bark commands at Quinn. It pained Eileen that her daughter went along with it; these days, Quinn didn't even flinch.

'Something's wrong, Eileen,' said Ed Delaney in bed that Christmas night. 'He treats Quinnie like she's a servant. I don't like it.'

'You're exaggerating,' his wife said. 'He's just obnoxious. Alec's always been a bit that way.'

'It feels different now,' said Ed, 'like there's been a power shift. She sits next to him like a scared rabbit and waits on him, fetching him beer after beer, agreeing with every idiotic thing he says. That's not Quinn.'

Eileen knew her husband was right but didn't want to fan any flames. She had heard Alec make fun of her daughter in a mean way several times. It gave her that same sick feeling she had on Quinn and Alec's wedding day, right after Linda Roberts mentioned her son's bad temper.

Chapter Thirty-Seven
QUINN

I was always tired. Everyone kept telling me what to do as if I was incapable of making my own decisions. I just needed more sleep, that's what was screwing me up. I read that sleep deprivation can do crazy things to your brain and make anyone act nuts, even have hallucinations.

My parents, sisters, Mike and Alec said I had bipolar disorder and that I needed to take my medication. The doctor at the clinic agreed, but I hated taking that stuff. The pills made me feel gooey like I was walking through thick, sticky syrup. Why would I have wanted that?

I didn't want to take crap that made me feel bad. Erin and Alec wouldn't take pills that made them feel sick. I needed rest, not meds. They all got mad at me when they found out I hadn't been taking what I was supposed to. It was my secret, for me to know and for them to find out.

Chapter Thirty-Eight

'Arrogance is tough to stomach, and a douchebag is annoying. Put them together, and you've got big trouble because an arrogant douchebag is fucking dangerous,' said Mike on the way home from their fifth and final visit to Avon. The weekend had been a disaster, and Erin and Mike both acknowledged that they were dealing with something really bad.

The minute they had arrived in Avon, they noticed a marked change in Quinn, for the worse. The last time Erin had laid eyes on her sister had been that past Christmas in New Jersey, close to seven months before. Since then, all communication between them had been on the phone.

Physically, Quinn had gotten extremely thin. The hollows of her cheeks were sunken. Her hair was stringy and uncombed, and her clothes looked dirty like she had picked them up off the floor. Erin detected dried food crusted on the front of her sister's sweater. Quinn had always been meticulous about how she looked. Now, her sister was tentative, nervous, and at times, confused. Her voice was flat, almost robotic. Her sister was fading away before Erin's eyes.

Conversely, from the moment Mike and Erin arrived, Alec was at high velocity. He knew everything. His opinions were right and theirs, if they differed, were wrong. When he spoke to Quinn, he was dismissive and condescending with a look on his face that screamed, 'I'm superior to you in every way'.

Between Alec's constant lectures and Quinn's withdrawn behavior, the weekend felt like a month to the two visitors from New Jersey. Mike endured Alec's opinions on politics, religion, guns and people at the university he thought were jerks. Erin and

Quinn spent most of their time in the kitchen cooking while Erin gently coaxed Quinn into telling her what was going on.

'Something's wrong,' said Erin. 'You're distracted, you're not acting like you. I'm worried, Quinnie. You've lost too much weight. Maybe you should be seeing someone.'

'I've got a lot going on,' said Quinn. 'If I can get more rest, I'll be okay. You don't always have to play big sister, you know.'

'That's my job,' replied Erin, more concerned than ever.

With the girls sequestered in the kitchen, Mike was left to fend for himself with 'the doctor'. He had long ago developed his survival strategy for Alec; agree with anything he said, no matter how ridiculous.

On the Sunday afternoon of that weekend, Quinn went upstairs to take a short nap, giving Erin a window to talk to her brother-in-law. She quietly asked Alec what he was doing concerning her sister's treatment. Alec looked at Erin with a smirk on his face.

'What am I doing?' he replied. 'You don't get it. I've been carrying your sister for years. I've done everything. You know how hard it's been for me? It's about time Quinn helped herself for a change. I can't fucking breathe for her.'

'*She's got an illness,*' Erin said, her voice rising. '*I live six hours away, or I'd take care of her myself. She needs a better therapist, not that crappy clinic you send her to so you can save money. Her medication has to be monitored and you have to make sure she takes it. You need to look after her. Alec, you need to take this seriously.*'

'Take it seriously?' said Alec. 'Screw you, Erin. You come up here, all high and mighty, like a Monday morning quarterback and tell me I'm not doing the right thing. Screw you.'

It took every part of Erin's being to keep from lunging across the room at her brother-in-law's throat. He was destroying her sister through neglect and he knew it, and didn't care.

When Alec verbally attacked Erin, Mike stood up, ready to pummel his brother-in-law. For a second, Erin thought they were going to go at it. Trying to bring the temperature in the room down, she pleaded with Mike to sit down and turned her attention back to Alec.

'I'm sorry I got so upset,' she said calmly. 'We all want the same thing, for Quinn to get better. We need to get her into better treatment and then make sure she follows exactly what the doctor prescribes. She cannot be left to her own devices.'

From the expression on Alec's face, she could tell her words were falling on deaf ears. It was obvious he no longer cared what happened to Quinn. That was when she understood everything. He only cared about her sister when she was beautiful, perfect, sexy Quinn. Unhinged and confused Quinn was of no interest to him. It didn't matter that she was the mother of his children and they had been together for twenty-three years. For better or for worse was not a vow he had any intention of keeping.

Part Three
OUR BREAK-UP

Chapter Thirty-Nine

It started out as a regular Saturday morning. Erin had just finished her first cup of tea and was reading a movie review online. The phone rang, it was Quinn.

'Hey, Quinnie,' Erin chirped into the phone. 'What's cooking up there in the boonies?'

'Nothing,' Quinn said quietly. 'Just hadn't talked to you in a few days.'

'What's wrong?' Erin asked, suspiciously noting her sister's flat voice.

'Nothing.'

'Quinn?'

'Well...' she began slowly, pausing slightly between every other word, 'I called to tell you that my husband of over nineteen years, Alec, has decided he doesn't want to be married to me anymore. He's determined he doesn't love me and thinks it's best that we get a divorce.'

'Divorce?' Erin shouted into the phone.

'He said he's not happy being married to me and has decided I should move out,' she continued, matter-of-factly.

'Are you sure he meant it?' Erin said. 'Maybe he was just upset about something.'

'Apparently,' said Quinn calmly, 'he's in love with one of his students from the university. He said that I'm fat, old and stupid and he's wasted enough of his life on me.'

'That bastard, like he's some kind of prize?' Erin shouted even louder, causing Mike to come racing into the room. Quinn began to cry and free associate with a string of questions and statements interspersed with sobs.

'I don't understand. What did I do wrong? I love him, Erin, I love him. I can't live without him,' she sobbed. 'I don't know what to do. Where am I going to go? I don't want to be alone. Why doesn't he love me anymore? I did everything I was supposed to do. What about my kids?'

As far as Erin was concerned, no one hurt her little sister, ever. Quinn's pain was palpable, and Erin's instinct was to protect her and make the pain go away. She wished she could reach through the phone and put her arms around her and tell her everything would be alright. Quinn cried and cried until she was too tired to weep anymore.

'He was never good enough for you,' Erin said quietly.

'You didn't like Alec?' said Quinn in disbelief.

'Not really.'

'But you were always so nice and friendly to him, always joking and laughing.'

'Because he was your husband,' Erin said. 'I made the best of it. We all did.'

'No one liked him? Oh my God,' said Quinn. 'Why?'

'When we were young he was okay but as he got older, he became more of an arrogant jerk,' Erin replied. 'He had all those whacky political ideas and the emotional mentality of someone with an arsenal of assault weapons in his basement.'

'How did you know? He does have assault rifles in our basement,' Quinn said, surprised that her sister guessed.

'Figures. Now I hate him even more.'

'What about Mike?'

'Mike can't stand him,' Erin said. 'After our last visit to Avon, Mike was done.'

'Why didn't you tell me?' Quinn asked.

'Because you seemed happy-ish. I thought he would take care of you. But he never did. Now, the gloves are off.'

'But I still love him,' Quinn wailed again. 'I don't want to be by myself.'

For over two hours Quinn went from tears to anger and back to tears. Her sister tried to comfort her by pointing out Alec's shortcomings. Now that she didn't have to hold her tongue, Erin let it rip and prayed they didn't reconcile down the road. If that happened, she would be *persona non grata* after all the smack talk she did about Alec that day.

Erin reminded her sister of an incident at their parents' house a few Christmases before. Alec, Quinn and Erin were in their parents' TV room. Quinn's kids were around fourteen and fifteen and were playing some kind of shooting and killing type of video game. Erin's kids were watching a movie in another room. Quinn's son, Jack, and a friend were blowing up and killing fictional people in their game.

'Do you think it's healthy for kids to play such violent games?' Erin asked Quinn and Alec. 'I don't let my kids play that stuff.'

Alec looked over at his sister-in-law, and she saw arrogance creep across his face. She knew he was about to enlighten her on something.

'When boys play video games it prepares them to defend our country, so they're ready if they are ever called to serve,' Alec said confidently. 'Video games hone weaponry skills and make them better and stronger soldiers.'

Erin started to laugh, thinking it was one of Alec's pranks. Even that deadpan look on his face was undoubtedly part of the joke, she thought.

'What's so funny?' Alec said. 'I'm not kidding.'

'Come on, Alec,' Erin said as she looked over at Quinn for support. 'Quinnie, he's joking, right?'

Quinn looked at Alec and then back at her sister.

'We both feel that video games develop young men's shooting skills and ultimately make them better soldiers,' Quinn had said, looking at her husband for approval.

'Do you remember that conversation, Quinn?' Erin said into the phone.

'I don't know what I was thinking,' said Quinn laughing a little. 'He had me so confused. He'd get so angry whenever I didn't agree with him, so I always did.'

'What do you mean he would get so angry?' Erin asked, antenna going up.

'He pushed me around and screamed at me all the time but mainly when nobody was around.'

'Did he hit you?'

'Not a lot.'

'What's not a lot?'

'He mainly shoved me against the walls and screamed in my face but sometimes he'd push me down onto the floor and pull my hair or twist my arms. One night, he locked me out of the house. Another time he locked me in the hall closet.'

Erin couldn't stop her once the floodgates opened, and Quinn's dirty little secrets came pouring out. That morning, Erin learned the truth about her brother-in-law and was thankful there were hundreds of miles between them, because she surely would have killed him, or at the very least, put him in a wheelchair.

Alec was dumping her little sister for one of his students. She hated her brother-in-law more than ever but at the same time, was relieved Quinn would finally be free.

Chapter Forty

Joan Hemmerly didn't feel like going all the way over to show the apartment if the woman on the phone was looking for a palace. It was just a plain vanilla box, but some prospective renters had such unrealistic expectations.

'It's nothing fancy,' she warned Quinn Roberts. 'Just your basic one-bedroom apartment but it has lots of closets, and the neighborhood is safe and sound.'

Quinn assured her that the location sounded ideal and the landlady agreed to meet her there later that day to show her around.

When Joan Hemmerly first laid eyes on Quinn, she thought the woman looked half-starved. Within the first few minutes, Quinn told the older woman that she was getting divorced and needed to find a new place to live, to start over.

'There's no shame in divorce,' the landlady said. 'Heck, I got divorced, too, before I married my second husband. Most of the people I like are divorced. No sense in staying with someone if you don't get along. Especially, if they're ornery like my ex. He was a bad one. Nasty and mean, especially after he had eight or nine beers.'

The two women talked a little more about the difficulties of marriage while they walked up the uneven wooden stairs to the apartment on the second floor. The landlady said the minimum rental was six months and she needed a two-month deposit up front.

The two women entered a spacious foyer, big enough to double as a dining room. The empty apartment had been freshly painted white. The kitchen was to the left and the living room to the right. On the far side of the living room was a hallway with two doors, one to the bathroom and the other to the bedroom. Quinn walked around the living room and then over to the windows and looked out.

'You get a nice view from here,' the landlady said, trying to sell the younger woman on taking the place. She'd already decided Quinn would make a great tenant. From the landlady's perspective, Quinn Roberts was mature and appeared to be quiet and clean, not like those two young hooligans she had in there before. Those two were a pain in the ass, she thought. They were always breaking things, making noise, and bothering all the other neighbors. At one point, her other tenants threatened to move out if she didn't get rid of those young guys. When their lease was up, she didn't renew. Quinn Roberts, on the other hand, wouldn't scare a mouse or make any trouble. She'd be a model tenant.

Quinn walked through the entire apartment and opened every closet and cabinet several times.

'Plenty of closet space, too,' Mrs. Hemmerly said, giving her the hard sell. 'And there's a little market in walking distance, so you don't always have to get in your car. Kenny's Kwik-Mart is just a few blocks over.'

'That's nice,' Quinn said. 'I like to walk.' She circled the apartment one last time and said she'd take it. She wrote the landlady a check for the first month's rent along with the deposit. Joan Hemmerly pulled out her lease, and they cut a deal right then and there.

'Well,' the landlady said, handing her the keys, 'I hope you make a great start here in your new life. I have a good feeling about you. I'm a southern girl, and in the south, we listen to our gut. My friends say I have a sixth sense about people and I have a good feeling about you. You're going to be just fine, honey.'

Quinn looked up at the landlady and flashed a big smile. Look how pretty she is when she smiles, thought the landlady. Her husband must be a real asshole. Most of them are.

Chapter Forty-One

Alec had chaired the History Department twice, and after twenty years of teaching at UR, he was considered by his peers to be an expert on twentieth-century European history. His dissertation was called 'The Rise of the Third Reich in a Complacent Europe'.

He'd never come out and say it, but weirdly, Alec admired what the Nazis had accomplished in only a few short years. That was a side to World War II that he wanted his students to understand.

'Germany had been ravaged and decimated after a massive defeat in World War I. An entire generation of German men had been killed leaving only old men and young boys,' Alec said to his freshman class. 'The Treaty of Versailles created economic sanctions and conditions that tied Germany's hands from moving forward economically. There was no money, work or food and the people were desperate until an Austrian artist told them there was a way out, and there was hope.

'In less than a decade, Hitler built momentum and Germany was on course to take over the entire continent,' Alec continued. 'If the United States hadn't finally gotten involved, and they might not have if Roosevelt, who was by nature an American isolationist, had gotten his way, Hitler would have been successful.'

'Why didn't Roosevelt want to get involved?' a student asked.

'Roosevelt wanted no part of it; as far as he was concerned it was a European war, and he had no plans to intervene,' Alec explained. 'If the Japanese, who were aligned with Germany, hadn't bombed Pearl Harbor, America probably would never have sent troops to Europe. You could say that it was the Japanese who caused the Third Reich to fall. When the Japs bombed Pearl

Harbor, America had to get in. At that point, Hitler was only weeks away from taking over Europe.'

Alec wanted his students to understand and appreciate the good as well as the bad.

'Good guys are not a hundred percent good, and bad guys aren't all bad,' he'd say every semester. 'To prevent the rise of another Hitler, we have to acknowledge the qualities and strengths that had enabled him to do what he did and amass so much power. The Germans didn't start out following a monster.'

The students loved debating this concept, and his classes got into some pretty wild discussions. Most of the kids liked his classes, and they filled up fast. His students told him he made them think about things from a different perspective.

'I guarantee you,' said Alec to one of his colleagues, 'none of these kids ever looked at the positive side of Adolf Hitler before. I can see it on their faces as their little minds grapple with that concept.'

That was one of two reasons Alec Roberts loved to teach. He enjoyed watching the light bulbs go on inside the students' heads and found it a real rush to mold a young person's mind.

The other reason was that he got to spend his days standing in front of a room filled with girls who were eternally twenty-years-old. No matter how old he got, the girls were always young, dewy, curious, thin and supple.

One or two female students per semester started the dance, resulting in at least one student 'relationship' each term. There were always plenty of willing volunteers and, it was common knowledge that spending a little extracurricular time with Dr. Roberts dramatically improved a girl's GPA. He didn't know it, but he was the easiest A on campus.

Chapter Forty-Two

QUINN

I didn't always know for sure, but eventually, I discovered my husband was cheating on me. I found out about 'Dr. A'. I may have had a mental illness, but I'm not stupid.

It was about seven or eight years before we separated. There was an opening of a new sports center at UR. Alec asked me to go, and we brought Hannah and Jack with us. The kids were around eleven and twelve then. I didn't attend many events at the school anymore, so no one knew who I was. During the reception, I excused myself to go to the ladies' room. I had just closed the door to my stall when I heard the main bathroom door open and two women enter. I could tell by what they were discussing that they were students.

They went into stalls on either side of me and continued their conversation. I think it's impolite to keep talking while you're peeing but that's just me.

'Are you going to the Sigma Tau party tonight?' said one of them.

'If I finish my History paper,' groaned the other.

'Who are you kidding? You know Dr. A will give you the A even if you turn in a blank page,' said the first girl, laughing.

'That's not true,' said the second girl coyly from her stall.

'We're talking about Dr. A,' said the first girl. 'Give him some ass, you'll be sure to pass.'

'Give him a lay, and you get your A,' giggled the second girl. Then both toilets flushed and the voices moved to the sinks and left. Frozen inside my stall, I collected myself and pulled up my pants.

Were they talking about Alec? They said a 'history paper'. It couldn't be Alec because they called him Dr. A. Alec would be Dr. R. There must be loads of other professors at the university whose last name begins with A. I remember Alec talking about a professor named, Dr. Abbott who teaches History. They must have been referring to him. I can't believe teachers give out grades for sex.

I walked back to the reception, got another glass of chardonnay and made small talk with some of the other guests. A few people gave speeches, and there was lots of applause. I casually asked Alec if anyone else from the History Department was at the party. He identified a few of his colleagues in the crowd.

'Everyone is here,' he said. 'The president wanted the whole department to show.'

'Point people out to me. It's been a while since I've been over here. Wasn't there a Dr. Abbott?' I asked. 'For some reason, I remember that name. Is he here?'

'What makes you ask about Abbott?' Alec said. 'She's right there, the one in the red jacket and black skirt.'

Dr. Abbott is a woman. Then she can't be Dr. A. Those girls were definitely talking about a man.

I asked Alec to tell me the names of all the professors in his department. He rattled them off, and Abbott was the only one whose last name began with A.

At the time, I convinced myself that Alec couldn't be Dr. A. Maybe those girls only called their mystery man Dr. A because they got an 'A' in the class. Deep down, I probably knew then it was my husband but couldn't admit it to myself. I wasn't ready to accept it until much later. Funny the things you can convince yourself of if you try hard enough.

Chapter Forty-Three

D ivorce is a messy business with lots of collateral damage. It's not for the faint of heart.

Most of Barbara Waxman's clients were so emotionally spent by the time she met with them that they didn't know what they wanted. Her job as a divorce attorney was to listen, advise and then help them figure out the best way forward.

At $325 an hour, people needed to decide pretty quickly what their end game was or it got expensive. If someone just wanted to get something off their chest, it was a lot cheaper to go to a therapist for $150 an hour. When it came to lawyers, every minute was billable. Don't ask a lawyer how they are, because they'll have to charge you for the time they take to tell you. Not Barbara Waxman's rules; the firm's.

The first time Quinn Delaney walked into her office, she was all fired up. That week, her husband of about twenty years had told her he wanted a divorce, no counseling, no negotiating, he just wanted out. Apparently, Alec had a girlfriend. Quinn had been suspicious of other women, but every time she'd point out a lie or bring something up, he was always ready with an excuse.

'He told me I was paranoid and crazy when I found his secret plane tickets to the Bahamas,' Quinn said that first day. 'He made me go to a shrink and then he put me in a mental hospital for observation.'

At first blush, Quinn Roberts' situation sounded like every other divorce Barbara Waxman had worked on. It was textbook, or at least that's how it looked in the beginning of their meeting. Pretty wife at home is taking care of the family, wrapped up in school and after-school activities. She's more focused on the kids than the husband, but the husband's ego needs stroking. He's out in the workplace where other women think he's the bomb and he starts playing around with a co-worker. Then the wife notices something. She wants to know why he's going out every night, or why he has a tan when he went to a convention in Minnesota in January. He turns everything around so that it's all her fault. Nine out of ten times, her husband is a liar. Make that ten out of ten. He's not the same sweet guy who got down on one knee and slipped a diamond ring on to her finger. He's evolved. He wants a second shot with a newer model so he can feel like he's twenty-five again. Barbara had seen it a hundred times – make that two hundred. But the hospital part, even with all the whacky marital stories she'd heard over the years – that was unusual. Barbara made a note to herself.

'I didn't think anything about him being out so often because he was so involved at the university,' Quinn continued. 'And then I'd find things like tickets or charges on our Visa bill that didn't jive with where he said he was.'

'I see,' Barbara said, running her fingers through her long, curly, salt and pepper hair as she wrote down a few more notes. She was listening to Quinn, but she was also thinking about what she was going to order for lunch. Big decision; tuna or egg salad.

'I was able to deal with his mood swings and even him being out all the time,' Quinn continued, 'but he started to push me around, and one night he knocked me down and tried to choke me. I thought he was going to kill me.'

Barbara stopped planning her lunch order and looked up at her client.

'He gets physical with you?' Barbara said.

'Sometimes,' Quinn said softly. 'In the beginning, it was only once or twice. Then it happened whenever he didn't like what I said or how I looked. Sometimes I didn't even know what set him off. He'd knock me down or twist my arm back or lock me in a closet. Is it considered rape when you're married?'

Barbara sat up tall in her chair and pushed herself back from her desk. When it came to spousal abuse or spousal rape, Barbara Waxman, Esq., loaded her gun and went into battle mode. Domestic violence was never okay. She often pondered how ironic it was that she spent her life untangling marriages while she herself had never gotten married.

'Quinn, listen to me,' said Barbara. 'I'm going to look out for you, do you understand?'

Quinn nodded.

'I'll deal with his lawyer but in the meantime, I want you to go meet with a domestic violence group here in town,' she said, handing Quinn a card. 'You'll see you're not the only one. Those women have been through the same thing you have, some much worse. They're a wonderful support network and they'll help you get through this. You've got to promise me you'll go.'

Quinn nodded again.

After hearing marital stories like Quinn Roberts', Barbara had zero interest in the institution. She would be Quinn Roberts' champion and provide her with her full attention and protection. Alec Roberts would have to go through her if he wanted to get to his wife, and Barbara Waxman was a force to be reckoned with.

Chapter Forty-Four

When the phone rang, and the caller ID displayed Quinn's number, Erin took a deep breath and reached for the phone. She never knew what state her sister was going to be in these days.

'Hey, sister-sister,' Erin said cheerfully. 'What's up?'

'I need to ask you a question,' Quinn said, her voice low and flat with no emotion. 'Do you know where I can buy a shotgun? Because I want to kill myself.'

'Talk to me,' Erin said, panicking. 'Did you take your medication today?'

'I just want to know if you know where I can get one,' her sister asked again.

'Listen to me,' Erin said. 'I can tell from the way you sound that you did not take your meds.'

Silence.

'Quinnie. Answer me, did you take your pills this week?' Erin demanded.

'I don't know,' Quinn said. 'Right now, I just need to find a gun.'

'Listen carefully,' Erin pleaded. 'You only feel this way because you didn't take your medication. We've talked about this. Remember that day you and I went for a hike up at Devil's Den? It was sunny and warm, and we were laughing and giggling like we did when we were little. You were happy. I told you I was grateful to have my sister back. You said you felt like yourself again. Remember?'

Silence.

'Quinn?'

'I need to find a gun,' she said for the third time. 'My husband of twenty years has a girlfriend. He doesn't want me anymore. I don't want to be alone.' Then she began to cry.

'Take a deep breath,' Erin pleaded. 'You already knew about Alec's girlfriends. That's been going on for years. He's a dick and one day he'll burn in a bad place. I personally will light the match.'

Silence.

'Try and remember all the bad stuff that Alec did to you,' Erin continued. 'He shoved you and pushed you around. He locked you out of the house and in the hall closet. That's why you went to the domestic violence support group.'

Silence.

'If Alec has a girlfriend, you should feel sorry for her. He'll do the same thing to her that he did to you,' Erin said. 'A leopard doesn't change their spots. Alec is a world-class leopard. Don't let that asshole define you.'

Silence.

'Look, what you're feeling now has nothing to do with him. It has everything to do with your medication. Think about what we said on our hike.'

'No,' said Quinn. 'I don't want to.'

At least, thought Erin, her sister had answered her and stopped talking about the gun. That was progress.

'You promised to remember how good you felt that day. You had been taking your prescriptions, and you told me you felt normal and happy. Do you recall that?'

'Yes,' Quinn said. 'I remember.'

Erin let out a sigh of relief. 'Then I'm asking you again. Quinn, have you been taking your meds?'

'I don't like the way they make me feel, so I take the ones I want and not the others,' she said sounding like a little child.

'Quinn,' Erin said, trying a little tough love, 'since when did you get a medical degree? Last time I checked you had a BA in Communications with a minor in English.'

Silence.

Then, Erin heard it. Very faint at first; it was laughter. Then the laughter got louder, and she knew the old Quinn was still in there trying to get out. Somehow, she had made her sister see the ridiculousness of their gun conversation and Quinn was actually laughing at herself. The crisis momentarily averted but Erin knew it was only temporary, the battle won but not the war.

After a long pause in the conversation, Erin tried to think of her next move.

'Erin,' Quinn said softly, 'I've been hearing voices.'

Shit, Erin thought. She's getting worse. It was crystal clear, her forty-something sister needed a babysitter, at least until she stabilized. If Alec hadn't moved her so far away from the people that really cared about her, Quinn would never have gotten so bad. Erin would have seen to that.

Fifteen minutes later, Erin was in her car headed to upstate New York to bring her sister back to New Jersey for a while. Quinn couldn't be left alone or they'd lose her forever.

Chapter Forty-Five

QUINN

I think my phone call freaked my sister out. I didn't mean to. When I called her, I really did want to get a gun to kill myself. I hated being alone in that stupid apartment in Newbridge. I wanted to be back in my house in Avon.

Alec wasn't perfect, but he was still my husband. At least when I was with him I had a place in the world and a family and a home. He wasn't bad to me all the time. He never punched me. He just shoved me a little or twisted my arms, pulled my hair. He did choke me that one time, but he didn't mean to. A few times he locked me out of the house, but he said it was because I got on his nerves. He was tired of my mood changes and sometimes I made him crazy. Could I really blame him? It was partly my fault he acted so mean. He said he was tired of taking care of me. He always apologized afterward and then we'd be happy for a while. Now he didn't want me at all.

I told Erin about the voices. She kind of bugged out.

'You hear voices, you mean like the Son of Sam?'

'Who's the Son of Sam?'

'That New York serial killer from the seventies,' Erin said. 'He heard voices from a dog telling him to kill people. You mean like that?'

'No,' I said. 'They're normal voices. They don't tell me to do anything or kill anyone. You really must think I'm nuts.'

'I don't understand,' Erin said. 'Can you explain the voices a little more?'

'I'll be sitting on my couch looking at a magazine, and I'll hear Mom's voice from behind me saying, "Quinn, can you help me with something in the kitchen?" I'll turn around, and of course, Mom isn't there.'

'So,' said Erin, 'do you hear these voices inside your head? Or do you hear them with your ears like a real sound?'

'I hear them with my ears. I hear sound, not from inside my head,' I said. 'They're not scary voices, they're people I know, like you or Colleen or Mom. When I hear them, they're about ordinary things. No dogs or killing. Nothing like that.'

'Does it happen often?'

'It used to be once in a while, but now I hear them almost every day. Do you think I'm crazy?'

Erin got very serious and assured me everything was going to be alright, that I just had a chemical imbalance. She made me promise to take my meds while she and Mike figured out what to do.

'I love you, Quinn.'

I promised her I would try and take my medication, but I didn't know if I would. The meds made me feel strange and gummy. Some days I felt as if I was going to explode, and other times I felt absolutely nothing. I wasn't sure which scared me more.

Part Four
AS MY MARRIAGE CRUMBLED

Chapter Forty-Six

QUINN

Our divorce lawyers had been fighting over the terms of our agreement and Alec had been particularly nasty the last time he and I talked. He always confused me. On the days my head was foggy, I wanted it to be over and was ready to give my husband whatever he wanted. My lawyer, Barbara, would find out I gave in to certain things and she'd reel me in. She'd call Alec's lawyer and tell him whatever I had said 'yes' to was off the table. Then Alec would call me up, screaming. Round and round we'd go.

Some days, I desperately wanted him back. I missed my old life with Alec and our kids. It wasn't perfect, but it was mine. Other times, when my thoughts were clear, I'd become furious and wanted Alec to fry in hell for how badly he treated me. He should feel the pain I felt and know what it was like to be thrown away like garbage. I flipped and I flopped. I was in the middle of my own mental shitstorm and couldn't find the exit.

Every day, I paced around my small, sad apartment trying to make sense of my new solo life. I couldn't hold on to a thought for more than a few seconds, and it frustrated me. What was the point of it all? I wondered, until I lost that thought too.

Erin picked me up and brought me back to New Jersey for a few weeks. When I stayed at her house, I think I was content. She was always around and made sure I got exercise, good food and took my meds when I was supposed to. My parents were around too and I felt safe again, something I hadn't felt in a long time.

Being in New Jersey was good, but I missed my kids and wanted to go back home. After a few weeks, Erin drove me back to upstate New York, so we could look for a new apartment in Newbridge, closer to my kids. Erin thought there would be more job opportunities for me there. Newbridge also put a little distance between me and you-know-who. After I found the place, my sister stocked my new apartment with food, bought me some plants and knick-knacks, put up some curtains and found me a new doctor and a psychiatrist. She stayed a few extra days to get me settled, but then she left, and I was by myself again. Alone.

The one question I asked myself over and over was, how did I end up here? This wasn't supposed to be how the great Quinntessa's life turned out. It wasn't supposed to be like this.

Chapter Forty-Seven

The first time Quinn went to see Dr. Judith Shapiro, she was in bad shape. Erin accompanied her and filled in all the missing pieces. Quinn didn't speak much that first day and presented as flat and distant. The doctor wasn't sure Quinn was even listening to what they were saying.

Physically, Quinn was gaunt and tired. Her movements were wooden and lethargic, and her body language screamed, 'I give up'.

'About a year ago, my sister's husband had her hospitalized for observation,' Erin explained to the doctor. 'The day Quinn was released, he told her he wanted a divorce.'

'Is he still actively involved in her care?' Dr. Shapiro asked.

'Not anymore,' said Erin. 'His idea of treatment was throwing her into a state mental hospital, so he didn't have to deal with her or spend any of his money. He's done it twice. I'm going to get more involved now. I live six hours away, but I'll figure it out.'

The doctor observed a vulnerability about Quinn, and despite her frail emotional and physical condition, her sweetness came through. She liked Quinn from the start and wished she could tell her everything was going to be alright but knew that chapter hadn't been written yet.

'I've never lived by myself before,' Quinn told her. 'My kids are away at college, and I never see Alec anymore. I don't know what I'm supposed to do or where I'm supposed to be.'

Every session Dr. Shapiro had with Quinn was a surprise. Some days, when Quinn stayed on her meds, she'd be feisty and funny and tell the doctor about the myriad of awful things Alec had done or said and how she was going to confront him during her divorce. Other times, when her spirits were low, she said she loved and missed her husband and wanted him to take her back. After those sessions, Dr. Shapiro adjusted her medication.

After a few months working with Quinn, one thing Dr. Shapiro was sure of was that Alec Roberts was a first-class son of a bitch. From her professional perspective, she figured Quinn's husband was probably a classic narcissist. Typical narcissists see themselves as entitled and perfect, always right, and consider that the rules for everyone else don't apply to them. No one is their intellectual equal, and they're always the smartest one in the room. They have no empathy for others. That profile fit Alec Roberts exactly.

Then another idea occurred to Dr. Shapiro. Alec Roberts could also be a psychopath. They live to manipulate and get one over on others, physically or emotionally. They have no regrets and no scruples. They'll become whatever they need to be to take advantage of a situation. They're chameleons who can be incredibly charming in their quest to get what they want. Once they have it, they'll leave their victim hanging out to dry. Their only concern is not getting caught.

Dr. Shapiro felt a pit in her stomach when it occurred to her that Alec Roberts might be both. It's rare, she thought, but it's possible he was a narcissistic-psychopath, a terribly lethal combination. She was relieved Quinn had moved out and warned her patient that she needed to keep her distance. In her opinion, Alec Roberts was a loose cannon.

Chapter Forty-Eight

When Erin called her nephew to tell him his mother was having severe mental problems, Jack Roberts was right in the middle of mid-terms. He listened quietly, saying little as his aunt sounded the alarm. When the call was over, he was dumbfounded.

Newsflash, Aunt Erin, you think I don't know my mother is nuts? She's my crazy mother. I lived with her. You're down in New Jersey and see her once a year. She's been whacked for years. You weren't around to see it, but Hannah and I were. You know how many times a day she calls me at school saying all sorts of crazy stuff? This has been going on since the middle of high school. I stopped asking my friends to come over to the house because I was so embarrassed. I'm sick of her and her conspiracy theories. It's not my job to take care of her. I'm the kid. She's supposed to be taking care of me.

When it started, it was just little things that didn't make sense to Jack and his sister. Then there were those long stories that they knew couldn't be true. Their mother was always cleaning, even places and things that didn't need to be cleaned, on an eternal search for mold. She convinced herself there was dirt where there wasn't, and things were growing where they weren't. And then she'd pace, back and forth for hours. She drove her kids crazy.

His mom's family and her friends thought his dad was the bad guy. Jack knew his father could be a dick, but he had to put up with a lot of crap from his mother. His father went to work every day to support the family, and he came home to Mom's crazy every night. On some level, Jack didn't blame his father for wanting to get divorced. At least things were peaceful now with

Mom out of the house in her own apartment. No more fighting. No more crying.

It always started the same way. Dad would stop at the gym on his way home from work. He'd walk into the house with his gym bag, and Mom knew just what to say to piss him off. She'd complain about him being late or something along those lines, and he'd say something nasty back to her. She'd start to whine, accuse or yell and then things would spiral downward.

Even though Mom usually had dinner cooking on the stove, they rarely ate together. When his parents would fight, which felt like every night, Hannah and Jack would go into their rooms. Jack would lock his door and turn up his music so he couldn't hear anything. Dad would grab a six pack and go into the den to watch a game or change his clothes and go out for the night. If he went out, Mom would corner her two kids and tell them how unfair and mean their father was. She'd carry on for hours. Sometimes, he wished she would just die and leave him alone.

Still, he knew it wasn't cool the times Dad locked her out of the house at night. Jack would hear her crying out on the front porch. After his father fell asleep, Jack would let his mother back in, and she'd go and lie down on the couch in the TV room. He'd put a blanket on her and go back to bed.

More than anything, he wanted his mother to be like she used to be. He wanted her to be old Mom, fun Mom, ukulele Mom. New Mom was wholly unglued.

Chapter Forty-Nine

Quinn refused to sign the divorce agreement Alec's lawyer had drafted. One week she was full of spit and vinegar, threatening to 'take him to the cleaners', and accusing him of hiding money. She said she was going to get a forensic accountant to 'blow the lid off everything'. Alec didn't want anyone poking around in his finances. It was none of their business.

The next week she was totally different; all whiny and teary. She called Alec twenty times saying she loved him and wanted their old life back. That's never going to happen, he thought. *The life you thought we had, Quinn, only you had it. For me it was hell. You should have gotten help years ago when I asked you to. Our marriage ship has sailed.*

A few months earlier, the courts had ordered Alec to send Quinn temporary alimony until they worked out their final agreement. His lawyer talked to him about the probable outcome of the divorce.

'I'll be honest with you, Alec,' said his divorce attorney. 'The courts will probably award lifetime alimony for your wife because of her mental illness. She has an existing, ongoing medical condition that will impair her ability to support herself.'

'Permanent alimony isn't an option for me,' Alec said. 'Do something. What am I paying you for?'

'You're paying me to advise you, and the laws are clear,' said his attorney. 'Unless Quinn waives her rights, which her lawyer will advise against, you'll likely be forced by the courts to pay lifetime alimony. It's the law.'

'Then I'll just have to convince my wife to waive her rights, I guess,' Alec said. His lawyer looked at him skeptically and shook his head, thinking his client was a pain in the ass.

Alec decided at that moment he would have to take matters into his own hands. Why is everyone so incompetent? he wondered.

The next day Quinn called, crying.

'I want us to get back together,' she sobbed, 'I still love you. We have two kids. We're a family. We need to try harder.'

'Look, Quinn,' he said gently, 'we both know it's over, for now. We had a good run. We have two great kids. I'll arrange for movers, and you can take anything in the house that you want. You keep the Subaru, too. But, in exchange, I need you to sign off on the alimony and the pension. I know what your lawyer is telling you, but do you really think it's fair I should support you indefinitely? Is that fair, Quinn?'

There was a long silence, and then he heard her meek voice. 'No, I guess not.'

'Now you're being reasonable,' he said. 'I'm perfectly willing to pay you alimony for the first year to give you some run room. But a year should be enough, don't you agree?'

'I guess so,' said Quinn, starting to whine. 'But I don't want to get divorced. I want us to get back together. I don't want to be alone. Why can't it be like it used to be?'

Here we go, he thought. Just when it looked like we were making progress, Quinn changed her mind. He knew he had to play this exactly right.

'Look, we might get back together,' he began slowly, 'down the road. But I wouldn't consider getting back with you if you saddle me with some long-term alimony and take my pension. I worked hard for that pension. If you want our marriage to have a chance, you're going to have to do the right thing on the money. Am I making myself clear?'

'Okay,' she said. 'Alimony for only a year.'

'And you'll give up all claims on my retirement funds and pension, too. Cause you didn't earn that, did you? I earned it. Right?'

'Yes,' she said. 'Retirement and pension are yours.'

Jackpot, he thought.

'We are a family,' Alec continued. 'The only way we might have a chance is for you to sign the documents. Then we'll start talking about rebuilding our relationship. But not with all these legal things hanging over our heads.'

Quinn agreed to only twelve months of support and to sign the agreement. Everything was all set until her lawyer, Barbara Waxman, got wind of it and went ballistic. She talked Quinn out of the whole thing and convinced her that she was entitled to all the money. When Alec heard that he was apoplectic. He had no intention of paying his wife alimony for the rest of his life. He was going to have to find another way to convince her.

Chapter Fifty

QUINN

D r. Shapiro and my lawyer made me promise to go to a domestic violence support group. I was terrified the first time. I walked into the room and wanted to sink into the floor, hoping no one talked to me because then I'd have to speak. I didn't want anyone to know my secrets.

As other women got up to talk, I realized most of them had been through the same things. Some, not as bad and some, much worse. One woman in the group lost an eye because her boyfriend beat her up so badly. Now she's got a glass eye and the boyfriend has disappeared. Believe it or not, she had a happy ending; she was free and clear and starting over.

Most of the women looked pretty normal but we all had one thing in common; we'd been abused by our partners. The group leader told us domestic violence could lead to a form of PTSD, post-traumatic stress disorder, the condition soldiers have when they come back from war. She explained that continuous physical and emotional abuse mirrors some of the things that troops experience in battle. I didn't know if I had that, but I knew I felt better after I started going to the group.

At my first meeting, a tall woman with long brown hair and a puffy face stood up to speak.

'Things got bad in my house. This one night,' she said, 'as I cleaned up the dinner plates, my husband started picking at me. He complained about the bills and the mess in the living room. It wasn't messy, I always made sure it wasn't.'

There was a murmur of understanding from the women in the room.

'It always started the same way,' the brown-haired woman said. 'He'd find one little thing and move to another and then another until he'd work himself into a rage. Sometimes he'd punch holes in the walls and sometimes the punches landed on my arm or my upper thigh. Always in a place where people couldn't see a bruise. Never my face. He was too smart for that.'

Another hum of support and camaraderie filled the room.

'That night when he started in on me,' the woman continued, 'I must have reached my breaking point. I called my two teenaged kids who were up in their rooms and told them to get in the car that was parked in the attached garage. My kids and I got into the car. Screaming, my husband followed us into the garage and told me to get out of the car. I pushed the automatic locks button so he couldn't open the doors. He came right up to my closed window and yelled at me through the glass. My whole body was shaking, and the kids were screaming for me to back the car out.

"You're not leaving," he shouted. Then he walked around to the back of my car and laid down behind my rear wheels so I couldn't back out of the garage without running him over. That's when it was clear; it wasn't me. He was certifiable.'

There was a collective gasp from the room.

'I grabbed my cell phone and called 911,' she said. 'Within five minutes, a police car showed up and found my husband lying under the rear wheels of my car shouting threats at me. They took him away, and I got a restraining order. That's when I started coming here.'

Midway through the meeting there was a cookie and coffee break and the brown-haired lady with the puffy face came over to me.

'Hi,' she said. 'Is this your first time? You don't have to talk if you don't want to. You get a lot from listening, too. What's your name?'

'Quinn,' I said softly.

'I'm Clare. If you have any questions,' she whispered, 'you can always ask me. The people who moderate this group are great, and the other women are extremely supportive. We've all been through the same thing. Different characters, same plot. You'll see.'

I nodded.

'It gets better,' Clare said, touching my arm gently. 'Really. Come to the next meeting on Thursday. I'll be here.'

I forced a half smile and nodded again. On Thursday, I did go back. Clare's face brightened when she saw me. We were all at different stages in our recovery, but somehow we understood each other. I was at the very beginning of the yellow brick road, and Oz was very far away.

By my fourth session, I decided to speak.

'My husband might start out teasing me,' I said, making eye contact with Clare. 'That would lead to criticism,' I continued. 'Then he'd bully me and get enraged when I didn't fight back. He didn't punch. He was more into mental and emotional abuse. Sometimes he'd give me an Indian rope burn on my arm or pull my hair hard or bend my fingers back where I thought they would break off. He was careful not to leave marks.'

'The smart guys never do,' Clare blurted out.

After a few months in the group, I started to see Alec for who he really was. My husband was trying to cheat me out of alimony and his pension. He insisted my meds were screwing up my body and mind. He didn't want me to take them. He wanted me to be confused and sign my financial rights away. *But guess what, Alec? Dr. Shapiro put me on some new medication, and it didn't bother me as much as the old stuff. I felt much better, more like my old self. I had energy. I was going out for walks, and that felt great. I even bought a chicken and cooked it. What do you think about that, dickhead?*

'You take so many pills,' he once said. 'You're no better than a drug addict. Get off all that crap, Quinn.'

'You think I'm a drug addict?' I said. 'I'm not taking opioids, you jerk. I'm taking mood stabilizers and medicine to keep me from hearing voices. I finally have your number, Alec. I know what you're trying to do and it won't work.'

'What won't work?'

'I'm going to take you for every penny I'm entitled to,' I said. 'If that means lifetime alimony, "Dr. A", I'm going to tell my lawyer to go for it. Buckle your seatbelt, buttercup, and hold on to your wallet. The Quintessa is back.'

Chapter Fifty-One

Forty-two and single, Alison Moore was still hopeful even though every relationship ended in disappointment. One forty-eight-year-old guy lived with his mother. Another thought a committed relationship included having other girlfriends. The most recent one couldn't decide if he liked women more than men. Men won. Despite the string of failed relationships, Alison continued to believe her prince would come eventually.

On her way home from the county mall one sunny Saturday afternoon, she stopped to get her car washed. While waiting in the lounge for her car to come out, she killed time by thumbing through greetings cards, stuffed animals and random car accessories. To her right, a long transparent Lucite wall separated the lounge from the car wash so you could watch your car on the conveyer belt being scrubbed by large soapy mechanical arms. Several plastic water pistols filled with different colors of neon soap stuck through holes in the wall so kids could shoot pink, green or purple soap at the train of cars. Today there were no kids, only a single, tall, dark-haired man spraying foamy rainbows at the string of moving vehicles.

The man shot the gun with the blue soap and then moved over to the orange and then to the pink. His intensity and enthusiasm made Alison laugh out loud. He must have sensed her watching because he turned and flashed a big grin in her direction.

'Don't judge me, I'm writing my name in soap,' he called over as he gestured for her to come join him.

'See,' he said as she approached, 'I try to write my name, Alec, before one of the sprays or scrubbers washes it off the car. If I get all four letters, I win. Try it,' he said, smiling. 'What's your name?'

'Alison,' she replied.

'Way too long. You'll get rubbed out before you get to the "o",' he said. 'Just try Ali. Which color do you want?'

'Pink.'

'You're such a girl,' he said, laughing.

'That's what they tell me,' she said, looking over at his left hand to see if he was wearing a wedding ring. She smiled when she saw his naked fingers.

Gingerly, she pulled the trigger on one of the guns, releasing shocking pink soap that splattered all over the side of a blue Mazda. The next time, she aimed higher, hit a window and drew a circle. She made an 'A' and started on the 'L' when a big soapy arm swooshed it away.

'Wait,' she cried out.

'Not so easy, is it?' Alec said as they both continued to shoot. 'It's very therapeutic, you'll see.'

Alison laughed and nodded.

'All those synchronized scrubbing machines and sprays,' she said, 'each one has its own job, like a big soapy ballet.'

For fifteen minutes they got very competitive, each trying to draw more elaborate shapes and words. The attendant at the register ended their shooting match when he signaled to Alec that his car was ready.

'My car is out,' Alec said. 'Before I go, I'm going to write your full name with my gun.'

Like an expert marksman, Alec wrote out 'Alison' just before a spray obliterated it.

'Six letters, nice,' he said, laughing as he put his arms in the air in a victory salute to himself.

'You're good,' Alison called out as he walked towards the register and left the building. A few minutes later, Alison went to pay.

'You're all set,' said the cashier. 'That guy you were talking to, he paid for you.'

Surprised, Alison quickly walked outside to find Alec and was relieved to see he was still there waiting for his car to be dried.

'Hey,' she said, smiling. 'You paid for my car wash.'

'Guilty,' he said with a sheepish smile that charmed her.

'You didn't need to do that, but thank you.'

'It was my pleasure. Hey, I was going to grab a coffee across the street at that Starbucks,' he said. 'Can I buy you a cup?'

'You bought me a car wash,' she said. 'The coffee is on me.'

For the next hour, Alec kept Alison laughing. The more he revealed, the more she was aware that Alec Roberts checked all of her boxes. He was kind of cute and appeared to be around her age. He was getting divorced from a woman, so he wasn't gay. He had kids which meant he understood responsibility and family. He taught History at UR, which said he was smart and had a steady job and he didn't live with his mother. The thing that hooked her was that he made her laugh.

'I'm sorry,' he said, glancing down at his watch. 'I've got to go. Gotta pick up my kids.'

When they stood up, Alison put out her hand. He shook it and at the same time leaned in and gave her a soft kiss on her cheek.

'Can I take you to dinner one night?' he said as they walked outside towards their shiny cars.

Alison smiled as she handed him her business card.

'Alison Moore, Director, Aventi Corporation. Sounds important,' said Alec.

'We're an Internet company. We sell data,' said Alison with a wink. 'I can find out everything about you.'

The following weekend they had their first date. Two weeks later, Alec spent the night at her place and they officially became a couple. His divorce wasn't final yet, but everything felt right to Alison. He treated her like a queen, laughed at all her jokes – even the lame ones – and marveled at her command of historical facts.

'I'm serious, Ali, the average person doesn't know anything close to what you know about history,' he said. 'I'm impressed. You're beautiful and intelligent. The perfect package.'

That was how it started. He made her feel pretty, smart and funny and she adored his sense of humor and spontaneity.

Everything flowed, and before long, she believed he was 'the one', the prince she'd been waiting for.

A few weeks later, Alec introduced Alison to his two kids. Hannah and Jack were suspicious of her at first, but eventually, Alison's good nature won them over.

Over time, Hannah shared stories about her mother with Alison. She described her as loads of fun, extremely kind, and incredibly loving, the polar opposite of what Alec had told Alison. Alec's version of Quinn portrayed her as a demanding, selfish bitch.

'My mom has this ukulele. She sings all the time, but she's really terrible,' said Hannah, laughing. 'She knows she's tone deaf and she doesn't care and just laughs when she hits a bad note. It makes us all crack up.'

Hannah told Alison how her mother used to take her camping with her friends and taught her how to bake homemade molasses bread and even sew her own clothes. The more Alison learned about Quinn, the less it jived with the person Alec had routinely demonized.

'I love my mom,' said Hannah, getting teary. 'I miss the person she used to be. It's been hard the last two years. She isn't herself. She cries a lot or just sits and stares at nothing. Other times, she paces for hours. She's still my mom, and I love her.'

Hannah pulled out some old photos and showed Alison pictures of her mother from when she was a teenager. Quinn was beautiful, thought Alison, prettier than me. Fighting back a wave of insecurity, Alison wondered if Alec noticed Quinn was better looking than she was and willed herself to push that thought out of her mind.

Eight months after their first date, Alec surprised Alison with a romantic trip to Scotland.

'It's one of my favorite places in the world, Ali,' he said when he presented her with the tickets. 'I can't wait to show you all the castles and the underground city in Edinburgh. Wait until you see High Street, Ali,' Alec continued. 'We'll see the sites of ancient battles, sabotage and bloody palace intrigue. You'll feel like you're stepping back in time.'

Alec was right. The old part of Edinburgh had cobblestone streets and castles with turrets like the ones in the fairy tales. They spent five magical days wandering around the old city, stopping intermittently in pubs to try the local beer and scotch and sample their revered fish and chips. Throughout the trip, Alec snapped picture after picture of castles and a laughing Alison.

They talked seriously about their future as a couple for the first time while in Scotland. Alec didn't use the word 'marriage', but he spoke of all the things they would do and places they would one day visit.

'Next year, Paris,' he said. 'I'll take you to the Palace of Versailles, you'll love it. The year after that, maybe Rome. Wait until you see the Colosseum. We could rent a house in Spain.'

Alison had only been to Europe once before. This vacation together was a big step in their relationship. It felt like a commitment. She liked that he had everything under control and decided that day that 'Alison Roberts' sounded right to her.

Chapter Fifty-Two

QUINN

D riving to the Red Tulip Cafe for lunch with the Avon Ladies, I felt my anxiety growing with each passing mile. I hadn't seen my friends in a while. They never called me anymore. I guess I never called them either.

I wondered if they still liked me or if they talked about Alec and me and our divorce when I wasn't around.

My mind was playing dirty tricks on me as I pulled into the restaurant parking lot, drowning in a sea of paranoia. *Your good friends are inside waiting for you. Get those negative thoughts out of your head.*

I willed myself to get out of the car and was halfway across the parking lot when I saw him, and I froze. Alec was walking hand in hand with a petite blonde woman towards the Red Tulip door. My heart pounded as I felt the adrenaline coursing through my veins. I couldn't get any air into my lungs. I thought I might be having a heart attack. As Alec held the front door open, the woman leaned over and quickly kissed him, and they disappeared inside.

My legs felt like lead, unwilling to move. The blonde had to be Alison Moore. Ali. I knew all about her from my kids. They said she was sweet. How nice could she be if she was stealing my husband? Skank.

Minutes later, I found myself driving back to my apartment in Newbridge. I called Viv from the car and told her I was sorry but my Subaru was acting up again, and I was afraid to drive all the way over to Avon. I bet the girls were probably relieved I didn't show, given that my husband was dining in the same restaurant with his new slut. They probably freaked when they saw him walk in with her, knowing I was about to arrive any minute. Maybe they planned it together? Maybe my friends knew Alec was bringing his girlfriend to the restaurant. Did they all want to humiliate me?

Lost in a labyrinth inside my own head, I nearly hit another car and pulled over to the side of the road, in a full blown panic attack. I shut the engine off and took deep cleansing breaths.

It had to be a coincidence. Alec lives near Avon, and he always loved the Red Tulip. There's no plot, no conspiracy. The Avon Ladies wouldn't betray me. They were my friends, right? Wrong.

Chapter Fifty-Three

An exceptionally long check-out line, an overcrowded doctor's waiting room or standstill traffic made Quinn restless. On those occasions, she'd routinely call her sister to pass the time.

'I'm sitting in my auto mechanic's garage, again,' Quinn complained. 'That damn Subaru is costing me a fortune. They said it was going to be over eight hundred dollars this time.'

Quinn's car had become the family joke, spending more time in the shop than on the road.

'What's wrong, now?' Erin asked.

'My brakes went out again.'

'Again?'

'Last month I almost hit someone. I kept pumping my brakes, and my car kept going. It freaked me out. When I brought the car into the shop, the mechanic said my brake pads were non-existent. Today, I nearly crashed into this car stopped in front of me at a red light. The same thing happened, my car wouldn't stop. The guy who looked at it said my brake fluid lines were completely damaged.'

The wheels in Erin's head turned, dark thoughts entered her mind. Alec knew how to take a car apart and put it back together with his eyes closed.

'Quinn, this is going to sound crazy, but do you think Alec did something to your brakes?'

'No,' Quinn protested. 'He wouldn't do something like that. He can be a bully, but he wouldn't hurt me.'

'What are you talking about? He *has* hurt you,' Erin shouted, 'and he knows everything about cars. Ask your mechanic if it looks like anyone tampered with the brakes.'

Convinced her sister was overreacting, but because she had promised, Quinn asked her mechanic to have a look. After a thorough going over, he told her the brake fluid lines were so corroded and banged up it was hard to know if someone had messed with them or it was just severe wear and tear.

Despite the inconclusive report, Erin was still concerned. Her brother-in-law was smart. He was also vindictive and knew his way around a car engine. She was confident that Alec would know how to make it look like the brakes failed on their own and it scared her.

Chapter Fifty-Four

Alison wasn't exactly sure when things with Alec changed, but they did. Right after they got back from Scotland, she saw a new side, a not so nice side. They'd had so much fun in Edinburgh, that his new behavior caught her off guard.

It was an ordinary Sunday afternoon, and they were in the supermarket shopping for dinner. Alec was reminiscing about their Scotland trip, opining about some of the historical aspects of the city and the walking tours they had taken.

'Remember when they told us how the medieval Scottish used to dispose of their shit,' he said, making a funny face and laughing. 'How they'd chuck it right out the window and onto the street below and shout "Garry Lay" to give the people walking on the street below a heads-up?'

'I think the word was "Gardy Loo",' corrected Alison, who continued laughing until she noticed he wasn't.

'It was "Garry Lay",' he said with a stern face.

'No, it came from the French word, "Gardez l'eau" which means "mind the water". I studied French in college, so that's why I remembered it.'

'Who's the historian here, Alison?' he said, with an edge in his voice.

'You are, of course,' she said. 'It's just that I took French.'

'It's just that I have a PhD in History. They said "Garry Lay",' he said again, ending the conversation and walking away from her with the shopping cart.

She stood alone in the market aisle, stunned. What had just happened? She ran the scene through her mind again. Were they really fighting about an ancient Scottish phrase? She'd never seen him act like that before and blew it off, chalking it up to him being tired. She rationalized that she could be bitchy from time to time too.

By the time they got home from the store, Alec was back to his usual self. They had a nice dinner, watched a movie and Alison convinced herself that their supermarket squabble was an aberration.

Later that night in bed, Alec leaned over and kissed her.

'I've got a cool idea,' he whispered. 'Hear me out before you say no. Why don't we make a video of us making love? Just for us to keep. We'd have fun, and it would be so hot.'

Inside her head she thought, 'are you freaking serious?' but replied calmly so she didn't upset or insult him.

'I'm not comfortable doing that.'

'C'mon, Ali,' he continued, 'let's just try it. It will be such a turn on.'

Alison considered herself an open-minded person but naked videos of herself floating around the universe was not something she was going to agree to. She worked for a data company, she knew all about information let loose on the Internet. She was firm, and Alec was disappointed, but he never brought it up again.

Over the next couple of months, Alec's mood deteriorated. Negotiations between his divorce attorney and Quinn's were not going well. He claimed Quinn was trying to 'suck him dry' financially and brought it up frequently.

'My piece of shit wife is holding out for more alimony,' Alec growled, reading a text from Quinn at the dinner table.

'Put the phone down, please. Let's enjoy our dinner without talking about Quinn for once,' Alison said.

'Don't you get it?' he said with a sneer. 'She's going to devastate me financially. You can kiss trips to Europe goodbye. She's a lazy, bloodsucking, piece of shit who wants to sit back on her fat ass for the rest of her life while I support her.'

'Alec, I hate it when you talk about her that way. Everything will be alright. Let the lawyers work it out,' she said.

'Lawyers are worse than cockroaches,' he said to her. 'All they care about is billing for extra hours. They'll drag this out for as long as possible just to make more money for themselves and who gets screwed? I do.'

'Maybe you should give her alimony for a little while, maybe four or five years so she can get on her feet,' Alison suggested. 'Your hard-line position might be what's holding things up. If you offer her five years, she might go for it and it will all be over.'

'When did you get a law degree?' said Alec with clenched teeth. 'I know what I'm doing. Stay out of this, Ali.'

After that, Alison kept her mouth shut on all things related to Quinn. It was hard because Alec constantly complained about the divorce and how greedy his wife was.

She never told Alec how she really felt. She didn't think his wife was asking for anything unreasonable. She understood that Quinn needed some money to get herself started. She had been a stay-at-home mom and finding a job wasn't going to be easy since she had been out of the workforce for so long. Alison thought, given the circumstances, that alimony for five years was fair and reasonable but said nothing more.

Chapter Fifty-Five

Aggravated and stressed out from the machinations of his yet to be finalized divorce settlement, Alec planned a day alone in the mountains to decompress and clear his head. It was still dark when he climbed into his car that Saturday morning. Overhead, a large moon cast a yellow glow on the deserted street.

He placed his hunting rifle and packed lunch on the back seat and checked the glove compartment; the Glock G-19 was right where it was supposed to be. He glanced over at the new telephoto lens on his camera nestled on the seat beside him. The manager of the electronics store had told him he could 'capture the detail on a butterfly wing from thirty yards away'. He'd take photos in the morning when the light was good and go duck hunting in the afternoon. No women. A perfect day.

Dutifully following the GPS, he paid little attention to the roads as he drove, putting his trust in the monotone female voice barking commands. Ahead on the right, was a single bright light. It was a bagel store, and it was open. He pulled over and parked in a dimly lit spot half a block past the store.

Minutes later, carrying a sesame bagel with cream cheese and chives and a large coffee, he walked back to the car and got in. It would be too messy to eat and drive at the same time, so he decided to finish his breakfast there and then continue his journey.

As he chewed the warm crusty bread, he looked out at the darkened sign on a bar across the street. The place was called the Dew Drop Inn. He smiled at the pun. A moment later, a small-framed, dark-haired man stumbled out of the closed bar. He staggered down the street about two hundred feet and got into a dented green minivan. Alec put his food down and turned on the camera to get a picture of the drunk guy's license plate. He zoomed in on the number.

After he snapped a picture of the plate, he turned on the video and pressed record. Holding the camera steady with his left hand, he reached for the phone with his right to call 911. Something caught his attention; a runner dressed in night gear sprinted by. Alec turned his head and saw the man was covered from head to toe in reflective clothing, a bright light strapped to his forehead. That takes commitment, he thought as he watched the runner continue swiftly down the road just as the drunk started his engine.

It all happened so fast as he watched the whole scene through the viewfinder. The drunk must have pushed on the gas pedal hard because his car lurched like a rocket out of its spot and within two seconds slammed directly into the runner. The runner went down. The car screeched to a stop. The drunk guy opened his car door and stared down at the man on the pavement. Alec pushed the lens on the camera to its highest magnification, continuing to record.

'What's a matter with you?' the drunk shouted at the fallen runner. 'I hardly touched ya.'

Silence.

A second later, he slammed his car door shut and sped away. Alec continued to record as the vehicle swerved down the street.

He started his engine and pulled up next to the runner to see if he was okay. He opened his door next to the limp body, saw the wide-open eyes and knew. He was dead.

Holy shit. That drunken asshole had killed this guy and just left him. He looked up and was still able to see the drunk's red tail lights in the distance.

He closed his car door and pressed the gas pedal all the way to the floor. *He isn't going to get away with this, I've got two loaded guns, and I'm going to get him.*

He raced after the van, adrenaline pumping through his body, his heart about to jump out of his chest. He was going to get this guy, make a citizen's arrest, call the cops and be a hero.

Driving sixty miles an hour down residential streets, Alec caught up with the van. He slowed down so his quarry wouldn't notice him following. The drunk was now only a single block ahead.

Then, without signaling, the van made a right turn. Alec followed, keeping his distance, filming with his right hand, steering with his left. The neighborhood grew seedier the further they went but Alec didn't care, he had his own arsenal.

Another mile and the drunk made a left onto Ashland Street. The road was lined with houses in various stages of disrepair, more than one car up on cinder blocks. Alec took a shot of the street sign as he turned so he'd be able to retrace his steps if he had to. The minivan slowed and pulled crookedly into the driveway of a small, beat up, yellow ranch house sorely in need of some tender loving care.

Alec stopped his car several hundred feet behind and turned off the engine. He carefully removed the handgun from the glove compartment and took a few deep breaths. The drunk got out of his van, stumbled across the gravel drive and fell onto the front lawn.

After a couple of minutes, seeing no further movement, Alec slowly got out of the car. He noticed he couldn't feel his legs underneath him as he moved silently like a panther towards the downed man.

In seconds he was alongside him, glaring down at his weather-beaten face. A streetlight flooded the yard, so he was able to get a good look. Lying on his back, the unconscious man appeared to be no more than forty and in need of a shave. The drunk reeked of booze, body odor and a faint smell of urine.

'Get up,' Alec commanded as he pushed the man with his foot.

'Who the fuck are you?' slurred the drunk coming to life, turning his head to focus his eyes.

'I'm the guy who's gonna turn you over to the cops,' Alec said, pulling out his phone and starting to dial.

'Fuck off,' the drunk said, closing his eyes again. 'Get the fuck out of my yard.'

'Maybe this will wake you up,' Alec said, pulling out his gun and waving it in the man's face, filming now with the camera on his phone. The man opened one eye, saw the gun and sat up on his elbows.

'Get that away from me,' he slurred. 'What the fuck do you want? I ain't got no money.'

'I don't want your fucking money, you piece of crap,' Alec said. 'You hit a man with your car, and you left him to die. I've got the whole thing on video.'

'Get the fuck out of here. I didn't hit nobody,' said the drunk waving him away.

'You're so whacked out on booze, you don't even know how screwed you are. Now, get up,' Alec said as he kicked the drunk in the leg causing the man to wince.

'Listen,' the drunk pleaded, 'it was an accident. He came out of nowhere. He shouldn't have been running at night, anyway. It was his own fault. Who runs in the dark?'

'You were smashed when you came out of that bar. I saw you. You hit him and left him to die.'

'I didn't leave him to die, he was already dead,' the drunk protested. 'That guy was cold. Get that gun out of my face.'

'You think I'm afraid to use this?'

Alec pointed his weapon at the guy's head. 'Ask yourself a question. Are you absolutely sure I won't blow your fucking head off?'

When the drunk finally realized he was dealing with a lunatic, he frantically offered money, apologies, and eventually, the sexual services of his girlfriend, hoping the deranged man with the gun would go away. Proffering the girlfriend made Alec laugh out loud. He was enjoying this little scene. He felt like the town sheriff. He was Wyatt Earp keeping law and order in Tombstone. Yeah!

'What's your name?' Alec demanded, still waving the gun.

The drunk guy stared at him, trying to devise an escape plan.

'Tell me your goddamned name or say goodbye to your head.'

'Calm down, man,' the drunk shouted. 'I got a kid.'

Alec smirked. *Like I care if this scum is somebody's daddy? Clearly, he doesn't know me at all. The cops might give me a commendation or put my picture in the paper for bringing this guy in. Maybe I'd get interviewed on* Good Morning America *or the* Today *show. That would be cool.*

He punched 911 into his phone and smiled.

Chapter Fifty-Six

Some people have good luck. Some have no luck. Victor Malecki had bad fucking luck which is even worse.

He'd gone out for a few drinks and laughs with some guys from his old neighborhood. When they were teenagers, they used to boost cars together and a bunch of other things he didn't like to talk about. Let's just say, cops weren't his friends and he knew first-hand what the inside of a jail cell looked like. He was no choir boy, he'd done some bad things in his life, some evil things.

It was supposed to be a nothing night, no business, just Victor and some guys hanging out at the Dew Drop. They had a bunch of beers and started playing pool. The shots began around midnight. By the third or fourth round, the drinks started going down real easy. Victor couldn't even remember what kind of shots he'd had. Maybe rum or tequila, or a few of each. After a while, he lost count. He and his friends closed the place at 2am. Then, the bartender locked the front door and let them hang out to continue drinking until four thirty.

When they finally left and were out on the street, Victor realized he'd left his wallet on the bar and told the guys to wait for him while he went back inside to get it. When he came out, his friends were gone, and the street was dark and deserted. Fuck them, he thought.

He stumbled to his car and stepped hard on the gas pedal when suddenly a runner was right in front of his headlights. His vehicle and the man collided. What the hell just happened? he thought, slamming on his brakes. He got out of the car to look. His headlights were right on the man lying in a pool of blood. Victor nudged the guy with his foot and decided he was dead.

If the cops came now and found him, they'd haul him off to jail, and he'd probably go down for manslaughter. With all his priors, he'd be looking at some serious time, maybe life. He was still on parole. He wasn't supposed to be drinking at all. He looked around, nobody was on the street, and he thought maybe, for once, his luck had changed. He got back in his car and pressed the gas pedal gently, easing his car slowly down the road, not wanting to attract any attention.

Relieved when he finally arrived in front of his rundown ranch, he got out of his car. He was home free. As he walked towards his front door, he tripped on a piece of concrete and landed on his back on the lawn. Exhausted, he decided to rest on the grass for a minute, grateful he had made it home without running into any police. Everything was going to be alright.

He lay on the lawn for a couple of minutes when he was interrupted by some crazy guy talking all kinds of smack. The stranger said he had witnessed him hit a runner and followed him home. He said he had a video of the whole thing and he was going to call the cops.

At first, Victor thought the crazy guy was full of shit and wished he would go away and leave him in peace. He had a pretty good buzz on, and he didn't feel like getting up and dealing with this maniac. Then the crazy guy started waving a gun around, telling Victor he wasn't afraid to use it and that he was calling 911 so the cops would come and make an arrest.

Victor indeed had terrible fucking luck.

Chapter Fifty-Seven

Everyone was looking forward to the Cranbury High twenty-fifth reunion. No one was more excited than Mark Miller because he had heard she would be there.

When the night came, everyone agreed that Quinn Delaney didn't look a day older than when they had graduated. In high school, every guy had had a crush on her and from the looks they gave her at the reunion, most of them still did. She was still the 'it' girl. In high school, Quinn had been funny and silly, always giggling. She made people feel good about themselves when they were with her.

Despite her popularity, she somehow was able to transcend gossip. Women could sometimes be ruthless about other women. Girls could be vicious, especially towards the real pretty ones. Mark had seen his wife and her friends rip another woman to shreds over the smallest transgression. In high school that had never happened to Quinn, probably because she was so darn nice, he thought. She had been a benevolent queen, routinely asking the shyest, nerdiest girls to sit at her lunch table like a majesty summoning them to court. The gawky girls thought they had died and gone to heaven when Quinn validated them with a luncheon invitation. She didn't do it for herself. She had a huge heart.

During high school, most of the guys were jealous of Mark Miller because he was Quinn Delaney's boyfriend for all of junior and senior year. He admitted now that he wasn't always the best boyfriend. He was only a kid when they started going out and still trying to figure out how to navigate a relationship. Given that his parents were divorced and his old man was a drunk, he didn't have many good role models.

When they were seventeen, Quinn grew more dependent on him and became clingy. Sometimes it felt suffocating to Mark. At other times, when she'd pull away, he'd get possessive. They were kids; neither one knew how to do relationships. Mark thought acting macho showed he cared. That behavior was what ultimately drove her away.

As the reunion approached, Mark thought about how much he had changed since high school and wondered whether, if he had been less controlling with Quinn, maybe she wouldn't have broken up with him. At one point, he'd thought he was going to marry her, aware that girls like Quinn came along once in a lifetime.

After they went to college, they both got caught up in their new lives, and Mark never saw Quinn again. He eventually married Annie. They'd been married for twenty-two years and had problems like most married people do. Now that their kids were in college, there wasn't much to talk about anymore except the bills, always plenty of those. They each did their own thing. She had her stuff, He had his. They co-existed.

Someone told Mark that Quinn was going to be at the reunion and that she was getting divorced. He was pretty sure he was still in love with her.

That night, he was nervous as he walked into the party. It was crowded, and he scanned the room for his old girlfriend. He looked from face to face for those twinkly blue eyes. He spotted Cathy Franz and Liza Columbo, Quinn's best friends, and figured she would be nearby. He looked to the left of Cathy and then to her right, and that's when he saw her. Quinn Delaney, once again holding court. She was wearing a long navy gown and had some kind of diamond thing in her hair. He thought she looked like a princess in one of those fairy-tale books. He took a deep breath, walked across the room and approached her from behind. He carefully put his hands over her eyes, cupping them to make sure he didn't mess up her eye make-up, something his wife had taught him to do.

'Guess who, my dear,' he said in a high-pitched voice and unidentifiable foreign accent.

'I don't know,' said Quinn, laughing. 'That's not fair, it could be anyone.'

Mark's heart beat faster as he lifted his hands and spun her around.

'Mark,' she squealed with a big smile and gave him a hug. 'Mark Miller, oh my God. You look great. Cathy, look, it's Mark.'

All the feelings for her came flooding back like a freight train. He was seventeen again, standing next to his girl. She looked exactly the way he remembered. Thrilled to be with her again, he didn't notice her underlying sadness.

That whole evening, Mark reprised his role as her boyfriend, fetching her glasses of wine or appetizers. He stayed by her side every minute. A few other guys tried to muscle in, but he held his ground and Quinn was genuinely happy to have him next to her, just like old times. Several of their classmates commented that seeing them together made them feel like they were all back in high school. That was how it felt to Mark, too. He liked that feeling.

He and Quinn drank more wine and hit the dance floor. In his arms, she felt the same way she used to. She even smelled the same. It felt like he had just arrived when the overhead lights flickered and someone shouted that they had to be out of there in fifteen minutes. Mark looked at his watch. It was almost one in the morning. Half the people in the room had already left, and those remaining were gathering their belongings.

Quinn kissed him on the cheek and said she had to go, that she was getting a ride to her parents' house from Cathy. When Mark offered to drive her home so they could chat a little more, she accepted. They walked to his car still laughing and talking about the highlights of the night. A half mile from her parents' place, Mark pulled over into a parking lot next to St. Gabriel's, the Catholic church she had been married in.

'What are you doing?' Quinn asked. 'Why are you stopping here?'

'Quinn,' he said, putting the car into park. 'I want to say something to you before I take you home. I'm just going to say it. Like ripping off a Band-Aid. Quinn, I'm still in love with you.'

Chapter Fifty-Eight

QUINN

You could have knocked me over with a Q-tip. I went to my high school reunion to have a good time, just wanted a fun night with old friends. I was hanging out with my former boyfriend, Mark, and he comes on to me. Tells me he's still in love with me. I haven't seen the guy in twenty-five years. How could he be in love with me? He doesn't even know me. I'm not the same person he knew in high school. I'm married with two grown children. I've lived a life since we knew each other. I'm different. I'm broken.

Mark stood next to me the entire night. I kind of liked the attention. It's been a while since I was the belle of the ball. It felt good to be that person again, the one all the boys wanted to dance with. Mark looked pretty good. A little older and grayer, a little heavier but he was still handsome. At the beginning of the night, it felt like old times. For a few minutes, I pretended he was my boyfriend, and then I remembered who I really am and where I was.

He offered to drive me home, so I accepted. All night our conversation had been about happy things we did in high school, this party or that football game. Light stuff, nothing profound. Then on the way to my parents' house, he pulled over by the church and told me he still loves me.

'I mean it, Quinn,' he said. 'I never forgot about you. I married Annie, but I never stopped loving you.'

That's messed up, I thought. You married your wife while you were still in love with me. I felt sorry for this Annie because I knew what it was like living with a liar and a cheat.

'We were so good together tonight,' Mark continued. 'Everyone said so. They said it was just like when we were a couple in high school.'

'But we're not in high school, Mark. I'm married and so are you.'

'You're getting divorced. I'll leave Annie,' he said. 'We don't spend any time together, anyway. Quinn, what do you say, we can make this work.'

What the hell? Mark may have been in love with me, but I haven't given him a single thought in twenty-five years. We were not on the same page. He convinced himself that I had the same feelings. I didn't.

He leaned over to kiss me for a second, and I pulled back.

'Mark, what are you doing?' I cried. 'Put the car in drive. Take me to my parents' house. I don't want to do this.'

He looked surprised, hurt and disappointed.

'Look, I know I'm springing all this on you,' he said encouragingly. 'Just think about it. We don't have to make any decisions tonight.'

When we got to my parents' house, he gave me a quick kiss on the lips. I let him because, well, I just did. It was easier. I had enough chaos in my life. I thought about calling his wife and filling her in on our conversation, but then I thought it would be mean, so I just put it behind me and hoped he never called. I wished I hadn't given him my phone number and address in Newbridge. Too late now.

Chapter Fifty-Nine

Alison and Alec lived over an hour away from each other. Because of the distance, they typically only got together on weekends. Weekday dinners were rare, except for the week Quinn died. That week Alison saw Alec every day. He had been preoccupied with work projects and said there were significant changes at the university and he was involved in the planning. He ducked out in the backyard on his cell phone several times that week to talk to colleagues about what he said were 'urgent issues'.

On Sundays, Alison usually left his place in the early evening so she'd be home to get ready for work the next day. That Sunday he begged her to stay longer, saying he was in the mood to barbecue, so she stayed until about ten. When she got home an hour later, he insisted on FaceTiming with her and kept her up video chatting until one in the morning. She remembered the next day she was exhausted.

On Monday, he called her at work and asked her to come over and watch a game. She balked, saying she was too tired but he dangled a home cooked lobster dinner in front of her. Alison could never say no to lobster and agreed. On Tuesday night, he called her around seven in a panic. He had a huge presentation with the president of the university the following morning and had accidentally left an important file at her condo the week before. He asked if she would bring it over and spend the night. She agreed but didn't stay and went home a little before midnight. Wednesday night he drove to her place to take her out to dinner as a thank you for bringing him the file. He stayed with her that night. Thursday, he got tickets for them to go to a lecture at UR.

Then they planned to spend the entire weekend together at his house.

Over that weekend, on Saturday afternoon, they found Quinn Roberts' body.

For a fleeting moment, it crossed Alison's mind that she and Alec had spent more time together the week Quinn died than any other week of their relationship. She brushed the dark thoughts away because she intended to marry Alec Roberts. She was in love with him and convinced herself he had nothing to do with it. After all, she was with him the whole week. Still, she wrote everything down on her calendar so she wouldn't forget the timeline. It's the kind of person she was, just in case, anyone ever asked.

Part Five
AFTER MY MURDER

Chapter Sixty

They had planned to make dinner and watch a movie on Netflix, but when Alison pulled up in front of Alec's house after a trip to the supermarket, a police car was in the driveway. When she opened the front door, Alec was seated on the couch with his head in his hands. Two police officers stood across from him.

'What's going on?' she asked. 'What's happened?'

'Who is this, Mr. Roberts?' said one police officer.

Alec looked up with tears running down his face.

'She's my girlfriend, Ali Moore,' he said.

'Alec, what's going on?' she asked.

'It's Quinn,' he said. 'She's dead.'

'Oh my God,' Alison said, sitting down next to him. 'I'm so sorry. You said she was very depressed.'

There was a long pause before anyone spoke.

'Ali, Quinn was murdered,' Alec whispered.

Murdered? Every nuance and detail of the past few months flashed through Alison's mind. Alec now had to go with the police officers to Newbridge to identify Quinn's body and provide some information.

'Call my parents,' he said as he got his jacket. 'Tell them what's happened. We'll figure out how to tell the kids when I get back.'

Five hours later, Alec returned, and they devised a plan. His parents would drive over to SUNY Geneseo to tell Hannah and bring her home while Alec and Alison went to Jack's school to get him. After the initial shock and disbelief, Jack sobbed softly in the back seat, barely speaking on the drive home except for a brief bit of anger directed at his father. Nobody talked much in the car. His mother was gone, and nothing was going to make it better except for time and not enough of that had passed.

Alec decided to make the service a one-day affair rather than two; a morning wake followed by a burial at the cemetery.

'I want this over as quickly as possible,' he said to Alison when they were alone. 'It's better for the kids.'

For a fleeting second, Alison wondered if Alec wanted only a single day to save money. She pushed the thought out of her head and felt guilty for thinking it.

That night, people gathered at Alec's parents' house; friends of the kids and neighbors from Avon streamed through the front door. Alec and Alison decided she should not attend the wake or the burial as it might be painful for Quinn's family to see their daughter's husband with his girlfriend.

'It seemed like the whole town of Avon showed up today,' Alec said the night after the funeral. 'I didn't think she knew that many people. I guess a lot of them were friends of the kids with their parents. Still, it was impressive.'

'The kids told me she did a lot of volunteering,' Ali said.

'I guess,' said Alec. 'Now that it's done, the cops will be all over my ass.'

'What do you mean?'

'They always go after the husband. You wait and see, they're going to try and pin this on me. They were just waiting for the funeral to be over,' he said. 'Fortunately, I have you, my little alibi. You're my Ali-bi. Get it? Ali-bi,' he laughed.

Given the gravity of what had happened Alison didn't find it humorous and didn't laugh.

'What's the matter?' he said, punching her softly on the arm. 'You don't think that's funny? Lighten up.'

'Alec, your wife was just murdered,' she said. 'So no, I don't think that's funny.'

'You were with me every night for the past week. During the days I was teaching class, and at night I was with you,' he said. 'It's airtight. They can't pin her murder on me. So, you're my Ali-bi.'

'You did plan something for us every single night last week,' said Alison, realising the coincidence for the first time. 'We normally only get together on weekends. That was lucky.'

'Good thing too,' he said. 'Those freaking cops tried to play mind games with me when I went in to talk to them. I played them, not the other way around. I thought they were going to lose their shit when I gave them my DNA.'

Little seeds of doubt crept into Alison's head after she learned of Quinn's murder. It was hard not letting her mind go to the crazy dark places. If he had given his DNA, she reasoned, he had to be innocent. Soon Alec would be cleared, and they could put this awful business behind them.

The next day, plans changed. Alec hired a criminal lawyer.

'My attorney told me not to take the lie detector test,' Alec said when Alison asked what day he was doing the polygraph. 'I don't know anything about Quinn's murder. The cops want to nail me for it, and I'm not going to help them crucify me.'

Two weeks later, Jack and Hannah returned to their respective schools and Alec and Alison tried to get things back to normal. Their relationship never gelled again. When Quinn died, everything changed, and Alison didn't know how to fix it.

Alec started drinking heavily after the murder. When he drank, he got nasty and said terrible things.

'At least I don't have to pay that bloodsucker alimony now,' he said to her one day a few weeks later, 'so there is a silver lining after all.'

Alison hated it when he said stuff that revealed an ugly dimension to his character. One she didn't like. She hung in with him for another six months, but then she wanted out of the relationship. She hated bailing on Hannah and Jack, but Alec wasn't the guy she had thought he was. He had become toxic and mean, and she still had unanswered questions about his wife's murder. And then there was the blackout thing. Alison wasn't a hundred percent sure, but she thought it was possible she might have been drugged by her boyfriend – more than once. She could never be sure because there were a few times when she just couldn't remember what happened. Alec had told her she had had too much to drink but she wasn't entirely sure she believed him. Now after everything that happened, she just wanted out.

Chapter Sixty-One

QUINN

The worst part of dying was knowing my kids were in pain and I couldn't comfort them or help them through it.

My son acted tough, but he was so vulnerable. From the time he was a baby he reminded me of Alec. He'd be playing cheerfully and then something tiny would upset him and he'd lose it, just like his father did. Once when Jack was only three or four, he was trying to put together a wooden jigsaw puzzle. I was nearby ironing and looked over at him. Sitting on the floor frozen, he held up one of the pieces and stared into space with an anxious and angry look on his face.

'What's wrong, honey?' I asked.

'Nothing. You shut up,' he screamed, throwing the puzzle piece across the room at me and running out of the room.

His outbursts took me by surprise, but I kind of knew this beast. Alec was the same way. Whenever my husband got stressed out, even over something small, he'd lose it. No warning. From zero to ten in three seconds, it made my head spin. Over the years, I learned how to handle my son. He was difficult but he was still my kid and I loved him, warts and all.

Hannah, on the other hand, was easy-peasy. She was always drawing pictures of flowers and rainbows and telling me she loved me. She had a sweet disposition but was also surprisingly funny and witty. I used to laugh to myself when she'd outfox her father or sidestep one of Alec's many life lectures. Most of the time he never realized it when she put one over on him. Probably because he was convinced he was always the smartest guy in the room. Breaking news, Alec; you weren't.

It was easy to love Hannah, easier than her brother. I loved my son, but it took a lot more effort on my part. If Alec had been a little gentler with him, Jack might be a happier, more secure young man. There was a sense of sadness about my son that he couldn't shake. Maybe he got that from me and my crappy genes.

Chapter Sixty-Two

After months of trying to get Jack Roberts to talk to them, he had finally agreed to come in. McQuillan got to work early that day because the Chief wanted a recap of their current highest profile murder investigation, Quinn Roberts. Before they could see the Chief, McQ and Crews went over their notes to make sure they were on the same page. They didn't want any mistakes in front of their boss.

'Why is the Chief bugging up our asses on this one,' said Jimmy Crews. 'This isn't the only unsolved murder in Newbridge. What about the Carla Carolli case? She's been dead for three years and nobody says jack about her.'

'Carolli was a seventy-four-year-old grandmother who regularly associated with lowlifes and was a drunk. Quinn Roberts was educated, young and beautiful. It's as simple as that, my friend,' said McQ.

Five minutes later the two detectives stood in front of their boss and painstakingly walked him through the details of their floundering investigation.

'Everyone in the Delaney family as well as old friends in New Jersey and newer ones in Avon were interviewed. Anyone who had contact with Ms. Roberts at her high school reunion was also interrogated,' said McQ. 'We found a couple of odd ducks in that group but nothing solid or conclusive. We subpoenaed phone records for Quinn, Alec, Hannah and Jack Roberts. All checked out. We also got a hold of cell phone tower data to see if the husband or son made any trips down to Newbridge the week the victim died. Again, everything checked out.' McQ looked over at his partner with a "help me out here" look in his eyes.

'We had a look at Alec Roberts' email and bank accounts,' said Jimmy Crews jumping in. 'No unusual emails from him, and his wife rarely used email. According to her sister and kids, Quinn Roberts preferred phone calls to texting. On money – he had it, she didn't. Her bank account was practically empty. Her only source of income was the check her husband sent to her – when he sent it. It barely covered her rent, electric bill and car insurance. I don't know how the lady ate.'

'We've sent DNA samples to the lab several times,' said McQ taking over again. 'We did get a match but it turned out to be the landlady and her son, which we anticipated might happen. We did find one other unknown DNA strand but so far haven't been able to match it to anyone. A buddy of mine over at the FBI prioritized my request and ran it through their CODIS database for me. No match.'

'What I'm hearing, Detectives, is you got nothing,' said the Chief.

'Don't count us out yet,' said McQ. 'We've got Quinn Roberts' son coming in this afternoon. That kid is ready to explode.'

'Don't make me look bad with the press,' said the Chief. 'The newspapers are snooping around and Mayor wants this one solved – yesterday. A beautiful mother of two murdered in the Glades has unnerved this entire community. People are freaking out. They think there's a lunatic walking around murdering people. I want this one put to bed.'

Four hours later, McQ and Crews waited in a conference room for Jack Roberts to show. The kid was already fifteen minutes late and McQuillan started to wonder if he was going to be a no-show.

From the beginning of the investigation, something about the Roberts kid was off, but McQuillan couldn't put his finger on exactly what it was. Sure, Jack was young, and his mother's death was traumatising, but he neither cooperated nor helped find out who did it. That didn't add up for the police. He was sullen, defiant and hostile and the detectives wanted to know why.

Twenty-five minutes later, Jack walked into the station belligerently and immediately took an adversarial stance. The police had been trying to get him in for questioning for months, but he never returned their calls. McQuillan wondered why he had decided to come in now, why the change of heart? He would let Jack tell him whatever it was that was on his mind, let him get it off his chest. McQuillan would be like a priest in the confessional, no judgments, just forgiveness of sins.

Jack sat across the table from McQuillan and Detective Jimmy Crews. McQuillan made a little small talk to break the ice and then asked the kid how he was doing.

'How would you be doing if your mother was murdered?' he answered, staring McQuillan down.

Oh boy, McQuillan thought as he and Crews made eye contact. *We're not off to a good start. Message clear kid, you're still pissed off about your mother's death. Got it.*

'I can't know how you feel, Jack,' said McQuillan gently. 'I want you to understand, we're doing everything possible to find the person who did this.'

'If you're trying to find the murderer, why do you spend all your time going after my father?' he asked. 'My dad didn't have anything to do with it. He didn't even know where she lived.'

'He must have known where she lived because he sent her alimony checks there every month,' McQuillan said. 'Some people told us your father wasn't very nice to your mother. We checked in with the Avon PD. They said your mother called them a few times when your father got out of control, but she never pressed charges.'

Jack glared at the detective.

'Anything you can tell us, Jack, even something you think isn't important might be what breaks this case open,' McQuillan said. 'I keep a picture of your mother on my desk. She has the kindest eyes. When you work a case like this, the victim becomes like family. Every morning I tell her that I'm still in her corner and I will find out who hurt her. I promise her I will see this through.'

A tear ran down Jack Roberts' face. Bingo, thought McQuillan.

'You don't understand,' Jack began. 'My whole family is screwed up.'

'Tell us what you mean,' Crews said gently.

Jack's face got very red.

'My father's a dick and my mother was a nut job,' he screamed. 'Every conversation I've ever had with my dad was like an oral exam. He's always looking for something to catch you with, to trip you up, to point out how you were wrong. Nothing was ever good enough.'

'It must have been rough,' McQuillan said.

'And my mother was bat shit crazy,' Jack continued. 'When she didn't take her pills, she was off the rails. Once, she drove up to my college and wandered around campus talking to herself. One of my roommates saw her and pulled me out of class to get her. Campus security detained her until I got there. I was so embarrassed.'

'I can imagine,' McQuillan said.

'She used to call and text me all the time saying she didn't want to live without my dad,' Jack said. 'How am I supposed to do a paper or take a mid-term when I'm getting texts like that?'

'It would be tough,' McQuillan said, feeling a little sorry for the kid.

'My dad can be a real hard ass but you've got to understand, my mom was off the rails. You never knew how she was going to be,' said Jack. 'My father tried in the beginning, but then he gave up when she didn't take her meds, and he couldn't control her. He deserves to have a life, too.'

'Sure, he does,' McQuillan said. 'Did you ever see your father hurt your mother?'

Jack looked over at McQuillan and his face got red again.

'He told me you would try to pin this on him and try to frame him,' Jack shouted. 'He said you were going to twist things around to make it look like he did it. He told me not to come here, he warned me.'

The detectives tried to calm Jack Roberts down, but the kid was spinning from a lot of pent up anger. He was mad at his father, but he defended him. He'd lost one parent and didn't want to lose the other, even if the other was a nasty piece of work. When Jack finished his rant, he stood up, walked to the door and opened it.

'Don't call me until you find the real killer,' he said. 'My father didn't do it, and I'm not going to help you frame him.' Then, he got up and walked out. That was the last time Jack Roberts ever spoke to the police.

Chapter Sixty-Three

The things Ed Delaney learned about Alec after Quinn's death kept him up at night. If he had known about it when it was happening, he would have gone to Rochester and beaten the crap out of his son-in-law. He would have stopped it. Now it was too late.

Dozens of unreturned calls to the Newbridge police made things even worse, all he heard were crickets. Ed was sure he was getting stonewalled but wasn't entirely sure why. When Alec lawyered up and wouldn't talk to the cops, Ed hired his own private investigator.

'The Newbridge police only know how to write parking tickets and march in parades, Eileen,' Ed said to his wife. 'Murder investigations are way out of their league.'

A friend from Philly hooked him up with Ben Patton, the famous cable news investigator. Patton was often a pundit on TV panels covering significant criminal cases. All the Patton's PI's were retired NYPD detectives and knew their way around a murder. Patton assigned former Manhattan detective Joseph D'Appolito, Joey D'App to his friends, to the Quinn Roberts case.

D'Appolito was a quintessential New York cop; sarcastic, suspicious of everything and everyone, methodical and thorough. The investigator was exactly what Ed was looking for.

'Newbridge PD is missing stuff,' Ed said to the investigator. 'They're amateurs.'

'Don't worry, Mr. Delaney,' said Joey D'App, 'I'll get to the bottom of it. When I was working homicide in the three-two on the west side, I usually knew who did it on day one. My job was to prove with hard evidence what my gut already figured out. They used to call me The Velvet Hammer. You don't hear me coming, but you feel it when I do.'

Ed gave Joey D'App what little documentation he had, and the private investigator went to the Rochester area to snoop around. A week later, he confirmed some things Ed had suspected. The big reveal was that the first cop to arrive at Quinn Roberts' apartment had assumed it was a suicide and didn't seal off the premises. Ed hadn't known that. Not surprisingly, the cops didn't share that tidbit with the Delaney family.

'Look, Mr. Delaney, none of the cops came out and said it, but it was obvious they had their eyes on your son-in-law,' said Joey D'App when he called Big Ed from Rochester. 'That's my gut. I've been doing this for almost thirty years, and it's almost never wrong.'

'What does that mean then?' Ed asked.

'From what I could tell, it sounds like they have a piece of evidence that's conclusive and pins it on your son-in-law,' said Joey D'App. 'But the DA excluded it, because of the way it was collected. If the crime scene was contaminated, that would do it. Every cop I talked to, off the record, thought your son-in-law was somehow involved. I'm sorry to say, it doesn't look like there's going to be an arrest anytime soon. In my professional opinion, Newbridge PD messed it up.'

'Now what?'

'I hate to tell you this, Mr. Delaney, but they may never make an arrest.'

And that was that. His beautiful daughter was dead, and an asshole was walking around without a care in the world. Over and over he asked himself why one of her kids hadn't picked up the phone and let him know what was going on? They should have looked out for their mother, he thought. He couldn't forgive his grandchildren, and at the same time, he couldn't forgive himself. His job was to always protect her, and he had failed.

Chapter Sixty-Four

His oversized shopping cart was loaded with gigantic packages of junk food and an apple pie big enough to feed an army. Long lines crisscrossed the large warehouse supermarket. Some were waiting to check out and others, like John McQuillan and his girlfriend, Marie, were lined up for some Costco free food samples. It had been a few months since Quinn Roberts' murder, and McQuillan was relieved to have his mind on something besides homicide. He and Marie would often make a morning out of Costco and eat enough so they could skip lunch entirely. Polishing off a mini taco, he saw a familiar face through the crowd but couldn't place the guy.

Somebody out of context can throw you. Your mailman in a bathing suit at the beach or your dentist eating a burger at TGI Fridays, it can take a minute. Usually, you'd recognize your dentist in a second, but in a strange location wearing different clothes, it can take longer. McQuillan stared at the faces across the floor, struggling to place them.

He nudged his girlfriend.

'See that guy over there? The one in the light blue sweatshirt.'

'Where?'

'The guy holding the big box of trail mix,' he whispered.

'Where?'

'Earth to Marie, over there,' he said, exasperated. 'The middle-aged guy in blue standing by the big containers of ketchup.'

'Yeah, I see him,' she said. 'What about him?'

'He looks familiar,' he whispered.

'Not to me,' she said, munching on her taco.

He begged his brain to kick into high gear. The older guy in light blue was with the twenty-something girl and boy. He knew them. He was sure of it.

Then, it hit him. The guy in blue was Alec Roberts. The smug little shit who murdered his wife. He'd been thinking about Roberts every day for the past four months. How could he not recognize that murderer right away? He hoped he wasn't losing his edge.

Every morning since it happened, he looked at Quinn Roberts' face. Her sister, Erin, had sent every police officer on the investigation a small framed picture of Quinn. Each cop also received a handwritten note from Erin begging them not to forget that her sister was a real person who was loved, not just a victim. McQuillan had her picture on his desk. As far as he was concerned, Roberts should be in maximum security instead of sampling andouille sausage at Costco.

Seeing Alec Roberts enjoying himself, moving freely around the store while that beautiful woman was in the ground churned up rage inside the policeman. He knew her husband killed her and that his own investigation was practically dead. All his leads were drying up.

'Watch the cart, Marie, I've got to do something,' he said as he walked directly over to Alec Roberts.

Alec was laughing as he ate a sample of macaroni and cheese out of a small paper cup. The detective planted himself directly in front of him and put his finger right in Alec's face, practically touching his nose.

'You murdered your wife, Roberts,' McQuillan spewed. 'Every cop in the department knows you killed her. You're not fooling anyone. We haven't figured out how you did it, but we will. And we're gonna get you, Roberts. You can count on it. Chew on that.'

The detective walked back to his girlfriend with a smile on his face and the two resumed their shopping.

'Feel better now that you got that off your chest?' asked Marie.

'A lot better although I'll probably regret it tomorrow. Not a chance Roberts is going to keep our conversation to himself.'

'You think he's going to file a complaint?'

'Absolutely, but I'll deal with it.'

As he had predicted, the following Monday, Alec Roberts' attorney filed a complaint with the Newbridge Police. McQ was summoned to the Chief's office shortly thereafter. He was given a slap on the wrist and told to shop at Walmart next time. Alec Roberts did not have any fans in Newbridge.

Chapter Sixty-Five

It was painful but at the same time therapeutic when Colleen, Mike and Erin put up the Memorial Page for Quinn on Facebook. They picked their favorite pictures of her from their photo albums and their phones and scanned them in. Some were from when they were little and others from when she was older. They found shots from each decade of her life to share with the world. The three sisters had been together for all of those moments, at every age, as kids, teenagers, young mothers. Sisters and best friends.

In their last face-to-face meeting with the Newbridge police, the cops suggested the Delaneys could help the investigation through their Facebook page by watching for any unusual activity; comments that were out of place or from people they didn't know.

'You never know where a lead will come from,' said Detective McQuillan. 'If you see anything odd, let us know. We'll take any help we can get.'

After a few months, they had over two hundred followers to Quinn's page; mostly cousins, high school and college friends and Quinn's neighbors from Avon. Around that time, Hannah told Erin that her father already had a steady girlfriend. Erin and Mike weren't surprised. They had since learned that Alec had cheated on Quinn for most of their marriage.

Erin checked the Facebook page often and one day a few months after it went up, she noticed two unknown men had started to follow Quinn's page. One was named Rich Morelle and the other, Devin Borke. She didn't remember Quinn ever mentioning those names, so she texted Mike and some of Quinn's college friends. Nobody recognized their names. They checked with Hannah and Jack and the Avon Ladies, too. Nobody knew them.

Erin did a deep dive into Morelle and Borke's Facebook profiles, examining their pictures, friends, and postings. Since Quinn died, she had become a master at forensic Facebook sleuthing. If she dug long enough and went down a bunch of rabbit holes, she'd find out a lot. It just took patience.

From their profiles, Morelle and Borke appeared to be in their forties, close to Quinn's age. Borke lived on Long Island, nowhere near Newbridge and seemed to be single. Morelle, on the other hand, lived in Buffalo, only about an hour and fifteen minutes from Quinn's apartment. He had pictures of himself with kids but no wife. Erin figured he was divorced.

Maybe the two guys amounted to nothing, but they stuck out as peculiar. She sent the information over to Detective McQuillan but never heard back on whether the cops checked them out. The cops were rarely transparent and only shared what they wanted claiming that they "would compromise the integrity of the investigation" if they told the Delaney's too much. The Delaney's usually interpreted that as "the cops had nothing".

About six months after Quinn died, Erin was poking around again on Facebook posting more pictures of her sister. She noticed her Facebook Messenger icon had a red alert mark on it. There was a message there from someone she didn't know. Her name was Denise Orrem.

Hi Erin,
I'm sorry about the loss of your sister. I found your name in a newspaper article about Quinn's murder. Last night, I met a guy in a bar, and we planned a kayaking date for later this week. During our conversation over drinks, he mentioned his wife had been killed three years ago. I told my friends about him, and they convinced me to Google him before I went anywhere. That's when I saw all the newspaper articles talking about the murder saying it

happened just a few months ago, not years. I'm positive he said it happened three years ago. Why would he lie about that? I hate to bother you with this, but I didn't know who else to ask. Am I overreacting? Should I be concerned or am I being overly suspicious? I really liked him, and he was never arrested, but I figured you would know better than anyone. Again, I'm so sorry to bother you and for the loss of your sister.

Thank you, Denise Orr.

Hi Denise,

Stay away from Alec! You are absolutely right, my sister didn't die three years ago; it has only been months. Alec is a world class liar and still a suspect in my sister's murder investigation. They were in the middle of a contentious divorce, and the police don't have enough evidence to arrest him. Whether he did it or not, he's not a nice guy. I would suggest stay away from him.

Erin

Hi Erin,

Wow, so scary. When I met Alec, he asked me how long I had been divorced, and I asked him the same. He told me he was a widower and that his wife had been murdered three years ago. I thought it was odd that he had this weird half-smile on his face when he said it but figured it was his way of hiding his pain. After I Googled him and read about the murder, I canceled the date. I want to meet a guy, but I'm not that desperate. Thank you for letting me know. I'm so sorry for your loss. D.

Chapter Sixty-Six
QUINN

Seriously, Alec? You told the woman in the bar that I died three years ago? It hasn't even been a year, who's the liar now? You smiled when you told her I died. She thought you were smiling to hide your pain. That's a laugh. You're not the person I thought you were. You're a narcissistic psychopath, just like Dr. Shapiro said. I'm starting not to like you at all.

Chapter Sixty-Seven

While Alec was seeing Alison Moore, he was also involved with another woman named Cindy Kelleher. Neither woman had any idea the other existed.

Cindy had joined an outdoor hiking group for singles online hoping to meet someone who shared her passion for nature and exercise. That was where she met Alec. The group met for an afternoon guided hike at a state park with marked trails. It was a beautiful, warm summer day, and Cindy was aware of him looking at her when the group started up the mountain. As they walked, she noticed he made a point of being near her. After about twenty minutes, they struck up a conversation.

He made her laugh and she liked that. She learned he was a History professor at the University of Rochester. She was a bit of a history buff herself and was drawn to intelligent guys. A man with advanced degrees was a huge turn on for Cindy. Towards the end of the hike, Alec asked her if she would like to go for a drink or a coffee afterward. They planned to meet at Canfield's, a wine bar near Rochester. The drinks and conversation went so well they decided to order dinner.

'I got divorced five years ago,' Cindy said. 'No kids, just me and Boo.'

'Who?'

It took Cindy a second but then she got Alec's little joke.

'Ha ha. Boo-hoo. She's a Maltese.'

'Why Boo?'

'Because she's white, like a ghost.'

Alec laughed. Cindy smiled. Not a naturally funny person, it made her feel good that she amused him. He told her about his grown son and daughter and mentioned his wife had died. As the evening progressed, he opened up more and said his wife had actually been murdered.

'The police are still looking for her killer,' he said with hope in his voice. 'It's been rough, especially on my kids.'

He looked sad when he told Cindy about his wife's death. He said she reminded him of her. Same height, dark hair and fair complexion. Cindy's heart broke for him. Poor man, she thought. How awful. No one should have to go through that.

After their fabulous first date, Cindy thought he might be 'the one'. Being with Alec was so easy. They started seeing each other even though they lived more than an hour apart. The distance made things challenging but they made it work.

After two weeks Alec spent the night at her place. He didn't rock Cindy's world in the bedroom department but she was in her late forties, and it was nice to have a man in her bed again. After their first overnight, Alec stayed over whenever they got together. Two months later, he suggested they go away for a weekend. That same weekend, Alison Moore was out of town at a trade show.

'It's only October, and it's still warm,' he said. 'I've got a tent, let's you and me go camping.'

That weekend they were completely in sync. They hiked, fished and cooked dinner around the campfire while singing corny country songs that neither could remember all the words to. At night, they zipped themselves into their tent and snuggled inside their sleeping bags. That weekend, Cindy fantasized about marrying Alec.

Everything was going great until Cindy accidentally discovered Alec had another girlfriend. She was playing around on Facebook and discovered Alison Moore. Based on the dates on Alison's posted pictures and comments, it looked like Alec had been seeing Alison for over a year, long before Cindy came into the picture. She discerned that he'd been sleeping with Alison while he was still married to his dead wife and while he was sleeping with her.

Cindy had already divorced a husband who two-timed her and had no tolerance for liars or cheaters. That was a deal breaker. Alec tried to lie his way out of it until she finally told him he was a jerk and never to call her again. Ever.

Chapter Sixty-Eight

QUINN

Sorry, Cindy. Guess you found out the hard way, just like me. It must have stung when you learned he was sleeping with another woman. You don't know the half of it. You only know about Ali Moore. Guess what? Dr. A was probably sleeping with two or three of his students, too. If I were you, Cindy, I'd get checked for STD's, you have no idea where that thing has been.

Chapter Sixty-Nine

All the Delaneys were frustrated. It had been ten months since Quinn had been found dead and nothing had happened. To make herself feel like she was doing something proactive, Erin trolled Alec on Facebook. She sifted through his contacts and their photos and their friends' pictures and comments for hours. Through her meticulous process, Erin figured out which women he was involved with. She copied every photo posted and saved them all to her hard drive. Alec didn't post much, but all his new girlfriends wanted their friends to know they had a new man in their life, even if he was a murderous shithead.

Once Erin figured out who they were, she was able to piece together some of Alec's romantic rendezvous. It was amazing what you could find on Facebook if you followed the strings. She wondered why all these women were willing to go out with Alec, given that Quinn's murder had been in all the newspapers and on local TV. These women only had to do a two-second Google search, and they would have known he was the primary suspect in his wife's unsolved murder.

When Erin found Alison Moore on Facebook, she hit the jackpot. Alison had posted tons of photos of herself and Alec hiking in the mountains and dozens more from a vacation they took to Scotland. Every pic posting had a time stamp and Erin was able to piece together the last year or two of Alec's life after he and Quinn split.

Erin wondered if Alison Moore had anything to do with her sister's death. From everything she saw online, Alison looked pretty normal. After an extensive search using Google and

LinkedIn, Erin decided the woman was most likely an innocent bystander.

Erin tracked Alison's Facebook page for months, checking it every day for anything new. One day, she noticed that Alison and Alec Roberts were no longer Facebook friends. The pictures Alison had posted of her and Alec had disappeared. Fortunately, Erin had made copies of all the pictures and had them neatly in a file on her desktop labeled, 'KILLER.'

If they were no longer friends on Facebook, Erin deduced, they probably broke up. She was dying to reach out to Alison to wring every juicy bit of information out of her but decided to wait, in case their break-up was temporary. Erin checked Alison's status every morning. Six months later, there was still no Facebook connection between Alec and Alison. Erin sent her an instant message through Facebook.

Hi Alison,
My name is Erin Delaney Danzi. I am Quinn Delaney Roberts' sister. I know you were seeing Alec Roberts at the time of my sister's death. I'm not suggesting you had any part in it. My family is frustrated with the lack of progress from the police investigation. We hoped you might remember something from that time that might help us. We would be grateful for anything, even something tiny. Thank you.
–Erin Delaney Danzi

A few weeks later, Alison Moore responded.

Hi Erin,
I am so sorry about Quinn. I had grown close to your nephew and niece when I was with Alec and learned much about your beautiful sister from them. The whole awful thing is so disturbing, and I too really wish they would solve her murder. As time passes, it bothers me

more and more. In fact, given that I was seeing Alec at the time of your sister's death, I was surprised the police never contacted me.

What day did they actually narrow her murder down to? I'm not sure I ever really got a straight answer on that from Alec. Weird things were going on the week before your sister was found, and I often reflect about them myself. If I knew anything, I would go to the police, but unfortunately, all I have is a bad feeling. I would be more than willing to talk with you although I don't think I know anything that would help. – Alison Moore

Excited that maybe this was a break they had been waiting for, Erin responded immediately. Despite Alison's initial offer to help, she never responded to Erin again. What were the 'weird things' Alison referred to the week before Quinn was found and why did she have a 'bad feeling'? Those two comments haunted Erin.

Also, Erin fumed, why hadn't the police interviewed Alec's girlfriend? Everyone knows when it comes to murder, it's always the husband or boyfriend. Watch any cop show, that's how it always happens. In her extensive research, Erin read that when it comes to murder, ninety-eight percent of the time, the killer is the significant other or someone the victim knows, not a stranger. Erin wanted to know why the police hadn't interviewed the woman her brother-in-law was sleeping with. Either the cops were hiding something, or someone screwed up. She was going to find out what happened.

Chapter Seventy

Detective Crews had talked to the owner of Kenny's Kwik-Mart ten months before. McQuillan wasn't sure there was much point in interviewing the owner a second time, but it had been almost a year since the murder, and he was out of fresh leads.

'That last time Ms. Roberts was in my store, it was crowded, and I didn't have a lot of time to talk like I usually did,' said Kenny. 'A couple of construction guys from that big apartment building going up over on Division Street put in a big sandwich order for their whole crew. My assistant manager and I were knee-deep in mayonnaise and Swiss cheese when Ms. Roberts came in. She looked nice, pulled together. Some days she didn't, but that day she looked good.'

'Was there anyone else in the shop that day?' McQuillan asked.

'Some construction guys nudged each other, they were watching her,' Kenny said. 'They spoke in a foreign language, like Hungarian or Polish. It was obvious they were talking about her. Guys can be real dogs, you know? I kind of felt a little protective of her even though I didn't know her that well.'

'Seems like she had that effect on people,' the detective said ruefully.

'When she came up to the register she asked me how I was like she always did. Before I finished ringing her up, I got an emergency call from my ex-wife. My idiot son had been suspended at his high school, and I had to go pick him up. I left right away.'

'Were there any other customers besides the construction workers in the store while she was here?' McQuillan asked.

'Yeah, there were two other guys in their thirties, not together and not my regulars,' Kenny said. 'I didn't know 'em.'

'Quinn Roberts didn't appear to know any of these men, correct?' McQuillan asked.

'Nah.'

'Was she on foot that day?'

'I don't know, but I got a security video if you want to see it. I'd have to find it and...'

'That's not necessary right now,' McQuillan said. 'I'll be in touch if we want to see it.'

'You know something, Detective. This murder scared the shit out of everyone in this part of town,' said Kenny. 'Right after it happened, every customer who came into my shop said something about it. Not so much anymore, but every once in a while, somebody brings it up. People are still nervous.'

'Yeah,' McQuillan said. 'We'd like nothing better than solving this one.'

'I don't think she even knew many people in town, she was always alone,' said Kenny. 'She told me once she was looking for a job, said she had to start over at the age of forty-four. I remember thinking she looked pretty good for forty-four.'

McQuillan thanked Kenny for his time and then headed back to the station. The truth was, it didn't matter who was on that security tape. He knew who killed Quinn Roberts. There was no point wasting time chasing after other people. They needed something concrete on Alec Roberts. Goddamn Yancy.

Chapter Seventy-One

Mike, Colleen and Erin were seated in the Newbridge police department conference room. The homicide team assigned to Quinn's case along with the assistant DA and the Chief of Police sat across from them. The Delaneys had asked for this meeting and were armed for a rumble. It had been one year since the murder, and the cops were nowhere. They told the family they were still following up leads but with each passing day, Quinn's killer was getting further away.

The Delaneys had stopped being politically correct with the police months ago and openly talked about Alec as the person they believed had killed Quinn. The detectives wouldn't confirm or deny it and used words like 'alleged' or 'person of interest'. Over time, the Delaneys began to understand 'cop-speak'. When dealing with the police they learned, it's not always what they said, sometimes it's what they didn't say that mattered. The cops never corrected the Delaneys when they talked about Alec being 'the killer'. For Erin, that alone was telling.

The thing that puzzled Quinn's sisters was why the cops weren't able to match any of the DNA samples from the apartment to anyone, and in particular, to Alec.

'I'm going to be direct,' said Mike. 'We're ninety-nine percent sure Alec murdered Quinn. You've got his DNA, why can't you match it? Don't you think he's the one who did it?'

'We've hit a wall with Alec Roberts,' said Bernie Gonzales, the assistant DA. 'You remember he came in that first day and spent a few hours with Detectives McQuillan and Crews. After that, he clammed up and hired a lawyer. All communication since then has been through his attorney.'

'Can't you make him talk to you?' Erin asked. 'He's a suspect, can't you bring him in?'

'Unfortunately,' said McQuillan, 'unless we have grounds to arrest someone, we can't force them to talk to us, it's up to them. That's the law.'

'It's a stupid law,' said Erin.

'If any of you can encourage him to come in, we'd be grateful.'

'Wouldn't a husband do anything he could to help find his wife's killer?' Mike asked. 'If someone were innocent they would volunteer as much information as possible, not shut down communication. Isn't that strange?'

'Yes,' said McQuillan.

'You think Alec did it, too,' said Colleen.

'All I can say is that Alec Roberts is a person of interest,' said McQuillan with a weary look. He would have loved to tell them that he thought their brother-in-law was a craven homicidal nut job, but he couldn't, the Chief would put his ass in a sling.

'If Alec is responsible, how come none of his DNA matched the crime scene? Why would he agree to give you his sample?' said Mike. 'He won't talk to you, but he gave you his DNA? It doesn't make sense.'

'Maybe he gave us his DNA because he knew we wouldn't find a match,' said McQuillan.

The detective was trying to tell them something without actually saying it. Exasperated, Erin wondered why the police had to be so obtuse.

Puzzled by McQuillan's comment, the Delaney contingency looked at each other for a moment trying to decipher what exactly McQuillan was getting at.

'Are you saying you think Quinn's murder was done by someone else but Alec may have been involved?' Mike asked.

'It's possible,' said Bernie Gonzales without emotion.

'It's one scenario,' McQuillan said. 'We're running down a few different threads. Nothing conclusive.'

It never made sense to Mike and Erin that Alec did the DNA swab and then refused to talk to the cops. Now they understood. They wouldn't find Alec's DNA in Quinn's apartment because he was never there.

This was even worse than the Delaneys had imagined. Quinn's murder wasn't because of an argument or a moment of passion. Alec didn't just lose his mind in a moment of temporary insanity or rage. He planned it. Erin felt dizzy and faint and she started to cry in front of everyone. She didn't care that the cops saw her cry; she wanted her sister back, and she wanted Alec to pay.

Chapter Seventy-Two

After they broke up, Alison Moore never contacted Alec again. She knew something was going on around the time of Quinn's death, but she couldn't put her finger on it. All she was sure of was that things were really strange the week before they found Quinn dead.

Right after the funeral and the first few weeks that followed, Alec had been remarkably calm. He'd busied himself with his hobbies like working on an old car or taking pictures and hiking. He was surprisingly content, which Alison thought was odd given the circumstances.

He took a two-week break from teaching when Quinn died and then went right back to work at UR. Hannah and Jack returned to school around the same time, and it was like Quinn never existed. Alison thought she was more upset about Quinn's death than Alec and she had never met her. Hannah and Jack used to talk about their mother all the time, and she had seen loads of pictures, so it felt like she knew her.

'This was Mom when she was a model in high school,' said a proud Hannah holding up an old magazine cover. There was a time when Alison felt insecure about Quinn's good looks. I'm attractive, Alison thought, but Quinn was crazy pretty. She couldn't help but compare herself to the woman who came before her. Despite all of Alec's nasty comments, she always thought Quinn was the kind of person she might have been friends with. They liked the same things like music and cooking. Quinn played the ukulele badly, and Alison was about the same on the piano. From Alison's perspective, Quinn had raised two good kids. She couldn't have been as bad as Alec made her out to be.

A few months after the funeral, Alec got mean and started to belittle Alison.

'Why are you wearing that dress?' he asked. 'It makes you look fat.' The little voice inside her head wanted to say, 'screw you'. But all she said to him was, 'Oh, it does, I'll change.'

It wasn't just because he picked on her appearance, although that should have been enough. He also started to chip away at her intelligence saying her opinions were 'uninformed' and even 'stupid'.

'I don't understand why you never support your opinions with facts,' Alec said on more than one occasion. 'You're worse than my students. Don't debate me, Ali, unless you know what you're talking about and can defend your position.'

Sometimes he'd raise his voice, and he always had to be right. Always. At some point, she was sure he used to make stuff up just to bully her.

At first, Alison chalked up the combative behavior to the trauma of his wife's murder. She figured Alec's new nastiness was a mask covering up his pain, and it would eventually fade. The police had leaned on him pretty hard, and Hannah and Jack were still in a dangerous place emotionally. Hannah almost didn't go back to school. Alison tried to give Alec the benefit of the doubt.

She toughed it out for a few more months but the relationship wasn't fun anymore. He scared her when his volatile temper emerged. She also caught him in a few lies and noticed how effortlessly twisting the truth came to him.

Then there was that other thing. She had blacked out a few times at his apartment after only a single glass of wine. When she woke up the following morning, she was naked with a whopping headache and no memory of the night before. When she asked Alec about it he said she must have had too much to drink and passed out. Alison thought it odd because she wasn't a big drinker and usually only had one glass of wine.

She cared about him and liked his kids, but things didn't feel right, and she finally ended it.

When she told him it was over, the smirk on his face turned into a sneer. She hadn't seen him look at her like that ever before. It sent a chill down her spine and reinforced her decision to break it off. Still, she had been in love with the guy and wished him and his kids well. Namaste.

When Alison got the that message from Erin on Facebook, it took her by surprise. It had been over a year since Quinn died. Erin's email dredged everything up. The week Quinn was killed, she and Alec were together every night, which was very unusual for them. They never saw each other on weekdays but that week, they did, and she remembered Alec got a lot of phone calls. She had teased him because he kept sneaking away whenever his phone would ring.

'Why do you keep going out in the yard every time you get a call?' she asked. 'What are you, CIA?'

'I could tell you, but then I'd have to kill you,' he replied with a grin, saying it was 'just university stuff'. She remembered thinking his behavior was odd, atypical. He was acting funny.

Maybe she shouldn't have communicated with Erin. Alec had been through enough, and she certainly didn't want to cause any hardship for his kids. Feeling a little guilty, she decided to call Alec. He was surprised to hear from her but was warm and friendly. They chatted like old friends, laughing and teasing each other like they used to, even flirting a little. For a second, she wondered if she had made a mistake breaking up with him. Alec was his old charming self, the guy she fell for at the car wash.

'So,' she said, 'the reason for my call is I got a message on Facebook from someone you know.'

'Oh yeah,' he said. 'Who?'

'Erin Delaney,' she said. Dead silence. 'She's your sister-in-law, right?'

'Yeah,' he said. 'She's a whack job just like my ex-wife. What did she want?'

Alison wondered why he called Quinn his 'ex-wife'. They never got divorced. She died. She was murdered before the divorce was final. Alison thought his choice of words was peculiar.

'She asked me if I knew anything that might help them solve Quinn's murder,' Alison replied.

'What did you tell her?' he said suspiciously.

'That I didn't know anything, but I had a bad feeling that week,' Alison said.

'You stupid bitch,' he screamed. 'Why would you say something like that? Why would you give her any ammo? They're all after me. They think I killed Quinn.'

'I didn't say anything, Alec. I just told her I had a bad feeling, that's all, like a sixth sense.'

'Keep your mouth shut and stay out of my business,' he shouted. 'If I find out you talked to any of them, you'll be sorry. I'll shut you down, you got that?'

She was shaking when she hung up the phone. Now she was afraid. A lot of people thought Alec was guilty of killing his wife. Alison had always defended him. Quinn's family and all her friends from New Jersey were convinced he did it. One of Alison's friends used to date a reporter for the *Rochester Bulletin*, and he told her all the cops thought Alec did it. That's why they weren't looking for anyone else.

Alison wondered if she had been sleeping with a murderer for all those months. She'd seen his temper, and it was bone chilling.

The next day when she got to work, she walked over to her manager without stopping at her own desk.

'Hey Ted,' she said, sticking her head into his office. 'You got a minute?'

'For you, Ali, always,' he said, closing his laptop. 'What do you need?'

'Remember last month you asked me if I'd consider relocating to run our office in Austin? I've changed my mind. I'll do it.'

Alison never communicated with Erin Delaney again. She didn't want to get mixed up with those people. Strange things *were* going on the week Quinn died. If the cops ever contacted her, she'd tell them to check Alec's phone records. She pulled out her calendar and added a few thoughts to the detailed notes about the weeks leading up to Quinn's death, in case she was ever asked about it down the road. For now, she didn't need any more trouble, and she didn't want Alec Roberts pissed off at her. Austin put 1,600 miles between them. Maybe now, she'd be able to sleep at night.

Part Six

THREE YEARS AFTER MY MURDER

Chapter Seventy-Three

Erin, Mike and some of Quinn's Jersey friends organized another vigil to mark the third anniversary of Quinn's death. They met in Newbridge on the street where Quinn had lived to do community outreach, handing out flyers followed by a march around the neighborhood. Somebody out there knew something, and they hoped this show of force might encourage that person to come forward. They even contacted local newspapers and TV stations to keep Quinn's name in the news, so she wouldn't be forgotten.

By the third anniversary, Jack and Hannah, who had somehow managed to finish college, had both found jobs in Rochester. They came to the vigil, too. No one invited Alec. None of the Delaneys had spoken to him since Quinn died. He'd never have the guts to show up at their event, anyway. He knew they all thought he did it and he stayed away.

'An innocent person would be looking for his wife's killer,' said Mike. 'Alec never spent one minute looking nor did he give any help to the police. That's all you need to know.'

They posted pictures of Quinn sealed in plastic sleeves all over Newbridge and hung purple ribbons around hundreds of trees along the streets of The Glades as a nod to domestic violence. Reporters came and took pictures, and they urged the public to come forward with anything they might know.

No one ever did.

Chapter Seventy-Four

Erin Googled her sister's name once a month without fail. She'd type 'Quinn Delaney Roberts' into the search bar and see what popped.

The first year after Quinn died, she got old newspaper articles from the *Newbridge Gazette* or one of the Rochester papers talking about the murder and the investigation. Sometimes there would be a new comment posted on a message board tacked to the bottom of an old article. Most comments were from kooks speculating about who killed her sister. There were a lot of creeps out there. One guy thought it was the Mafia. Another thought it was al-Qaeda. She hated reading them but it was necessary, you never knew what could be significant. Anything could be a lead.

Mike begged her to stop Googling Quinn's name.

'It's been more than three years. Every time you do it, it's like you drag your heart through shards of glass,' he said gently.

'I'm not giving up on her. She would never give up on me.'

The next day she ignored her husband and typed 'Quinn Delaney Roberts' into the Google search bar and scrolled through pages of results. The news coverage on her sister was extensive.

She checked every link until she saw one she hadn't seen before. It was brand new. Her fingers trembled as she clicked on the document. It took her to an article on some political conspiracy news magazine. The report was about U.S. Supreme Court Justice Alexander Roberts. Erin wondered if it showed up in the Google results because the judge and Quinn were both named Roberts.

That wasn't it. Erin had typed 'Quinn Delaney Roberts' in quotes, so Google search looks for all three words. She kept reading. At the bottom of the article there were hundreds of reader comments ranging from thoughtful to insane. She read through every posting until she found it.

One commenter called himself 'Tater', and the other was named 'Tot'. Tater and Tot obviously knew each other. Also, it appeared that they knew her sister and not in a good way.

TATER: And as a perfect example I'll give you a point for the war on growth hormones in the meat supply. But first, could the ladies on this site do some online shopping for a moment? This next part is just for the guys. I'm almost 50, and one of the things that always stuck with me is the lack of Female Blouse Basketballs in junior high and high school. As I'm getting old enough to be an old geezer myself, my memory ain't what it used to be, and neither are the Bra Sizes on today's fairer Sex. But one thing I've never forgotten is the names of the only two girls in junior high AND high school who you'd want to be pressed up against on a Japanese Subway on the way to work (DOES that make any sense to you people? WAKE UP.) Quinn Delaney and Julie Gardner.

As Captain Snarky Face has already reported: The hottest chick in our high school class was murdered by a husband who must have lost it after the birth of a few kids and the wreck and ruin of what used to be inside her bra. That's just a guess, I don't have any hard evidence on the motive.

But I digress...

Think how boring life would be if there were no lemons to leer at behind the lemonade stand. Or no fresh melons at the Farmer's Daughter Food Stand.

TOT: I don't know what happened to Julie Gardner but Quinn Delaney married Roberts and moved near Rochester. She was murdered there a few years ago.

TATER: You are absolutely correct, Captain. She and her breasts were murdered by, at the time, an unknown assailant, I have no doubt that Roberts did it. It was the year of my (mostly flat chested) twenty-fifth High School reunion. I had scoped the ballroom out as soon as I got there for a chance peek at an old fantasy that had never come true and never would. Did you happen to dig up anything on rack number two, Julie Gardner, Tot? Or is that her on the fat girl pop up ad? I never got to go out with her and my best friends of the time have all moved on to divorces from their Fat Wives. Only one of my friends is still with his Fat One.

But I'll never forget the memories of those mammaries and having to cover my pants crotch with my Math book when called to the front of the room after a secret staring contest between me and Quinn Delaney's Chest from across the room.

TOT: I don't believe that Roberts has been charged. It may have something to do with him being on the Supreme Court and having one of their cleaners erase traces of him from the crime scene. From the reunion, I thought Quinn appeared to retain much of her attractiveness up to the time of her demise.

TATER: Never forget what Roberts did to Quinn Delaney.

Erin froze, barely able to breathe.

Who the hell were Tater and Tot? Why were they talking about my sister, her breasts and her murder on a message board, years after her death?

She copied and pasted everything and sent it to the police. If these two creeps had something to do with her sister's death, maybe it wasn't Alec after all. What if they killed Quinn, and this was the only place they could brag about it?

Chapter Seventy-Five

L osing three hundred dollars was nothing, if there was the slightest chance Erin could communicate with her sister. She punched James Vance's address into her GPS and drove south for two hours until she reached a small town outside of Philly. Vance was a well-known psychic who had come highly recommended. He had worked on many criminal cases with police all over the country. Even though she was skeptical, she had nothing to lose – 'except your money', her husband pointed out when he learned of her intention to go. She wouldn't tell the psychic anything. If he were legit, he would know why she was there.

She drove to the end of a leafy country lane in the rural town and pulled past a gravel driveway. There were several cars parked on the side of the house, one behind the other. A sign hanging on the front door said, 'Office in back'.

Erin had never been to a psychic before and wasn't sure what to expect. When she entered the office, she heard New Age music quietly playing. Every inch of wall space was filled with shelves of books and spiritual knick-knacks, all for sale; crystals, candles, and stuff she couldn't identify. She sat down and thumbed through some old magazines, anxious about whether her sister would come through and wondering if the whole thing was a bunch of bullshit.

A few minutes later, a door opened, and a man in his sixties with long white hair, rimless glasses, and wearing what looked like blue medical scrubs entered the waiting room. He smiled.

'Erin?' he asked.

Erin nodded with a puzzled look on her face.

'I'm James Vance,' he said, grinning more. 'You're wondering about my clothes.'

She blushed.

'Am I that transparent? Clearly, I need to work on my poker face.'

'I wear these clothes because they're comfortable,' Vance said. 'I like to keep things loose. You don't get much looser than scrubs. I don't have to decide what to wear in the morning. I'm always in my blue uniform. Come on back to my office.'

They walked down a hall into a small room with two beige couches facing each other. She sat on one and he on the other.

'Every psychic is different, and no encounter I have is ever the same. Some days I hear the spirits with my ears. Sometimes I see them with my eyes and other times they send information and messages that pop into my head like on a billboard. I want you to understand how they come through to me. It varies, okay?'

Erin nodded, although she had no idea what he was talking about.

Almost as soon as they sat down, James began talking about all her deceased grandparents.

'It's your mother's mother,' James said. 'She likes the scarf you're wearing. She's admiring your accessories. She approves and says you're a chip off the old block and have inherited her sense of style.'

His comment took Erin by surprise. Her grandmother had been a clothes horse and loved accessorising. Grandma always used to say 'less is less and more is more and more is always better'. On any given day her grandmother would have on four or five rings, an arm full of bangle bracelets, a scarf, earrings, a pin and something sparkly in her hair. Still, Erin wasn't sold yet. A lucky guess, she thought, everyone must have one grandmother who liked to dress up.

'There is someone I want to talk to,' said Erin. 'She died a few years ago.'

'What was her name?' he asked.

'Quinn, her name is Quinn.'

James closed his eyes, then opened them, cocked his head to the side and looked down at the floor. There was a long silent pause.

'She's here,' he said softly. 'I can feel her. I can't see or hear her yet, but I feel her presence.'

'She was murdered,' Erin blurted out and immediately kicked herself for volunteering too much. 'I miss her. I worry about her being hurt and alone.'

James started to laugh.

'Okay,' he said, still chuckling and looking across the room over Erin's head. 'Yes, I see you, calm down.'

Silence.

'Yes, they're very nice,' James said, still smiling at an open space on the other side of the room. After a moment, he turned back to Erin. 'I see your friend Quinn,' he said, laughing again. 'She's funny. She wants you to know, she's okay. She's pointing to her chest and neck and showing me everything is good. She wants you to know that she's not hurt anymore. That she's healed.'

Tears streamed into Erin's eyes. James handed her a box of tissues.

'She says she misses you but that she's alright,' he continued. 'She said wishes she could hang out and drink margaritas with you. She's pretending to make a drink in a cocktail shaker.'

Erin started to laugh and cry at the same time. Maybe this was the real deal, she thought. Quinnie loved margaritas. How could he possibly know that?

'Can she tell you anything? We're trying to find out who killed her,' Erin said. 'Was it her husband?'

James turned his head a few times, looked down and then looked up. He shook his head, confused.

'I'm having trouble hearing her,' he said. 'I can't see her face, no wait, now I can. She's frustrated. She says she doesn't know why the person who killed her did it. She says that her last day isn't clear. She didn't know him or why he wanted to hurt her. She begged him not to do it.'

The session went on for a full forty minutes and Erin got more information about the murder.

'It wasn't her husband?' Erin gasped near the end. 'Are you sure?'

James looked over Erin's head again. 'Her husband might have known about it,' James said. 'But he didn't do it. Quinn's showing me a deli or a supermarket. I can see the sign outside the store, it's blue and white. She's pointing to the camera over the register.'

'She must mean that little market near her apartment. I went there once with her,' Erin said. 'I think their sign was blue and white.'

James turned his head again and zoned out, then he began to nod.

'I'll ask her,' he said, looking over Erin's head at the wall, still nodding.

'Ask me what?' said Erin.

'Quinn wants to know why you didn't tell me that she's your sister?' he said.

Erin lost it. This was *real*. Her sister was there.

Chapter Seventy-Six

QUINN

Everything is so weird now. I don't know where I am or where I'm supposed to go. I'm always walking, always moving. There are others around me, but they've got their own agenda. I often find myself at a playground, riding on the swings. I'm waiting for something, but I don't know what. How will I know I've found it if I don't know what I'm looking for?

Today, if it even *is* today, I was suddenly yanked from the park and found myself in a strange room. There was a man there with white hair and rimless glasses. He must have been a doctor because he had on blue scrubs like the kind they wear in operating rooms. Erin was sitting across from him. She was crying and talking about me. I went right up to her face.

I said, 'Erin. I'm here.' But she couldn't hear me. No one ever hears me. I screamed into her ear. 'Erin, I'm right here next to you. Don't cry.'

Nothing. Then I saw the doctor look over in my direction almost like he had heard me. I tried to get his attention by jumping up and down and shouting, 'Doctor, here, doctor, I'm over here, can you see me?'

He was looking the wrong way. I grabbed at my shirt and lifted it up to show him my boobs and then stood directly in front of him, dancing. He'll notice these, I thought. Within seconds, I saw a glimmer of something in his eyes. He saw me. He could see me. Yay! I did a little victory dance.

He laughed when he saw what I was doing and told Erin I was there. I pointed to each of my naked breasts and laughed with him because someone finally acknowledged me. The doctor told Erin what he saw.

'That's Quinnie,' Erin said to the man in the scrubs. 'Always outrageous, always wanting to have fun. I miss her so much. I'm afraid she might be scared and alone.'

I didn't want my big sister to worry, so I showed the doctor that I was all better and pointed to my neck and chest, so Erin would know I was healed. He told her and she started to cry again.

'She wants you to know she's okay,' the doctor said.

'Please don't cry, Erin,' I shouted. 'Let's have a margarita together.' I pretended I had a martini shaker and acted out making a drink, pouring it into a glass and having a sip. The doctor saw me do it and laughed too.

Chapter Seventy-Seven

E rin sobbed while she told Mike about her session with the psychic causing Mike to cry too. After they composed themselves, they laughed about Quinn making margaritas and flashing her breasts. It was so her.

'You know I don't believe in this kind of stuff,' Mike said to his wife, 'but I have to admit, James Vance kind of nailed your sister. And, Kenny's Kwik-Mart does have a blue and white sign. How could he have known that and how did he know Quinn was your sister?'

Although the cops would probably think they were total flakes, they decided to write a recap of sections from the recording Erin made of her session with James Vance and send it to the police. They wanted the cops to check the security video from that market.

The session with Psychic, James Vance

Erin: I want to talk to my friend Quinn, she died.
(Long pause)
James: (Vance laughing) I can see her. She's showing me her breasts, pointing at them and smiling. There's a lot of bright light around her. She's okay. She's in a good place. She says she had a feeling something wasn't right, not at first but near the end, she knew. It happened quickly. Her chest was hurt, and so was her neck. But she's restored now and looks good. (Pause) Now, she's making herself a

cocktail and mouthing the word 'margarita'. (Pause) She wants you to know she's alright and she loves you. That you shouldn't worry about her.

James: (Long pause) She can hear you by the way. She says she didn't expect things to get as out of hand as they did. She's showing me a man walking up to her house with a dog. (Pause)

Erin: Is it her husband?

James: She says her husband is useless.

Erin: He wouldn't talk to the police.

James: She thinks the person who did it is somebody she had seen in a store. She's showing me a small store that sells eggs and bread and has a blue and white sign. She's pointing to the camera over the register. She says that last day is fuzzy. Everything is upside-down. She didn't know the person who did it.

Erin: But, we thought it was her husband.

James: She says her husband's not the brightest bulb, but he thinks he is the smartest. She's telling me her husband is someone who could have blood on his face, like war paint and still say he's innocent. Lying comes easily to him but it wasn't her husband. The person who did it was jittery and nervous. (Long pause) Avon. There's some connection to Avon, NY.

Erin: Quinn lived in Avon with her husband and kids.

James: She says her husband didn't kill her, but all connections lead to Avon. Her husband may have a piece of information you need. Quinn's telling me she felt like she had been under surveillance, that a stranger had been watching her. She's showing me the security camera at the store. The killer was there when she was.

Chapter Seventy-Eight

Candace Burrows, head of Victim's Rights for the Newbridge PD cornered McQuillan in the department's break room. She was the point person between the police and DA, and victims and their families. She was Erin's primary contact, and she wanted to know if McQuillan had seen the email from Erin about her meeting with the psychic.

'Yeah, I read it,' he said as he poured himself his third cup of coffee.

'And?'

'C'mon, Candy, a psychic?'

'McQ, what have you got to lose?' she said. 'Some police departments work with psychics all the time.'

Candace knew which of McQuillan's buttons to push. She slathered him with guilt, and eventually it worked. Though the detective was convinced it was a big fat waste of time, he decided to go get the video from Kenny's Kwik-Mart and have a look at it.

'I had a feeling you'd want to see it one day,' Kenny said with a satisfied smile when McQuillan walked into the market. 'It's in my safe. I've looked at it at least fifty times. There's no audio, only pictures and the images aren't that clear. I only have the system to prevent shoplifting. It ain't HBO. You know what I mean?'

'Thanks for saving it, we'll give it a good look down at the station.'

'How come you want to see it now, after all these years?'

'We got a tip. Figured we shouldn't leave any stone unturned.'

McQuillan took the video back to the station and popped it into a player. He saw Quinn Roberts standing at the register talking to Kenny while two construction workers were nearby talking to each other. They must be the guys Kenny told him about who spoke Polish, McQuillan thought. A third guy was in front of Quinn paying for his things. It was hard to make him out because of the quality of the video. That guy paid and left. Another man stood behind Quinn but again, it was impossible to get a good visual on him. Kenny was right, the pictures were poor and grainy. One thing the detective was sure of, unless Alec Roberts was standing inside Kenny's Kwik-Mart that day, this video showed him nothing he could use to nail anyone. So much for the psychic, he thought.

Chapter Seventy-Nine

E rin figured it would happen one day, but when it did, it hit her hard. Hannah had called to tell her the news. Quinn had been dead for more than three years but hearing that Alec was getting married again, that he was happy, while her sister was in the ground, knocked Erin on her ass.

Hannah said her father was marrying a woman named Melissa who was in her twenties. Alec's soon-to-be new wife was practically the same age as Hannah. He always liked them young, thought Erin. That was my sister's fatal error; she got older. How careless of her.

'How do you feel about your dad getting married?' Erin asked her niece.

'It's weird,' Hannah said, 'but he's happier, so I guess it's a good thing for all of us. She's nothing like Mom. She thinks my father is the greatest guy in the world. That's a joke.'

Erin tried to get Hannah to explain what she meant, but as soon as she pried, Hannah clammed up and said she had to go. It happened whenever Erin tried to talk to either Hannah or Jack about their father.

The cops never told the Delaneys precisely what the cause of Quinn's death was. According to them, only the killer would know the exact way Quinn Roberts died and they wanted to keep it that way. Mike and Erin tried to read between the lines. From the bits and pieces they had gleaned from countless conversations with law enforcement, they believed Quinn had been beaten and strangled. In their research, they also learned that the leading cause of death from domestic violence was strangulation. At least that was their theory.

'Do the math,' Mike said to his wife. 'Two plus two equals four.'

'But what about the psychic? He said it wasn't Alec.'

'But he said Alec knew about it. Whether Alec did it himself or he got someone else to do it, he's behind it. He's a killer and now he's marrying some other unsuspecting person.'

'Why would any woman go out with Alec?' Erin said. 'If I met a guy whose wife was murdered, I'd run in the other direction. Quinn's case was all over the news. All you have to do is Google "Alec Roberts", and hundreds of articles come up that ask a lot of unanswered questions.'

'Maybe Alec getting married is a good thing,' said Mike. 'I hate to say it, but with all the time that's passed, the only way we're going to get him is if he hurts someone else.'

Chapter Eighty

QUINN

My husband, Alec, has a brand-new wife. Didn't take him long. He got over me pretty quickly. Now that I think about it, he had plenty of girlfriends even before I died. The new wife, what's her name? You think I don't know? I know a lot. It's Melissa, and she looks like she's about fourteen. That's my husband for you, always going for the teenagers. The younger, the better, as far as he's concerned. He stopped looking at me as a sexual being around the time I turned thirty. Well, Miss Melissa, you'll get older, too. Better start watching your back around your twenty-ninth birthday, if you make it that far. Does he slip pills into your wine too? Tickety-tock.

Chapter Eighty-One

Candace Burrows called Erin to let her know about the arrest of Ronny Hemmerly, the landlady's son. The police had just picked up and charged Ronny with assault and rape. Allegedly, he beat up a woman and then sexually assaulted her in her apartment. They said he nearly killed her.

Because of this, the police were taking another look at Hemmerly for Quinn's murder, but Candace warned Erin not to get her hopes up.

'They did look at Hemmerly when they began the investigation,' said Candace, 'but ruled him out. Given what just happened, the police are going to give him another look. But it's a long shot.'

'Do you think we were wrong? That Alec is innocent?' Erin asked her husband that night.

For the first time, Mike wasn't sure about anything. Was it possible that maybe his brother-in-law wasn't guilty after all?

Chapter Eighty-Two

When she signed up for Alec's class, Melissa D'Souza had no idea the kids at school called him 'Dr. A'. She heard the rumors later on but she didn't believe them. The buzz on campus was that Dr. Roberts was an outstanding teacher and was very popular with the students. Melissa D'Souza was an Accounting major, and History was a requirement, so she had to take his class.

Not particularly fond of history, she deliberately sat in the front of his classroom because her mind wandered when she wasn't interested in a subject. She figured if she sat in the hot seat, she'd be forced to focus. The first day of class, Dr. Roberts walked into the room carrying a leather backpack. Right away she found him attractive in an older, mature, dashing professor sort of way.

'Good morning, everyone,' he said. 'Hope you all had a nice summer. I'm Dr. Alec Roberts, and this is History 210, Effects of Twentieth-Century Politics on the Twenty-First Century. Everyone in the right classroom?' he said, grinning. One red-faced student stood up, collected his things and left as Dr. Roberts and the rest of the class chuckled.

'There's always one,' said the professor. 'Let's get started. The year is 1917...'

That first class was still vivid in Melissa's mind. She'd seen Alec walking on campus before, but she hadn't connected the name with the face. He was old but not ancient. He was cute, not classically handsome but appealing, unusual-looking, exotic even. He looked like he might have been South American or Italian. She later learned he was half Korean and half English; the Korean was the exotic piece. What she found most appealing was his curious mind and his self-assuredness. She was intrigued by the unique way he examined the world and found his confidence really sexy, probably because she had so little of it herself.

From then on, Melissa always sat in the front of the room. Midway through the semester, Alec assigned a term project that was worth seventy-five percent of their grade. Wanting to ace the class, Melissa approached him at the end of the lecture after everyone else had left the room.

'Dr. Roberts,' she said. 'Do you have a minute? I wanted to discuss the theme for my project with you.'

He looked up at her and smiled knowingly.

'Sure, Melissa,' he said. 'I was about to get a coffee so I don't fall asleep in my next class. If you're free, why don't you join me and we can talk about it.'

They walked across the quad to one of the coffee bars on campus. He asked a lot of questions like where she grew up, how many brothers and sisters she had, and so on. Melissa was surprised by all the personal questions but didn't mind. His interest made her feel special and she was flattered.

'You're an Accounting major. Graduating next spring?' he asked.

Melissa nodded.

'So, what are you, twenty-one, twenty-two?'

'Twenty-one,' she said. 'I'll be twenty-two in March.'

'That's a great age. Believe it or not, I was twenty-one once,' Alec said with a wink.

'About how long ago was that?' she asked, vaguely aware that she was flirting.

He grinned at her and cocked his head as if he had picked up a signal she hadn't realized she had sent.

'It was a long time ago,' he said with a rueful smile.

'Exactly how long?'

He grinned and shook his head.

'If I tell you, I might have to kill you. I was twenty-one about twenty-six years ago.'

Melissa thought for a few seconds. 'That would make you forty-seven.'

'Bravo, Melissa, it appears your Accounting classes have indeed paid off,' he said, winking again. As they laughed, she was vaguely aware that something was happening between them.

They talked for almost an hour until they both had to leave for their next class. Two days later, he invited her for coffee again. Coffee led to lunch and lunch to dinner. Within a week, it led to bed. They were a couple. She'd never dated a man as old as Alec before. It was exciting, and of course, the fact that it was a secret, made it more intoxicating. During the school day, Melissa was his student, and he, her professor. After school, she'd drive to his place, and they were lovers.

He never tired of telling her she was beautiful and frequently complimented her body. Melissa worked out regularly and taught Pilates part-time. If her body looked good, she figured she earned it. Alec also took care of himself and was in great shape for someone his age. She thought he had the body of a much younger man. Truth be told, she thought Alec looked better than most of her male peers in their twenties who didn't exercise and consumed nothing but junk food and beer. Age is just a number, she told herself.

When the semester ended, Melissa got an 'A' in Alec's class, but she wasn't in the relationship for the grade. She really liked him and before the end of the term, like turned into love. Only a few of her friends knew about the relationship with Alec. She didn't tell a lot of people, but she did tell her two best friends. One thought Alec was 'decrepit' and the other thought he was cool and a little bit hot.

It wasn't until the semester was over that Melissa first heard the rumors about Alec. People said his wife died, that she had been murdered and that maybe he had something to do with it. She didn't believe any of it. Alec was the kindest man she knew.

'If you knew him the way I do, you'd know it couldn't be true,' she said to one of her friends who cautioned her. 'I've read every article online that I could find. There wasn't a single thing that proved Alec had anything to do with his wife getting killed. He told me all about it.'

'But, aren't you just a little concerned?' asked her friend.

'He and his wife were getting divorced. Why would he have killed her if they were already getting divorced? Besides, it was so many years ago. If he did it, the police would have arrested him by now. He told me the cops only questioned him one time. If he had done it, they would have talked to him more than once.'

The Alec she knew was playful, charming, thoughtful and treated her like a princess. He was always telling her how smart and sexy she was. He'd regularly bring her little gifts and buy her clothing and jewelry. There were always little surprises waiting for her. The sophisticated professor was so different from the guys her own age who spent their weekends playing drinking games. Alec treated her like a lady and taught her about photography, fine wine and art. She fell for him hard, and they got married the summer after she graduated.

A couple of years later, when Melissa reflected on their relationship, she realized Alec started to change right after they got married. Until then, she was 'perfect, beautiful and hot'. Once she'd fallen for him, he very subtly started to chip away at her self-esteem. She didn't notice it at the time, but now she could see it clearly for what it was. What do they say, she thought. Love is blind, and hindsight is twenty-twenty. So true. I should have had my eyes checked.

Chapter Eighty-Three

Mike walked into the house with three overflowing bags of groceries, barely making it to the counter before he dropped one of them on the floor. Erin came racing into the kitchen when she heard the commotion.

'You're not going to believe this. McQuillan just called,' Erin said breathlessly. 'Alec may not have done it. We may have been all wrong about him.'

'What happened?' Mike asked, picking up a loose apple on the floor. 'Last time you wanted to give Alec a pass when we thought it could have been the landlady's son. When that didn't pan out, I moved Alec back to the top of my list.'

'There's this serial killer named Wayne Carden,' said Erin. 'Carden was in upstate New York the year Quinn was killed. The cops are checking right now to see if Carden was anywhere near Rochester or Newbridge.'

'A serial killer might have been in upstate New York the year Quinn was killed? Do you know how big the state is?' he said. 'Where's Carden now?'

'In jail,' said Erin. 'They're going to check his DNA against the samples they took from Quinn's apartment. Mike, we might have been wrong about Alec.'

'I know you don't want to believe Alec killed your sister,' said Mike. 'It would be better for the whole family if it wasn't him, especially his kids. But look at the facts. He was abusive and refused to give her any money when she moved out. He only sent her checks when he felt like it. Your parents had to buy her food a few times, remember? We even sent her money. Did you forget that the cheap bastard left her in an unmarked grave because he didn't want to pay the fifty dollars for a freaking cemetery marker?'

'That crushed my parents.'

'We bought Quinn's headstone. Everything with him is always about money,' said Mike. 'You think a random stranger appeared out of nowhere and for no reason arbitrarily killed Quinn?'

'No.'

'Alec is mean to the bone, and he had a motive,' said Mike. 'I predict there won't be a match with the serial killer's DNA.'

'It would be so much better for our whole family if Alec was cleared,' Erin said. 'My parents haven't spoken to Quinn's kids since she died because they stuck by their father.'

'I know. The whole thing sucks,' Mike said quietly.

'Things will never be the same,' said Erin. 'When Quinn died, our whole family disintegrated. There's almost nothing left of us.'

Part Seven

FIVE YEARS AFTER MY MURDER

Chapter Eighty-Four

From the first day of the Quinn Roberts investigation, McQuillan never wavered on who he thought the guilty party was. He remembered how his inner truth meter went nuts the first and only time he interrogated Alec Roberts. His intuition always pointed towards her husband even though there were other possible players on the board.

There was the son, Jack Roberts; one angry kid. In shock when he found out his mother had been killed but also looked relieved. His mother had been leaning heavily on him for emotional support, and the kid didn't like her hanging around him and his friends. He wanted to party at college, not babysit for Mommy. Sometimes he wanted her gone, and the more he pushed her away, the clingier she got.

The police had looked at Jack Roberts from every angle. They ran his prints, checked his DNA, and talked to all his friends and girlfriends. They put the squeeze on him but ultimately decided he was a dead end. The kid was a bundle of raw nerves. He was damaged goods who couldn't get out of his own way. They ruled him out.

Next, there was the high school boyfriend, Mark Miller. For a while, he was number two on the cops' hit parade right behind the husband. Miller was an interesting character. Some of his old high school friends remembered Romeo being too possessive of Juliet when they were teenagers. Some of their classmates said Miller still carried a torch for Quinn Delaney after all the years. People who attended their reunion said Miller was practically on top of her that night, and wouldn't leave her alone. He acted like the two of them were a couple again, and people saw them exit the party together. Miller was definitely a person of significant interest.

At first, the cops thought the Mark Miller theory had legs if they expanded the scope beyond the husband. Old boyfriend meets up with the love of his life and puts it all on the line. He goes for broke and then she cock-blocks him. Things get out of hand, and someone ends up dead. Also, the cops discovered Miller's wife once called the local Cranbury police on him during a domestic dispute. Turns out Miller had a bit of a temper, too. It was looking interesting until they learned Miller had an airtight alibi for the week Quinn Roberts was killed. He was on vacation in Hawaii with the wife he wanted to dump for Quinn. He had the plane ticket and time-stamped photos of he and the Mrs. drinking mai tai's on a beach in Kauai. Aloha.

A couple of years into the investigation, the police got a tip on a serial killer named Wayne Carden currently doing life for the murder of a man in Buffalo. Carden was bad news and over a ten-year period had left a string of bodies up and down the east coast. He had no discernible pattern, except that they were usually young men in their twenties, but not always. He strangled, stabbed, smothered and caught people by surprise. Carden didn't know his victims and seemingly killed for sport. Some aspects of the Roberts' murder were a fit with him. Carden's methods were so random and diverse though, almost any murder could be his handiwork. When the cops learned that the serial killer might have been in the Rochester area around the month Quinn Roberts was killed, he made it onto their list.

McQuillan personally called Erin, to give her a heads-up. He wanted to provide her with some good news for a change.

'You really think it's possible this Carden is the one who killed my sister?' Erin asked.

'I don't want to get your hopes up,' McQuillan said. 'DNA will rule him in or out. I'm sending people up to Attica tomorrow to get a swab from him. Then we'll see what happens.'

The lab finally called back with the results — no match; Carden wasn't the killer, at least according to the DNA.

'Probably wouldn't have been able to use it, anyway,' said McQuillan to Crews when they got the news. 'Goddamned Yancy strikes again.'

Erin Delaney started to cry when McQuillan told her it wasn't Carden. She had thought the nightmare was finally over, but it wasn't. After the detective hung up, he chastised himself for getting her hopes up.

They had also investigated Tater and Tot, the losers from the online discussion board. Once they figured out Tater was Morelle, they were able to identify Devin Borke as Tot, his partner in perverted crime. Both men had been high school classmates of Quinn's. Crews and McQuillan had interviewed each of them.

'You think I had something to do with Quinn Delaney's murder?' said Morelle, surprised but oddly smiling when the two detectives showed up at his office.

'We've got to rule people out Mr. Morelle, and your comments on the *American Witness* website were somewhat alarming,' McQuillan said. 'Why would you be talking about a dead woman you hadn't seen in over twenty-five years, now?'

'I don't know, my buddy and I were just riffing,' said Morelle. 'Quinn Delaney was hot.'

After interviewing Morelle, they went to talk to Tot, aka Devin Borke. Morelle was a jackass, but at least he had a brain. Borke on the other hand, thought McQuillan, was a card-carrying idiot.

'Your friend, Morelle, said you two were just free-associating when you talked smack about Quinn Delaney, her body and her murder,' McQuillan said.

'Yeah, that's right,' said Borke. 'It was nothing. She just popped into our heads.'

'Except,' McQuillan said, 'you discussed her murder more than once over several years. That doesn't fit a pattern of a random thought, does it?'

'I have random thoughts all the time, and sometimes I think them again.'

'Mr. Borke, did you see Quinn Delaney Roberts at your twenty-fifth high school reunion?'

'Yeah, she was still hot.'

After years working on Quinn Roberts' case, McQuillan had become protective of her. He didn't appreciate this ass jockey talking about her like this.

'Let's stick with the facts,' said McQuillan.

'Oh, it was a fact alright, she was smokin',' Borke replied. 'But she was also a stuck-up bitch. Once in high school, I tried to talk to her on the lunchroom line. She was in front of me looking at desserts on the cake shelf. I took a chance and spoke to her highness. I told her she should try the carrot cake because it was really good. She said carrot cake was disgusting and it would make her puke. Then she grabbed a brownie and walked away. She didn't even look at me. Like I didn't exist. Totally shot me down. I could never eat carrot cake again, and it was my favorite.'

What a fucking moron, McQuillan thought. That's when he decided Borke was too stupid to kill anyone and ruled him out.

It appeared the only reason Tater and Tot went to the reunion was to get a look at Quinn Delaney Roberts. Turns out neither had the balls to speak to her or even make contact at the event. Quinn's friends confirmed that, so did Mark Miller. In the end, they both had solid alibis the week Quinn was killed. Borke was playing golf in Ireland with friends and Morelle was at a trade show in Indianapolis the whole week.

The last suspect on the murder hit parade was Ronny Hemmerly, the landlady's son. He'd been in her apartment a few times and had even struck up a little friendship with Quinn by bringing his dog over; she was a sucker for dogs. For a while, some of the team thought it could be Hemmerly, especially after he was picked up for another assault. The only catch was, the week Quinn Roberts was murdered, Hemmerly was in the hospital passing a kidney stone.

'No way he could have killed her,' McQuillan said to Crews. 'I had a kidney stone once. Trust me, you're not killing anyone when you've got one of those bad boys moving through you.'

That left only one person, Alec Roberts. All roads always led back to him.

The police saw no point in pretending to pursue other actors like Tater and Tot, or the high school boyfriend when new crimes were happening in Newbridge every day. Their department didn't have the money or the manpower to run after bogus leads just to appease the Delaney family, especially when the cops were certain it was her husband. They just hadn't figured out how he did it. For McQuillan, Quinn's murder had become a waiting game, waiting for someone to come forward and roll on Alec Roberts. It would take time. One day someone would step up and spill it. McQuillan hoped it happened before he retired or died.

Chapter Eighty-Five

A few months after the fifth anniversary of Quinn's murder, the Delaney family asked for another meeting with the Newbridge police. Mike, Colleen and Erin were led into a meeting room with a U-shaped table. Ed Delaney had recently had a heart attack, preventing him and his wife from attending. The Delaney group sat on one side of the U and a few minutes later, ADA Bernie Gonzales, Detectives Crews and McQuillan and Rights Advocate Candace Burrows filed into the room and sat on the other side of the U.

It looked like a war room with everyone silently staring at each other from across the table waiting to see who would make a move first. Mike noticed the police looked uncomfortable, and they should, he thought; his sister-in-law's murderer was still walking around teaching History in Rochester.

The cops started the meeting, telling them there hadn't been any new leads in a while. Then they dropped the bombshell. They were moving Quinn into the Cold Case Unit. They assured the family that this was a good thing. They said the cold case team would put a 'fresh pair of eyes' on Quinn's investigation. That sometimes, cold case investigators found things that were initially overlooked. The cops sold the concept hard. Mike didn't buy it. From his perspective, the police had failed miserably, and now they were bailing.

'If a doctor does something wrong, you sue him for malpractice. With police, there's nowhere else to go, no one to sue and they don't have to tell you anything they don't want to,' said Mike the night before. 'They keep saying it's still an open investigation and only the murderer would know certain pieces of information so they won't tell us anything more.' After five years, the Delaneys still didn't know how Quinn died or the exact day it happened.

After Bernie Gonzales finished his politically correct speech, Erin pulled out pages of notes and started firing. At this point, she had nothing to lose and didn't try to be polite. She wanted answers.

'Detective McQuillan, did you interview Mark Miller, Quinn's old boyfriend? Might there be DNA you can collect from Miller to rule him in or out? He wanted my sister to run away with him, and she refused. I'm sure he was angry.'

Detective McQuillan looked weary but knew it was his turn up at bat.

'We talked to Mark Miller a few times but he's got a solid alibi,' he said.

'Detective, it's been more than five years since Quinn died. You really think there's still a chance for an arrest? Doesn't look that way from where we sit.'

McQuillan was about to give her a canned response when she interrupted.

'What about those creepy guys we found online, Tater and Tot, the ones who posted all that crazy sexual stuff about my sister? Did you talk to them?'

'We interviewed Devin Borke and Rich Morelle aka Tater and Tot,' said McQuillan with a sigh. 'Both men apparently went to high school with your sister and admitted having a thing for her back then. However, they each had a solid alibi for the week Quinn was killed. Rich Morelle even has his picture in a newsletter from the conference he was attending that week. It's all been documented. I'm sorry, those two were cleared.'

'But they posted things recently about how sexually turned on they were by Quinn,' cried Erin, 'and about my sister being dead. Don't you think that's weird?'

'It's strange behavior for sure,' said Gonzales jumping in. 'There are a lot of whackos out there, but it doesn't mean they're killers.'

'Did Tater and Tot break any laws writing those perverted posts about Quinn?' she asked.

'It's not against the law to be a creep,' Gonzales said. 'Half the guys in this country would be in jail if that were the case.'

The room fell silent waiting for Erin to continue.

'Did you ever interview Alec's girlfriends – those women I found on Facebook, Alison Moore and Cindy Kelleher?' she asked. 'The last time we asked you about Cindy Kelleher, you said Detective Crews had "attempted to contact her but had no luck". Have you since spoken to her?'

'I reached out to Ms. Kelleher several times,' said Crews, 'but she never responded and…'

'Excuse me,' said Erin, 'Cindy Kelleher is a vice president with an insurance company. I think she would return a call from the police. Also, Alison Moore was sleeping with Alec at the time of Quinn's murder. She was never interviewed. Why?'

'Our officers talked to all material witnesses and took full statements from everyone,' said Crews. His answer sounded like a bullshit party line, and Erin was having none of it.

'I'm sorry, Detective, but we know that's not true,' Erin said. 'Alison Moore sent us a message saying she was "surprised the cops never questioned her", and that "weird things were going on the week of Quinn's murder". We don't know why but we think you're lying to us and you've missed a lot of important things. We want to register a formal complaint.'

Bernie Gonzales stared at McQuillan and Crews with a 'what the hell just happened?' look on his face.

'Officer Yancy took a statement from Alison Moore,' said McQuillan, stepping in. 'It was taken right after the murder to corroborate Alec Roberts' alibi. As I recall, when the investigation picked up steam, Yancy did a follow-up with Ms. Moore. I'm not sure why she said we didn't contact her, but I'll look into it.'

McQuillan's response landed like a lead balloon. The Delaneys were sure the cops had missed something and now didn't want to own up to it. Erin hoped after this meeting that the cops would finally talk to Alison Moore.

Chapter Eighty-Six

After meeting with the Delaney family, Gonzales and McQuillan walked back to the DA's office in silence. Finally, Gonzales spoke.

'What the hell happened back there, McQ?' You didn't interview Alec Roberts' girlfriend?'

'We did,' said McQuillan shaking his head. 'I know we've got a statement from her. I'm not sure what happened. I'll circle around with Yancy on the follow-up that he did. Our paperwork doesn't jive with what Erin Delaney told us.'

When McQuillan got back to the station, he let dispatch know he wanted to speak to Officer Yancy the minute he got off patrol. An hour later, Yancy strolled up to McQuillan's desk.

'You wanted to talk to me, McQ?' he said cheerfully.

'Just had a meeting with Quinn Roberts' family,' said the detective. 'They said no one ever interviewed Alec Roberts' girlfriend, Alison Moore. According to the files I have here, you interviewed Ms. Moore twice. You did interview her a second time, right? We specifically asked you to do that, to reconfirm everything.'

The squirmy expression on the patrolman's face told McQuillan everything he needed to know before the kid opened his mouth. Busted.

'I c-called her,' Yancy stammered, 'but she never called me back. Things got busy, other cases were thrown at me. To keep things moving along, I picked up some sections from her original statement and used it in my second report. I thought it would be okay. She didn't know anything anyway.'

'Get out of my sight,' McQuillan said with disgust. 'This isn't over,' he shouted as the young officer slinked out the room. That afternoon, McQuillan wrote up an official grievance report on the young officer and handed it into the brass. Shortly after that, Paul Yancy was suspended.

The following week, the Chief told McQuillan to shut down the Roberts' investigation.

'After all this time, why are you so sure the husband is good for it?' said the Chief.

'First, Alec Roberts had a history of physical and emotional abuse. The victim's sister said he might have also drugged his wife. We know for sure Quinn sought help from a domestic violence group. Second, he had a motive. He was on the hook for lifetime alimony and she was going to get a big chunk of his pension and he wasn't happy about it. Third, Alec Roberts is a word-class shithead.'

'All circumstantial,' said the Chief.

'The husband had a history and a motive. While we didn't get any DNA matches from the apartment, that little scrap from the university newspaper with her address written on it ties his place of employment to her apartment. There's your connection.'

'And, you believe he wrote her address down for someone else,' said the Chief. 'That's why he gave his DNA so quickly. He knew he'd never been there but someone else had.'

'That's my theory.'

'It's possible but without anything more than your theory, we've got nothing,' said the Chief. 'We've got over sixty thousand people in this city and new crimes that need our full attention. I have to put our limited resources into investigations we can actually solve. There hasn't been a shred of new evidence or a lead in years. I'm sorry, the Roberts case is over. I'm moving it to cold case.'

McQuillan was now officially off the Quinn Roberts' investigation, the case that had consumed his life for five years. He had made her a promise, and he had let her down.

Chapter Eighty-Seven

In the five-plus years since her sister died, there had been several new murders in Newbridge. Now that Quinn was moved to cold case, no one was interested in her any more. That's why Erin was surprised when she got a message about Quinn through Facebook.

> Hello Erin,
>
> I'm part of a group who works on cold cases in New York State. We are not investigation professionals but more concerned citizens. Our goal is to bring about justice for families. We read about your sister, Quinn Delaney Roberts, and want to help.
>
> We decided to look into her case, and we're hoping you might share what you've know and what theories you may have. Any information would be helpful.
>
> We're very sorry for your loss. Our group is comprised of Rochester professionals. Quinn lived near where many of us have families, and we care about our community, which includes your sister.
>
> We look forward to hearing from you.
>
> Sincerely, Tom Franken

Erin didn't have a ton of hope that a group of hobbyists playing weekend detectives were going to crack the case when the police hadn't, but she had nowhere else to turn. She and Mike decided to talk to them. It would probably piss off the cops, but at this point, she didn't care. *Carpe diem.*

Chapter Eighty-Eight

When Melissa started dating Alec, he was a perfect gentleman. Smart and funny, he made her laugh all the time. Maybe it was because they maintained the student/teacher roles even after they started seeing each other. It worked for them, and they were happy. It occurred to Melissa that this arrangement felt good because she might have been looking for a 'replacement dad'. She had always felt she had been cheated out of having a father when her own died when she was twelve. She convinced herself that she liked Alec for the man he was and pushed that other idea out of her head.

In the two years they had been married, their dynamic had changed and deteriorated. A few months after their wedding, Alec started picking at her – little things at first. He wanted her to wear different clothes, tighter tops, shorter skirts. He corrected her grammar and finished her sentences. She couldn't even tell a joke without him jumping in with the punchline. He always had to be the center of attention. At first, she blew it off. While she was insecure about a lot of things, she was confident about her looks. She had her own personal style and didn't need a guy telling her how to dress. Still, he pressed her on those things. After the first year of marriage, he brought up new sex things he wanted to do with her. Melissa Roberts was, for the most part, a white bread girl. She didn't go for kinky stuff, and she told him so after he said he wanted to make a sex video.

'We'll record ourselves while we make love,' he said. 'We can watch it together later on. It will be so hot.'

'I don't want to do that, Alec,' she said, 'I'd be self-conscious. I don't do things like that. Besides, what if someone else saw it?'

'No one's going to see it,' he said. 'It will just be for us to keep. Come on, do it for me. It'll be fun. You'll see. Think out of the box, Melissa.'

'I don't want to do it,' she repeated. 'I'd be uncomfortable.' And she refused. Alec brought it up a few more times, but she always said no and finally told him to stop asking her. He never brought it up again.

Chapter Eighty-Nine

Tom Franken and his band of weekend private eyes also sent Jack Roberts a message through Facebook. Jack thought they sounded like a bunch of 'loser armchair detectives' and didn't trust them. He also wasn't sure he wanted to talk to anyone about his mother. Not yet.

It had been over five years. He had tried to move on with his life and put it behind him, but it wasn't easy being the guy whose mother was murdered. People looked at him with a mixture of surprise and pity. He hated when that happened. He could feel it, even from behind.

Talking to Tom Franken would only stir up all the pain again and wouldn't bring his mother back. If the police don't know who killed my mother, he thought, how are these amateurs going to find out?

He called his father and told him about the cold case hobby group and asked his dad again why he wouldn't talk to the police or take a lie detector test. It had been a while since Jack had brought it up and he never got a satisfactory answer from his father.

'Ever watch a police show, Jack?' his father said over the phone. 'They always pin the murder on the husband or the boyfriend; it's classic cop noir. I'm not going to put myself in a compromising position. I didn't touch your mother, and I don't want the cops to railroad me. It's that simple.'

'But you could at least talk to them,' Jack said. 'It might help find Mom's killer.'

'Don't you get it?' his father replied. 'The dumbass po-po doesn't have a clue about who killed your mother. If they knew anything, they'd arrest somebody. They want to pin it on me so they can close their case. I'm not that stupid, and I'm not gonna play.'

'But maybe you know something that would help, Dad,' Jack urged.

'Are you listening to me?' Alec said, getting angry. 'Those cops have been out to get me from day one. I'm not going to help them hang me. And, don't talk to those half-assed would-be private eyes, either. They sound like a bunch of pathetic losers with nothing better to do than get into other people's business. Stay away from them, is that clear?'

Jack was silent.

'Jack,' shouted his father over the phone. 'Did you hear what I said? Stay the fuck away from them.'

'Yeah, I heard you,' his son said, barely audible.

The next morning Jack called Tom Franken and said he'd meet with him and his group. They asked him a lot of questions about his father. Some he had the answers to, some he didn't.

Months later, Jack checked in with Franken to see if he had made any headway. Franken only uncovered what they already knew, no new information. It was a bust.

'I'm afraid we've hit a wall,' said Franken. 'Don't know how much further we can go. I hate to tell you this, but circumstantially, your father looks like the most likely suspect.'

Tell me something I don't already know, thought Jack as he hung up the phone.

Part Eight

MY SWAN SONG

Chapter Ninety

It was a Sunday night, and Alec had been drinking since lunchtime. He started with beer and then switched to bourbon around four o'clock. When he got drunk, he became demanding, obstinate and nasty. Melissa steered clear of him to avoid getting caught in his crossfire. He hadn't been like this at all when they first met. After almost three years of marriage, he had changed a lot and not for the better.

Later that night, she lay next to him in bed unable to move. Tears ran from the corner of her eyes into her ears. Her husband had just raped her.

He had been snarky and belligerent all day. By nine o'clock that night, he was inebriated and grabbed her and pulled her to the bed.

'Leave me alone, Alec,' Melissa said, pushing him away. 'Let go of me.'

She tried to get away from him, but his grip was firm, he was much stronger than she was. He pulled her down onto the bed and forced himself on her. She screamed as he climbed on top of her. He put one hand over her mouth and the other around her neck and started to squeeze. She couldn't breathe and believed he was going to kill her so she let him do what he wanted so it would be over faster.

When he was done, she heard him panting next to her. Without looking over, she knew he had that self-satisfied expression on his face. She had seen it a thousand times. She wondered what all his precious students would say if they knew the esteemed Dr. Roberts had just assaulted his wife. He would rationalize that a husband can't rape his wife, but she knew what he'd done He had raped her.

She heard him pour himself another glass of bourbon from the bottle on the nightstand on his side of the bed. He was babbling about how great he was, but she wasn't listening, still lost in the trauma and violence of what had just happened. He was drunk and slurring his words. He reached for her, and she cringed when his hand touched her arm.

'Gimme a kiss,' he said as he pulled her towards him and grabbed at her breast. She pushed him away. He turned to pick up his drink on the nightstand, and she jumped off the bed and moved across the room.

'Don't ever touch me again,' she screamed and ran into the bathroom and locked the door. She could hear him shouting, saying how ungrateful she was, that she was a bitch and a whore and a whole lot worse than that. She didn't want to hear him so she turned on the radio in the bathroom as loud as it would go to drown him out.

Chapter Ninety-One

'You don't have to be such a bitch, Melissa,' Alec shouted at the closed bathroom door. 'You're only a goddamned Pilates instructor. I'm the one with all the fucking degrees. They call me doctor. You're nothing.'

He could hear her radio playing through the bathroom door. Who the hell does she think she is, he thought. She's a nobody. If I want to have sex with my wife, I damn well will. Fuck her and all women. They're all whores, anyway.

He poured himself more bourbon and looked at the bottle. He had almost finished the entire thing. What the hell, he thought, might as well have it all. He emptied the rest into his glass.

'If you won't talk to me,' Alec yelled at the closed bathroom door, 'I'll fucking talk to myself, then. Better company, anyway. I don't need you, Melissa. I got options. You hear me?'

He took another swig of his drink. He could barely feel his body, it was numb from all the booze. It felt nice.

'There are loads of women who want to be with me,' he shouted. 'I've got dozens of women who would go out with me in a heartbeat. You think I need you?' he screamed. 'You're nothing but dead weight around my neck. From now on, when I say jump, you ask how high. You hear me, Melissa?'

Chapter Ninety-Two

Melissa put some towels in the bathtub and laid down in there while she waited for her husband to pass out. She stayed in the locked bathroom for over an hour. She could still hear him shouting and muttering, but with the noise from the radio couldn't make out what he was saying.

After about an hour, there was quiet in the other room. Melissa waited another twenty minutes to be sure he was asleep before she crept out of the bathroom. The lights were still on in the bedroom. Her husband was passed out on the bed with the bourbon bottle lying next to him. What a pretty picture, she thought. She considered taking a photo and posting it online but decided she didn't need any more trouble. Alec could be vindictive.

She went to sleep in the guest room, as she had done any times before. Thankfully, her husband was going on a business trip to Atlanta in the morning. She decided to leave the house before he woke up to avoid having to see him. She needed time to think. She needed an escape plan.

When the alarm went off at six thirty that Monday morning, Alec thought his head was going to explode. He felt like crap and asked himself why he had drunk so much the night before when he knew he had to get on a plane to Atlanta. He stumbled to the bathroom searching for aspirin and his toothbrush. His teeth felt like they had hair on them. Melissa was already up and gone. Odd, he thought, his wife was never up this early. He looked at his face in the mirror. He felt like shit and looked even worse.

Twenty minutes later, the aspirin started to kick in. Random images flashed through his mind. Did he and his wife have sex the night before? He couldn't remember. He had a vague memory that maybe they did and that she had given him a hard time. He couldn't think about her now. He'd deal with his wife and her nonsense when he got back from Atlanta.

He showered, packed his things, took a few more aspirin and drank a full quart of water. Before he walked out the back door, he wrote Melissa a note and left it on the refrigerator.

Chapter Ninety-Three

Alec had to leave for the airport at nine. Melissa deliberately left the house at six thirty and went to her Pilates studio before he woke. She didn't want to see him that day and wasn't sure if she ever wanted to see him again. He'd be gone for three nights, and she needed the time and space to sort things out. It couldn't continue like this.

When she went back to her house a few hours later, she quietly opened the back door, for fear that he might still be there. He wasn't. Tears ran from her eyes as she got into the shower and let the hot water run over her head and body for almost an hour. No amount of soap and water was going to make her situation better. Her husband was a bully and he had hurt her more than once. She knew now that he wasn't going to stop, and it was getting worse.

After what had happened the night before, the feeling of anything touching her body was unbearable. She put on the loosest fitting clothes she could find and went into the kitchen to make some herbal tea. That was when she saw the handwritten note pinned by a red ladybug magnet to the refrigerator.

Be back on Thursday around 6. Clean the fucking house. It's a sty.
A.

She stared at it for a moment, numb. It was the dismissiveness of the message that got to her. Alec had treated her like a piece of garbage the night before and then left her a note as if she was the hired help. All the rage that had been bottled up from the night came pouring out, and she knew what she was going to do.

Chapter Ninety-Four

He didn't know why but McQuillan's ears were itchy all day. His usually reliable inner alarm was warning him to pay attention to something he might otherwise overlook but he hadn't figured out what that was.

He was at his desk about to bite into a corned beef on rye with extra Russian when a call came in from the front desk sergeant.

'McQ, there's a woman out here who says she's been raped,' said the officer.

'What are you calling me for?' McQuillan asked. 'I'm homicide. Call Janine Nash in special victims.'

'The lady is asking for you by name,' the officer said. 'She said she only wanted to speak to Detective McQuillan. She's pretty banged up, got discoloration on one of her cheeks, and she's highly agitated. Says her name is Melissa Roberts.'

Melissa Roberts? Holy shit, thought McQuillan, that's Alec Roberts' second wife. He called Detective Nash and gave her a one-minute rundown on the woman they were both about to meet and asked her to follow his lead and trust him.

There had been nothing new on the Roberts case in years, it was bone dry. The only new thing was that Alec Roberts got remarried to a Melissa D'Souza now, Melissa Roberts, a former student, and part-time Pilates instructor. The wedding happened after the case was moved off the active list to cold case. McQuillan had never met wife number two in person.

Melissa Roberts was pacing nervously in conference room C when McQuillan walked in. Immediately he noticed how much she looked like the first Mrs. Roberts. Like Quinn. Long dark hair, sparkly blue eyes, pale skin, petite. Even though the investigation had moved to cold case, McQuillan still had Quinn Roberts' picture on his desk. When he was actively working on her investigation, she had come alive for him, the beautiful woman with the dancing blue eyes. He couldn't bring himself to put that picture away. Every morning he looked into her eyes and promised her he hadn't forgotten.

McQuillan's attachment to a victim had happened to him before. It was a strange phenomenon for cops who worked homicide. If the vic was a scumbag, you did what you had to do because it was your job. But, if the vic was a good person, someone who had a family, someone people cared about, you sort of fell in love with them a little. Quinn Roberts had become a part of McQuillan's life, and a tiny piece of him had fallen in love with her. Even though she was in cold case and nothing new had happened, he was always on the lookout for that break. It would come one day. Sometimes it took forty years, but it almost always happened if you waited and were lucky enough to live that long. His red vibrating ears told him the wait might be over.

Janine Nash and McQuillan sat across the table from Melissa Roberts. Ms. Roberts was visibly upset, and her cheek was turning purple.

'Ms. Roberts, this is Detective Nash from the Special Victims Unit, and I'm Detective McQuillan.'

Melissa's left hand was in her mouth as she unconsciously bit her thumbnail. Her eyes were red and filled with tears She was barely holding it together. In addition to the small bruise he could see on her face, he noticed a couple of other discolorations on both of her wrists and forearms.

'Front desk said you've been attacked,' McQuillan said gently. 'Can you tell me what happened?'

'Last night,' she said softly while holding back tears, 'my husband, Alec Roberts, raped me.'

That arrogant little prick was at it again, thought McQuillan. This might be the break he'd been waiting for. Melissa Roberts had McQuillan's full attention.

Melissa reached into her pocket, pulled out a piece of paper and laid it on the table.

'This was the note he left for me this morning before he went on a business trip,' she said starting to cry.

The two detectives read the note.

Detective Nash handed Melissa a bottle of water and a box of tissues.

'Melissa, we're going to be with you every step of the way, okay?' she said.

Melissa nodded and chewed on her thumbnail.

'Would you start at the beginning?' McQuillan said calmly, trying to hide his excitement.

'Alec says that a husband has a right to have sex with his wife whenever he wants,' she continued, 'even if she doesn't want to. But I don't think because you're married, it means you can do whatever you want, whenever you want. Don't I have rights, too?'

'Of course, you have rights and no,' McQuillan said, 'being married doesn't give anyone the right to do whatever they want. Rape is rape.'

Melissa swallowed and nodded her head.

'Last night, he was drunk again,' she said. 'I told him to leave me alone, and he told me to shut up, that he could do whatever he wanted. I screamed for him to stop. I tried to get away but he held me down and put his hand over my nose and mouth, and then he choked me. I thought he was going to kill me. I couldn't breathe. After a while, I stopped fighting, there was no point. He's much stronger than me, and I just wanted it to be over, so I let him do what he wanted. When he rolled over, I got up and locked myself in the bathroom.'

'Ms. Roberts, has your husband done this before?' Detective Nash asked.

'Yes.'

'Do you want to press charges?' McQuillan asked. 'Legally, you would be within your rights. What he did, it's not okay.'

'I don't know,' she said. 'What would pressing charges mean? Would Alec be arrested?'

'That depends,' McQuillan said. 'Where is your husband right now?'

'He went to Atlanta this morning for work. He'll be gone for three days.'

'Do you have another place to go?' Detective Nash asked.

'No.'

'We can help you with that,' said Detective Nash. 'We've got temporary housing for this kind of situation. I can make the arrangements for you.'

The two detectives spent the next half hour collecting details from Melissa Roberts. Clearly, thought McQuillan, Alec Roberts still got his jollies from beating up defenseless women.

Detective Nash took Melissa Roberts to another room to get photos of the bruises and abrasions while McQuillan filled out the required paperwork to open the rape and assault case.

With Alec Roberts out of town until Thursday, the plan was for Melissa to go home tonight and pack her things. Tomorrow, Detectives Nash and McQuillan would take her to a safe house until they could sort things out.

'Ms. Roberts,' McQuillan said, 'we'll give you a lift home tonight to make sure the house is vacant. I'd also like to get a look at the room where the attack happened, take some pictures and collect whatever evidence there might be. Are you okay with that?'

Melissa nodded.

Chapter Ninety-Five

Half an hour later, the three of them walked into the dark house and Melissa turned on the lights in the living room. The house was messy with papers piled everywhere. McQuillan took out his camera and took some pictures. He needed to play this legit. He was here to get the goods on a rape but hoped he might find something that might open a crack in the Quinn Roberts murder case. As long as Melissa Roberts had willingly let him into the house, he was going to take full advantage and take his shot. He'd look around for as long as she'd let him, knowing he'd never have another chance at the inside of Alec Roberts' house again. This was his moment. It was show time.

Melissa led the two detectives upstairs to her bedroom. An empty bottle of bourbon lay its side on the nightstand. Nice, thought McQuillan.

'This is where it happened,' Melissa said with no emotion in her voice. 'He raped me on that bed and then I ran into the bathroom over there and locked the door.'

McQuillan and Nash made a few notes, bagged all the sheets and blankets as well as grabbing a few pieces of paper along with the bourbon bottle. McQuillan took photos of the bedroom and bathroom from every angle.

'Mind if I look around your house?' McQuillan asked.

'Do whatever you need to do,' Melissa said. 'Is there something, in particular, you're looking for?'

'I don't know exactly,' McQuillan said. 'I'll know it when I see it. In a case like this, it could turn into a he-said-she-said. I need something concrete to make sure we nail him.'

'If I file the complaint, he might not go to jail?' she asked, starting to tear up. 'If he doesn't go to jail, he'll come after me. You don't know him.'

But I do, thought McQuillan, I know him very well.

Janine Nash gave McQuillan a 'what's going on' look but continued to play along. It was a small Cape Cod house with no basement. They started upstairs and systematically went through dressers, closets and all the bathroom cabinets. Nothing. McQuillan poked around the kitchen, opening cabinet doors and then moved into the TV room/office.

The desk was littered with paper so that the detectives could barely see the wooden top. McQuillan pulled at the top right-hand drawer, but it wouldn't open.

'He keeps that drawer locked,' said Melissa. 'I always wondered why. I asked him once, and he told me it's where he keeps all of his financial information and to mind my own business.'

McQuillan's ears were itching and getting hot again.

'Do you have a key to this desk?' he asked nonchalantly while doing high kicks inside his head.

'He never lets me near his desk.'

The detective was about to suggest they bust the lock open when Melissa Roberts had an idea.

'Wait a minute, there's a little glass bowl on the top of Alec's wardrobe filled with coins. I looked in it once, and I remember now, there was a small key mixed in with the coins. I didn't think anything of it, just figured it was one of the many random keys floating around that didn't belong to anything.'

Melissa ran upstairs leaving Janine Nash and McQuillan alone. Nash looked at the detective skeptically.

'What's going on McQ?' Nash whispered. 'We're way out of SVU territory right now. What have you got up your sleeve?'

'It's my only shot,' McQuillan whispered. 'Work with me, Janine. I ran the Quinn Roberts murder investigation for over five years. We're okay, remember, she invited us in. No harm, no foul. If we find something, then we do. If we don't, we don't.'

Melissa came back into the room with a smile and a small key in her outstretched palm.

'I fished through the coins. It looks like the right size for the lock on the desk drawer, don't you think?'

She handed the key to McQuillan. He sat down at the desk and pushed the key into the lock. The key turned, and he slid the top drawer open. It was practically empty. He had hoped to find packets of stolen money, drugs or kiddie porn, anything that would be incriminating.

'There's nothing in here,' he said disappointedly as he picked things out of the drawer. 'Just a couple of notepads, a UR key ring, three pens, and some tape. You said he always keeps it locked, right? Why would someone religiously lock an empty desk?' McQuillan said, his mind racing.

'Let me have a look,' Melissa said. The detective got up, and Melissa slid into the chair. She reached her thin arm to the very back of the top drawer to a section they couldn't see. Then, she looked up at him and smiled.

'I feel something,' she said and pulled out a pack of Marlboro Lights and a big box of kitchen matches.

'That's why he locked it,' she said. 'He started smoking again and didn't want me to find out. I hope he gets lung cancer.'

'Is there anything else in the back of the drawer?' McQuillan asked. Melissa fished around again.

'No, that's all.'

McQuillan had thought the desk was going to be a criminal treasure trove. He opened the pack of cigarettes. Three left. Then he picked up the box of kitchen matches. It felt heavy. The little voice in his head told him to open the box. He pushed the cardboard tray out. Instead of big wooden matches with red tips, the carton was filled with a couple dozen SD cards, like the ones you have in your camera or phone for storing videos or pictures. He wondered why Alec Roberts kept all these SD cards in a matchbox in a locked drawer.

'Melissa, do you recognize these?' McQuillan asked. 'Do you know what they're from?'

'Alec is into photography,' she said. 'He's pretty good, he even won an award at a local art show. He's always taking pictures of nature and birds. That's probably what's on the cards.'

'Why would someone hide pictures of birds in a matchbox in a locked drawer?' said Detective Nash. 'That doesn't make sense.'

'Do you have a computer I could use?' McQuillan asked.

While Melissa went upstairs to her bedroom to get her laptop, McQuillan poked through the matchbox.

'You think it's something?' Janine Nash asked after Melissa left the room.

'My gut and my itchy ears don't think it's nothing. Why keep a desk locked when there's nothing in it?' he said.

Chapter Ninety-Six

Melissa came back with her computer, placed it on the desk and McQuillan plugged in one of the SD cards.

The three of them watched Alec Roberts have sex with a variety of women captured from the same vantage point in his bedroom. McQuillan recognized a couple of the women. One was Alison Moore, Alec's old girlfriend and the other was Cindy Kelleher, another one of Alec's women. There were many videos of women, dozens of them, mainly young. Some were active participants, but many appeared to be unconscious or severely impaired. Most of them looked like they could be college students. Melissa Roberts stared at the videos, tears running down her face, but said nothing.

McQuillan plugged in card after card and the same tawdry yet familiar episode started again and again.

'Most of them were filmed in my bedroom,' said Melissa. 'They have timestamps, and they're from before I knew Alec. I can tell because all the bedding is different now. The videos of the other women had his old bedspread and pillows, the stuff he had before we got married. I bought all new sheets and a comforter after our wedding. I guess my husband is only a liar, rapist, peeping Tom, and pornographer but not a cheater. Lucky me.'

McQuillan inserted a new SD card. A video of Melissa Roberts in bed with Alec appeared on the screen. She sat next to the detective silently, covering her eyes, face bright red, periodically gasping.

'Can you stop the video, please?' she said, 'I can't watch it.'

McQuillan stopped it.

'I didn't know he filmed me. I'll bet the other women didn't either. If he videoed them without their consent, is that a crime?'

'Oh yeah,' McQuillan said. 'If they didn't know about it, it's absolutely a crime.'

'I want to find out how he did this,' Melissa shouted as she bolted up the stairs with Nash and McQuillan right behind her. When they got to the bedroom, they fanned out to determine the exact angle from where the videos were taken. McQuillan walked around the bed until he thought he had found the spot.

'It looks like they were recorded from somewhere on that chest of drawers,' he said.

The detective reached up to the top of the chest. There was a bowl of coins and a digital clock.

He picked up the clock, shook it and pushed some buttons. A little door on the back of it opened. Inside was an SD card. It looked like all the others they had found in the matchbox.

'That's how he filmed everyone,' said McQuillan. 'Through this fake clock.'

'He's a pig,' said Melissa. 'I can't believe I married him.'

The three of them went back to the first floor, and McQuillan put the new SD card into the computer. The video started to play. Timestamp: last night. They watched Alec Roberts knock Melissa down and get on top of her and put his hands around her neck and over her mouth. They could see how badly Melissa was trembling and heard her plead with Alec to stop. She fought but he overpowered her and then her whole body went limp when she realized there was no way out.

McQuillan looked over at Melissa crying in the corner. She wasn't watching the video any longer.

'I hate him,' she said through her tears, 'and I feel sad for the woman on that video crying on the bed. Me.'

McQuillan turned back to the video. Alec climbed off his wife and poured himself another glass of bourbon. When he reached over to get his drink, Melissa jumped up and then ran into the bathroom and locked the door behind her, just like she'd told them. Alec remained on the bed in a drunken stupor, still shouting at the closed bathroom door.

'You're a bitch, Melissa, I don't fucking need you. You think I give a rat's ass about you,' he shouted, 'cause I don't. You're just a weight around my neck. When I say jump, you ask how high. I'm the king of this fucking castle. You got that?'

Alec was quiet for a moment and then almost as if he got a second wind, started again.

'You better shape up, Melissa,' he continued, slurring his words, 'I got rid of wife number one, and I can take care of wife number two the same fucking way. I still got the goods on Malecki. That's right, I'll call my man, Victor.'

Alec laughed to himself so hard that he choked on his own saliva. Too bad he didn't choke to death, McQuillan thought. He didn't know what Alec Roberts was talking about, but he was going to find out. Who was Malecki? Was that a person? McQuillan understood the 'wife number one' part though, that was loud and clear. It was judgment day, thought McQuillan and Alec Roberts was going down.

'You hear me, Melissa,' Alec began again. 'I'll get Malecki to shut you down the same way he did with that other bitch. She thought she was so great. She was a pathological liar. She deliberately got pregnant. She thought I didn't know. All it takes is one word from me, and you're gone, Melissa. Forever. Just like that lazy, crazy whore. She was trying to bleed me dry. Wanted all my money. She got what she deserved. Wanted me to pay her for the rest of my life. It's my fucking pension, not hers. She had no right to it. Never worked a day in her life and expected me to keep paying.'

Alec took another gulp of his bourbon, smiled and looked over at the closed bathroom door again.

'You better get your act together,' he shouted, 'or I'm going to call my buddy and have him pay you a visit too.' He took one last swig of his drink and a minute later, passed out.

McQuillan looked over at Melissa. She was curled up in a fetal position on the couch under a blanket. The detective dumped the remaining SD cards on the desk and played and fast-forwarded through each one. There were twenty-three, each loaded with numerous videos taken covertly in Alec Roberts' bedroom.

One last SD card remained that looked different from the others. The rest were black, but this one was green. McQuillan pushed the card into the port of the laptop. This video was different, it wasn't recorded in a bedroom. It was taken outside at night.

A light flashed on the right side of the screen. Something moved by fast. McQuillan couldn't tell what it was. Two seconds later, a car pulled out onto a road and screeched to a stop. The car backed up and turned a little as its lights flooded the street in front of it. It looked like the car had hit something, there was a person on the ground. The headlights reflected off the shirt of a man lying on the pavement. The man was wearing night time running gear. The flash at the beginning of the video had been the runner's headlamp and the reflectors on his clothes. The driver of the car got out and looked at the man on the ground. The video zoomed in close on his license plate as the driver got back in his car and drove away.

A few seconds later, the video went dark, and they could only hear the audio. They listened to the sound of a car door opening and then Alec Roberts' voice saying, 'Oh my God, he killed that guy.' The video came back and flashed on the head of the fallen runner in the road. The man was bleeding, his eyes were open, and he was dead. They heard a car door slam and a car engine roar. The video went black again, and they couldn't see anything, only the sound of Alec shouting like a cowboy. He was making whooping noises as he drove. That mental case was enjoying this, thought McQuillan.

'You fucking bastard,' they heard Alec scream. 'You killed that guy. I'm going to get you and make a citizen's arrest. You thought you were free and clear, woo-hoo, but Dr. Roberts saw the whole fucking thing.'

The video was dark, and McQuillan and Nash could only hear sounds. They figured the camera must have been on the seat or the floor of the car. After about fifteen minutes of Alec's endless shouting and threats, the engine stopped, and everything went quiet.

Chapter Ninety-Seven

The two detectives and Melissa Roberts stared at a black screen. They heard something open and close, and then it sounded like Alec said, 'Come on, my little friend, let's go pay this asshole a visit.'

With only audio, McQuillan wondered who Alec Roberts was talking to. Was there another person in the car? A few moments later, the video came back on again and was slowly moving towards a house. As the shot got closer, they detected a man lying on the grass in the front yard of a ranch style house.

'Get up,' they heard Alec's voice shout at the man.

'Who the fuck are you?' said the man on the ground, barely opening his eyes.

'I'm the guy who's gonna turn you over to the cops. It's called a citizen's arrest,' Alec said.

'Fuck off,' said the guy on the ground, closing his eyes again. 'Get off my fucking lawn.'

'Maybe this will wake you up,' Alec said. McQuillan saw the end of a gun barrel in the corner of the video frame. Roberts was waving a gun in the other man's face with one hand while filming with the other.

'You were smashed when you came out of that bar,' they heard Alec shout. 'You hit him and left him to die.'

'He was already dead,' said the guy on the ground, starting to wake up. 'The guy was cold. He shouldn't have been out running in the dark.'

The banter between Alec and the drunk went back and forth for several minutes with more of the same.

'You're wasted. I saw you come out of that bar. You couldn't even walk,' Alec shouted, waving the gun again. 'What's your name?'

'Watch out with that thing. Don't shoot me,' the man pleaded.

'Tell me your fucking name or say goodbye to your head,' Alec yelled again, pointing the gun right at the man's scalp.

'Malecki. Victor Malecki.'

That's when the video ended.

'Do you have any idea where this is taking place?' McQuillan asked Melissa, now sitting up and watching.

'Something looked familiar,' she said. There was a long pause. 'Once, Alec took me to this bagel shop when we were in Metaire doing an errand. He said they had the best bagels in the world. We bought a dozen to take home. I'm not sure, but I think it's the same street as in this video. That little pub at the beginning of the video, the sign said, Dew Drop Inn. When we went to the bagel store, we parked in front of that place. I only remember because I thought the name was funny.'

McQuillan looked at the time stamp. The video was taken almost six years ago, a few weeks before Quinn Roberts was killed. McQuillan thought he finally had Roberts and his ears were in flames.

'Melissa,' he said. 'Why did you come to West Plain PD and ask specifically for me? You don't even live in Newbridge, and I work homicide, not SVU.'

'I know,' she replied. 'Every time my husband had a few drinks, which lately was every day, he'd start ranting about a Detective McQuillan in Newbridge and what a nasty SOB you were. You really got under his skin,' she said.

'I'm told I have that effect on people,' McQuillan said smiling.

'What Alec did to me,' she continued, 'I knew you were the person to go to, that you would listen to me. I guess I was right.'

A minute later, McQuillan placed a call to the Metaire PD to confirm what he had seen on the video was legit. They patched him through to the homicide detective on duty. McQuillan asked him if there had been any unresolved fatal hit and run of an adult male from about six years ago near the Dew Drop Inn.

'You must be talking about Christopher Marshall. He lived here in town, was training for the NYC marathon. Used to go out early before he went to work and run in the dark. Wore two flashing lights and was covered in reflector material,' the homicide detective said, 'you couldn't miss the guy. We always thought the "accident" was either deliberate or a DUI.'

'Did you ever find out who hit him?'

'No,' said the Metaire cop. 'No witnesses. According to everyone who knew him, Chris Marshall was a stand-up guy. No enemies. Great family. Good people. The whole town was really broken up when it happened. He used to coach kids' soccer.'

'Do you know the name Victor Malecki?'

'No. Should I?'

'Oh yeah,' McQuillan replied.

His next call was to Assistant DA Gonzales.

'Are you sitting down?' he said. 'I think we've got the goods on Alec Roberts for his wife's murder.'

'You're shitting me,' said Gonzales. 'How the hell did you pull that one out after all this time?'

'We always knew it was him because of that piece of school newspaper with her address written on it. Our murder for hire theory was right; Alec Roberts must have written his wife's address down on that scrap of paper for the killer,' he said. 'The evidence we found also unmasks the perp of a hit and run six years ago in Metaire. We got a double whammy.'

He told Gonzales to sit tight as he was personally going to walk the evidence over to him. After watching all the videos, Gonzales knew the detective wasn't blowing smoke. This was evidence he could take to the grand jury.

'I guess Alec Roberts has finally been "hoisted by his own petard", as we like to say in legal circles,' said Gonzales. 'That asshole was so intent on seeing his naked white ass having sex with all his little girlfriends that he incriminated himself.'

'Yeah,' said McQuillan, 'and even more intent on being some kind of vigilante hero with Malecki, that he implicated himself in a murder for hire. From his soliloquy on the video, it sounded like he thought he was going to end up being famous.'

'That might still happen, only not for the reason he thought. More like infamous, I'd say. His next photo is going to be a mugshot,' said Gonzales. 'I won't even have to show up in court to win this case.'

Within minutes, the DA's office had called Judge Montgomery to get an arrest warrant for Alec Roberts. Game, set, and light the fucking kitchen match.

Chapter Ninety-Eight

One of Atlanta's most decorated detectives, steely yet diminutive Anita Blalock, was headed across town to arrest Alec Roberts. During her phone call with Detective John McQuillan, his euphoria was palpable and contagious. She knew all too well what it was like to finally nail someone you'd been chasing for years. Some cases get under your skin, and this one was under his. She had heard her grandmother say on more than one occasion, 'Honey, you lie down with dogs, you get up with fleas.' The way McQuillan had described him, she thought, Alec Roberts was most definitely a hound.

By eight o'clock that night, Blalock received the arrest warrant from the judge in Rochester, grabbed two uniformed deputies and headed over to the downtown Marriott. She had promised to let McQuillan know when Roberts was in custody. After hearing all the particulars of the case, she was looking forward to making that phone call.

Wanting to avoid commotion with the other hotel guests, she and the two officers entered the property through a side door and spoke privately with the night manager.

'We're going to need a key to Alec Roberts' room,' said Detective Blalock. 'Don't want to go breaking down no doors if I don't have to.'

The three police officers took the elevator to the fifth floor and knocked three times on Room 506.

'Go away, Señorita. *Estoy muy cansado,*' said a laughing male voice inside the room. 'Come back tomorrow, I'm sleeping.'

Better wake up, hound dog, the detective thought. She knocked harder. Roberts was a bad guy, and she smiled to herself contemplating how his world was about to come crashing down around him.

'Occupado,' said the male voice snickering. 'Come back mañana, por favor, Señorita.'

A woman giggled inside. 'Alec, just answer it,' the woman said.

Blalock knocked a third time, heard some commotion and the door swung open.

'I told you to come back,' Alec said, standing in the doorway with only his pants on. Confused and annoyed, it took him a second to realize the group was not housekeeping, nor were they señoritas.

'What's going on?' he asked, noticing the police uniforms. 'Is there a problem in the hotel?'

'You Alec Roberts?' the detective asked, knowing for sure that he was.

'What's this about?' he said.

The detective grinned and held up a warrant.

'Good news. You've won a free trip to New York, compliments of the Newbridge PD and the District Attorney of Monroe County,' she said as the two deputies moved in to handcuff Roberts.

'Alec Roberts, you're under arrest for the murder of Quinn Roberts,' she said. 'You have the right to remain silent. Anything you say can and will be used against you in a court of law. You have the right to an attorney. If you cannot afford an attorney, one will be provided for you.'

The two officers led Roberts towards the door as the half-naked young woman in the bed stared, mouth agape, clutching the sheets around her neck. Knowing Roberts' history, the irony that she had arrested him while in bed with what looked like another student wasn't lost on the detective.

'Alec, what's going on?' the girl shouted as one of the officers opened the door.

'Can I see some ID, Miss?' the detective asked the girl.

'You don't have to say anything to them, Vanessa,' Alec shouted over his shoulder.

Rolling her eyes, the girl reached for her bag on the nightstand, dug out her wallet and handed her student ID and US passport to the detective.

'Vanessa Rivera. 601 Argyle Road, Rochester, New York,' Detective Blalock read aloud, leaning heavily on her southern drawl for her own amusement. 'You're a long way from home, Ms. Rivera.'

'Thanks for the geography lesson,' said the young woman.

'Your passport says you're only fifteen years old,' the detective said as she looked at Roberts and gave him some shade. Alec's eyes widened.

'Yeah, so what?' said Vanessa defiantly.

'I guess, in addition to murder, Mr. Roberts,' the detective said, looking directly at Alec, 'we're going to have to add statutory rape.'

'But you're a college freshman,' shouted Alec to the girl.

'I skipped two grades,' she said, shrugging her shoulders. 'I'll be sixteen in December.'

'Gotta stay away from the smart ones, Roberts. They'll take you down every time. You know what happened to Al Capone? They got him on tax evasion. You probably thought you were giving Ms. Rivera a charitable contribution, but I'm afraid fifteen is against the law in the great state of Georgia.'

'This is bullshit, this is a set-up,' Roberts said. 'I want to call my lawyer.'

'They are going to extradite you to New York, but because of Ms. Rivera being only fifteen, the state of Georgia may want a little piece of you, too,' the detective said. 'Make sure you catch a glimpse of the sky when you walk outside tonight, Roberts. It's a full moon. Might be the last time you see one of those.'

The two deputies walked Roberts out of the room, and the detective turned her attention back to the young woman in the bed.

'What's your relationship with Alec Roberts?' she asked her.

'He's my History prof at the University of Rochester.'

'I need you to come down to the police station to make a statement,' the detective said.

'I don't want to,' Vanessa replied.

'I'm going to have to insist. Get dressed, Ms. Rivera. I'll be waiting right outside the door.'

Detective Blalock stepped into the hallway and phoned McQuillan just as she had promised.

'Guess who's on his way to central booking,' she said to him.

'We've been after him a long time,' McQuillan said. 'I wondered if I was going to retire before we nailed him. This is a good day, a great day. I don't know how to thank you.'

'You're gonna love this part,' Detective Blalock said. 'When we got to the hotel to make the arrest, he was in bed with a teenager, one of his students.'

'A leopard doesn't change their spots,' McQuillan said. 'Quinn Roberts' family used to say that about him all the time. They figured if they waited, he'd screw up again. I'll be on the 6am flight to Atlanta tomorrow morning to pick him up. Looking forward to shaking your hand in person, Detective.'

'Same here,' she replied, 'same here.'

Chapter Ninety-Nine

The traffic between the Atlanta airport and downtown was brutal. McQuillan's taxi was stopped in a sea of immobile cars filled with angry drivers. It was almost ten o'clock, and he was already late for his meeting with Detective Blalock.

The car finally started moving and arrived at Peachtree Street stopping in front of the Atlanta Police Department headquarters. Over six years had passed since he had first heard the name Quinn Roberts.

When he received that phone call from the Atlanta detective the previous night, McQuillan felt lighter, like a humongous weight had been lifted off of him. He walked into the building, flashed his badge and was told Detective Blalock was waiting for him outside conference room twelve.

Anita Blalock was an attractive, petite woman with eyes that cut right through you. She may have been small, but you knew instantly that she meant business.

'Detective McQuillan, I presume,' she said, reaching out her hand and flashing a big white toothy smile.

'Detective Blalock,' he said, shaking her hand. 'You are my hero. So, where's our filmmaker?'

'Mr. Roberts is right on the other side of that door,' she said, pointing to one of the conference rooms. 'He's hog-tied and ready for transport to New York.'

'I can't thank you enough. I mean it; this was the big one. Roberts was kind of my white whale.'

'Glad to help you reel him in, Detective,' Blalock replied. 'You'll do me one, someday. Go on in, he must be dying to see you.'

McQuillan took a deep breath as he thought back to the one time he had interviewed Roberts where he'd copped an attitude with the way the detective had mispronounced his name. McQuillan turned the knob on the clouded glass and wood door and went in.

'Hello, Alex,' he said. 'Been to Costco lately?'

Chapter One Hundred

Victor Malecki was no snitch. He'd been in tight spots before and he'd never ratted on anyone, until he crossed paths with Alec Roberts, the guy who had ruined his already shitty life.

Since the night he hit the runner, Alec Roberts had put the squeeze on him and played him like a puppeteer with a marionette. Alec had stood over him waving a gun while he put his phone on speaker to call the cops. It rang twice but before anyone answered, Alec disconnected the call. He continued to stare down at the man on the ground. Fifteen silent seconds later, a half-smile crept across Alec Roberts' face.

'Get up, asshole,' he finally said. 'I have a proposition for you.'

Since Alec had the gun, Victor complied and clumsily stood up. Alec could see from the way the drunk man moved that he was still very intoxicated. He guided Victor to the front door and demanded his phone number.

'I'm going to call you tomorrow when you're sober, asshole. No point trying to talk to you now, you won't remember anything,' Alec hissed. 'When I do call, you answer, is that clear?'

Victor nodded in agreement. A minute later Alec Roberts was gone.

The next morning, Victor woke up because his phone was buzzing. His head was pounding and his mouth was dry. He didn't recognize the number but answered anyway. Big mistake.

'Good morning, Victor,' said a man's voice. 'It's your friend from last night.'

Victor rubbed his eyes and scratched his head. He wasn't completely awake yet.

'Who is this?'

'Oh, Victor, I'm hurt that you would forget me so soon, after all that we shared.'

An image was triggered in Victor's mind of a man with a gun and he realized it wasn't a dream. *How the hell did he get my number? Shit.*

'What do you want?' Victor demanded, still half asleep.

'To meet with you,' the man said.

'What for?' Victor asked.

'I have a little job for you,' Alec said.

'No thanks, I'm busy.'

'You might want to reconsider, Victor. Remember, I have that video of you hitting that runner with your car last night. Would be such a shame for it to end up in the hands of the police,' Alec said.

That was when Victor saw another image of a dead guy in the road. Shit.

'What do you want?' Victor asked.

'I'll tell you when I see you,' Alec said. 'Meet me at three o'clock by the carousel at Ontario Beach Park.'

Victor met Alec at three. Alec told him to call him 'Doctor', leading Victor to assume his tormenter was some kind of medical doctor. That afternoon by the lake, Alec told Victor he wanted his wife 'removed' and expected Victor to take care of it.

'Do this for me, Victor,' Alec said, 'and I'll destroy that awful video of you running that poor man down. So sad, I read in the paper he was training for the New York City marathon.'

Alec held out his phone and played the video of the accident for Victor. As Victor watched, he knew he was screwed.

His first thought was to kill Alec Roberts and be done with the whole mess. When he was in a gang he had killed a few people, and he had liked some of them a lot more than Alec Roberts. He'd never whacked a woman and wasn't sure he wanted to. He was thinking over his next move when Alec boxed him in.

'If you're considering harming me in any way,' Alec said, 'don't. If anything happens to me, I've got copies of the videos with dates, times, names and addresses all locked and loaded to go to the police and the FBI.'

Victor didn't want to kill her, he didn't even know her, but he started to think he had no choice. He was on parole, and he had a kid now. He wasn't going back to prison. He had to get that video.

'I need it to happen within the week,' Alec said. 'When you finish your task, I'll destroy all copies of the video, and you'll never hear from me again. Sound good?'

After that day, they never met in person again and only communicated by phone.

Alec told Victor that his wife, Quinn, went for long walks every afternoon between two and four and usually stopped at a local market called Kenny's. He said his wife was a sucker for dogs. Victor needed to get a dog, wait down the street in his car and when he saw her, start walking with the dog on a leash.

'I guarantee she'll stop and talk to you,' Roberts said. 'My wife can't pass up a dog. Never could. They are like catnip for her. Let her start the conversation so she's the instigator and she won't suspect anything. Let her walk with you for a while. Her guard will be down if she initiates contact. Once she trusts you, when you get to her place, ask if you could get some water for your dog before you head home. She'll agree. She'd do anything for a dog.'

'What if somebody sees me?'

'That neighborhood is like a ghost town during the day,' he said. 'Everyone is at work. My wife used to complain there were never any people around to talk to. She should have gotten a job like everyone else instead of bleeding me dry.'

Victor's mind raced trying to figure a way out of his predicament and came up with nothing.

'I don't care how you do it, just get it done. Make it look like a drug addict robbery or something like that,' he said. 'You're a resourceful guy, Victor, you'll figure it out.'

'Where does she live?'

Alec reached into his bag, tore a piece off the corner of a newspaper and handed it and a pen to Victor.

'She lives at 1404 Brookside Drive, Apt B in the Glades section of Newbridge.'

Victor scribbled the address down on the scrap of newspaper. Alec showed Victor a picture of his wife so he could identify her. Victor thought she was pretty and wondered why the 'doctor' wanted to get rid of such a hottie.

Chapter One Hundred One

After numerous phone calls with Alec, and seeing no way out, Victor agreed to do it. He tucked the little slip of newspaper with her address on it into his jacket pocket and drove over to Brookside Drive to case the neighborhood. He double checked the number and parked two hundred feet down from #1404 to get a sense of the area before his big move. No mistakes.

Victor didn't want to kill her but it was either his life or hers and given the choice, he would always pick himself. An hour later, Quinn Roberts stepped out of her front door to go for a walk. He followed her in his car for a while, careful to keep a safe distance. She walked for about half a mile and went into a small market with a blue and white sign out front that said, Kenny's Kwik-Mart. He pulled over and sat there for a few minutes while she was inside. That's when he had a creative brainstorm and knew exactly how it would go down.

The next afternoon, he borrowed a little white dog named Macho from his cousin and drove over to Newbridge. He waited down the street from the Kwik-Mart for about forty-five minutes. Like clockwork, Quinn Roberts showed up and went inside. He got out of his car and walked up to the store with Macho on a leash. He tied the little terrier up right outside the front door of the shop and went in.

Quinn Roberts was at the checkout. A couple of construction guys stood by the deli counter waiting for an order. Victor grabbed a Snapple from one of the fridges and stood in line to pay. The woman chatted amiably with the store manager for a moment, picked up her small bag of groceries and left the store. Victor surreptitiously watched her go, waiting to see if his bait worked. Just like her husband had predicted, when Victor exited, Quinn was outside squatting down scratching Macho's ears and talking to him.

'Looks like you have a new friend,' he said to her. 'He doesn't take to everyone. He must know you're good people.'

'Is he yours?' she asked. 'He's so adorable.'

'His name is Macho,' Victor said.

'That's a great name. Hi, little Macho,' she said to the pup. 'You're adorable.'

The three of them walked along cheerfully talking about different breeds. Victor didn't give a shit about dogs or the difference between a schnauzer and a retriever, but on that walk, he laid it on thick. He noticed the woman kept repeating herself and was a little disoriented. He continued to bring the conversation back to Macho hoping to maintain her comfort level. After walking a while, they ended up on her block.

'Well, this is my street,' she said, starting to turn towards her house and ending their walk.

That was when he made his move.

'We've got a long walk back,' Victor said. 'Do you think we could come in for a second so I could give him some water before we start for home?'

Once he was inside, he did what he came to do. When he was finished, he made a mess. He opened up cabinets and closets, throwing a bunch of her pills around to make it look like an addict broke in and ransacked the place for money and drugs.

He didn't want to kill her. She was kind of nice, but that doctor had boxed him in. Later, when the cops offered him a deal, he rolled. If he testified against Roberts, they'd go easier on him. If the doctor had kept his part of the bargain and destroyed the video, they wouldn't be in this situation. Now, he was looking at manslaughter for the runner and a murder rap for the wife. He wasn't ever getting out.

The DA said he'd probably go to a maxi somewhere out in Wyoming, that it was one of the worst prisons in the country. If he were out there, he'd never see his kid. His boy was only five and his ex-girlfriend sure as hell wasn't going to drag her bony ass out there so he could see his son. He just had one choice. If he gave up Roberts, the DA would recommend a jail close to Rochester. At least then he'd get to see his kid. The decision was easy.

Chapter One Hundred Two

Ten years after losing Quinn, the Delaney clan made their last trip from New Jersey to Rochester for Alec's sentencing. The trial had started almost two years to the day after his arrest. The lag time between the guilty verdict, the appeal and this day took another two years. But this was the end of the road, it was finally over.

There had been many witnesses and lengthy testimony. Alison Moore, Cindy Kelleher and other women who had been in relationships with Alec testified, as did a number of his former 'student girlfriends'. Even Denise Orr, the woman he asked out and lied to about how long his wife had been dead, told her story. At the sentencing, Colleen, Mike, Erin and Ed Delaney, each had their turn to speak publicly, before the judge passed out his ruling.

'The loss of our daughter has been the most excruciating experience of our lives, Your Honor,' said Ed Delaney gripping his wife's hand, his voice catching with each word. 'This evil snuffed out a beautiful light. She was someone who brought immeasurable joy to all of us and showed kindness to everyone. Our lives will never be the same. As her father, I have to live with the guilt. You see, Your Honor, it was my job to protect her, and I failed.' Eileen Delaney put her arms around her husband as he broke down into tears.

It was Erin's turn. At last, she would say out loud what had been bottled up inside her for so many years. She wanted Alec to hear every biting word.

'You killed my sister, the mother of your children,' Erin began, trembling, words pouring out, 'for your love of money, your arrogance, and selfishness. I will pray every day that you live a long time so you can rot in jail as your evil devours you from the inside out. You will never have another moment of peace, and you will die old, alone and terrified. You took away my sister's future, now this is yours.'

Alec didn't look at any of them; he couldn't, still a coward.

He was convicted of orchestrating a 'murder for hire,' and he received a sentence of life in prison with no parole. Instead of lining up his next girlfriend for the new semester, Dr. A was going to spend the rest of his life in prison.

Since the arrest, Quinn's kids and the Delaneys had slowly rebuilt their relationship. Hannah, now thirty and Jack, thirty-one, were there in the courtroom that last day. Hannah stood to Erin's left and Jack to her right, all three holding hands as Alec's sentence was read. That was the moment they started to heal.

Quinn's actual killer, Victor Malecki, was to be sentenced a few months later. The Delaneys had to wait their turn until after Malecki's first trial for the manslaughter of the runner Chris Marshall before he would be sentenced for Quinn's. The Delaneys went to the Marshall trial and got to know his family. They were nice people, still shattered from losing their husband and father. The Marshalls and the Delaneys would be forever connected by death, Alec and Victor Malecki. Both families promised to return to Rochester when Malecki was sentenced.

When the Delaneys finally arrived home to New Jersey, they were exhausted from the long physical and emotional trip. Eileen asked everyone to come in for coffee. Mike, worn out from driving, begged off, telling Erin he'd meet her at home. She stayed for half an hour and then it was time to leave.

'We did it,' Erin said, tearing up and hugging her parents and sister goodbye. 'We did right by her. We got him.'

'Don't you start crying,' Colleen said, her eyes filling, 'or you'll make me cry and I'm just too tired. But yeah, we got him.'

'The Quinntessa would approve,' Erin said, grinning and feeling lighter.

Driving home, she passed the park where she and Quinn had played when they were kids. Images of the two of them flashed in front of her. It was dusk. Something made her stop and get out of the car. She walked into the park through an opening in the fence. It was dinnertime, the air was chilly, and the playground was empty. The old swings and slides had been replaced with new, modern recreation equipment. Oddly, everything was in the exact same place it had been when two sisters, one tiny, with dark hair and blue eyes, and the other a tall strawberry blonde, soared on their swings up to the sky.

Erin wished the past would come to life for just one moment, but the park remained quiet. Six empty swings hung forlornly from thick plastic-coated chains. All were still, except one that was blowing in the breeze. She walked over and sat down on the swing next to the one that was swaying and closed her eyes.

After years of fighting for justice for her sister, it was time to let her go. Erin pumped her legs once to get her swing moving, and as she did, she felt the seat lift on its own, almost as if someone was pushing her. Something warm gently encircled her shoulders, and she thought she heard Quinn's voice, 'Go higher, Erin, higher.'

Erin smiled as she soared through the air. Her sister was with her. Quinn was still there, she could feel her presence. Best friends, always and forever.

Chapter One Hundred Three

QUINN

I am a mother, a daughter, a sister, a friend. I *was* a wife. I love to skate and ski and hike in the woods. I like to bake cookies and eat them while they're still hot and gooey and sometimes even before they're cooked. I play the ukulele badly while singing as loud as I can. I don't care if I hit a sour note, it's part of my charm. I love a good margarita with extra salt, and I think mustard tastes good on everything.

I am Quinn.
I may not be there, but I'm still here.

Acknowledgements:

I'd like to thank my first readers who read Quinn at different stages and provided invaluable input, guidance and cheered me on. Leslie Arkin, Patricia and Heather Bellomo, Jill Chaifetz, Anne Fitzpatrick, Julie Garcia, Lisa Goodman, Jamie Holt, Madalyn Barbero Jordan, L.A. Justice, Charles "Chuck" Kanganis, Faye Kim, Marlene Pedersen, Tina Reine, Emily Shaw, Julie Saunders, Jessica Sitomer and Regina and Bob Turkington. An especially big thank you goes to my very smart and patient sister, Diane McGarvey, who sees everything before anyone else and has waded through really rough drafts. And finally, to my husband, Peter Black, who read it twice...a prince among men.

Made in the USA
San Bernardino, CA
23 May 2019